# TAKEOUT

## DONALD KINGSLEY

### A Sam Dancer Novel

# Copyright

Takeout is a work of fiction. The characters, incidents, and dialogue are drawn from the author's imagination and are not to be considered real. Any resemblance to actual events or persons, living or dead, is entirely coincidental.

# Dedication

To my wife Mary Jo: Thanks for your support and help.

To Stephanie: Thanks for your invaluable insights.

# Table of Contents

TAKEOUT 1

Copyright 2

Dedication 3

Table of Contents 5

Prologue 8

Chapter 1 13

Chapter 2 20

Chapter 3 34

Chapter 4 39

Chapter 5 53

Chapter 6 66

Chapter 7 73

Chapter 8 92

Chapter 9 100

Chapter 10 108

Chapter 11 114

Chapter 12 126

Chapter 13 139

Chapter 14 145

Chapter 15 153

Chapter 16 170

Chapter 17 174

Chapter 18 181

Chapter 19 186

Chapter 20 193

Chapter 21 203

Chapter 22 216

Chapter 23 228

Chapter 24 239

Chapter 25 261

Chapter 26 276

Chapter 27 289

Chapter 28 295

Chapter 29 301

Chapter 30 332

Chapter 31 334

Chapter 32 342

Chapter 33 346

About the Author 347

# Prologue

*Philadelphia Enquirer, City and Local, May 6: (Picture)*
*Local doctor an avid coin collector. Dr. William Dancer shows his*
*extensive coin collection of early US coins at the US Coin Show at*
*the Philadelphia Sheraton Convention Center this week.*

\*\*\*\*\*\*\*\*\*\*

The three men dressed in black crept silently through the suburban Philadelphia woods in the dusk of late July. Mosquitoes attacked them at random. Cicadas buzzed noisily in the background. The heat was an oppressive ninety degrees and ninety percent humidity.

"Goddam bugs," swore one of them.

"Shut up. We're almost there," the tallest whispered.

The woods stopped at a row of large cedar bushes. The three pushed their way through them. The rear of a large two-storey brick house stood before them with a well-groomed lawn leading to it. To the left a high brick wall connected the back of the house to what appeared to be the back of a garage. To the right a brick patio with lawn chairs stood in front of French doors leading into the large house.

"No one's at home," the shortest of the three commented.

"They'll be there soon. They have a regular routine on Saturday nights. Put your ski masks on. Keep quiet." They approached a gate in the brick wall. The tallest quietly opened it. Tall bushes surrounded a path from the gate to a path from the garage to the house.

"Okay, Rafi, you take the lady as she goes into the house. Make sure she has turned off the alarm. Lamont and I'll take the man." The tallest and Lamont silently crept behind a series of tall bushes next to the garage on the left. In front of the garage was a cobblestone driveway and courtyard surrounded by a brick wall. Two iron gates blocked the driveway. A driveway leading to a street in front of the house was visible through the gates.

Suddenly the gates in the driveway wall began to open. Lights in front of the garage came on along with a light over a door leading into the house. A late model Mercedes pulled slowly through the gates into the courtyard in front of the garage. The garage door opened, and the car entered the garage. Car doors opened and shut. A door leading from the garage to the house opened, and someone began to walk through. The three shrunk back into the bushes.

"Angela, open the back door. I'll bring in the food boxes. Those ribs were great, but I just can't eat a whole rack anymore."

The woman walked the short path to the house, unlocked the door, and entered a security code into a keypad on the wall as she walked into a corridor to the kitchen. The garage door began to close.

As the man walked toward the house, suddenly the two in the bushes attacked him. The taller hit him at the base of his skull with a blackjack; the other grabbed him as he sank to his knees. At the same time the one called Lamont rushed into the kitchen and knocked the woman to her knees with a punch to the head.

The man and woman awoke to the three men in ski masks facing them. They were duct-taped into their dining room chairs.

"Okay, people," the tall intruder announced, "we can make this easy or hard. We want your coins. Tell us where they are, and we leave. No one gets hurt."

The man in the chair said, "They're in a safe. I'll show you where."

"No, you tell me where, and give me the combination."

"Okay, just don't hurt us."

*********

Monday morning at 7:00 A.M. the maid opened the kitchen door, as she did each week, and entered the kitchen prepared to start breakfast. Something was wrong. She walked through to the dining room where a terrible sight confronted her. She moaned as she staggered back to the kitchen. She took a deep breath and dialed 911.

*********

At 10:00 A.M. the police lieutenant walked through the front door. "What have you got so far?"

The uniformed officer replied, "It looks like a home invasion. We got here about 7:45. The perps entered through the rear yard, overpowered the couple as they came into the house, and then ransacked the house. Jewels and cash maybe, two wall safes: one upstairs in a bedroom closet and one in the den. It looks like they cooperated with the perps and gave them the combinations. It wasn't enough to save their lives. Both of them have their throats cut. It's not pretty."

"Any idea when this happened?"

"The maid said they have a regular Saturday night routine. If they followed that, they ate at a local restaurant, left about 8:30, got home about 9:00. From the looks of the dried blood they were attacked on Saturday. The alarm was turned off, probably by the couple as they entered. We don't have a lot of forensics. No fingerprints. The perps apparently left as they came—through the woods. There are some tracks through the woods, but we don't have any good shoe impressions. We're checking to see if anyone on the other side of the woods saw anything. The perps appear to be very professional. They were waiting for the couple to come home. Must have been planning this for a while."

The lieutenant thought for a minute, "any relatives we need to contact?"

"The maid said the couple has two sons, one lives in Arizona. The other is in the Navy. I have a phone number for the one in Arizona."

"I'll call him right now."

*********

*PHILADELPHIA – Tuesday, July 28 (PVI)* – William Dancer, a prominent surgeon in Havertown, and his wife Angela were found dead in their home on Monday morning, apparent victims of a home invasion. Police said the bodies were found by their maid. Police have asked for anyone having information regarding this crime to call the Police Hotline.

# Chapter 1

When his parents were being robbed and murdered, Sam was sailing from Grenada in the Caribbean toward Puerto Cabello, Venezuela on a Vagabond 47 sailing yacht. He and Rico were on a "reward" mission. They had been part of a team that had taken out a terrorist lord in Yemen. The mission had been particularly difficult because of the need for non-attribution, or better yet, attribution to a specific terrorist cell opposing the terrorist lord. Their team of six parachuted into the area and set up an ambush leading directly to the opposing cell. It went off without a glitch. After they were extracted, the two terrorist factions began attacking each other. The mission was a success. They were congratulated for their proficiency; however they were immediately presented with a new mission.

A year before, an undercover Colombian agent stationed in Venezuela had observed several Iranians coming and going through the Simon Bolivar International Airport. He worked as a baggage handler and had seen the same three individuals coming through the terminal several times over four months. He photographed them and passed the information on to his Colombian handler.

The Colombians in turn passed copies of the photographs to the CIA station in Bogota. The wheels turned a bit slow, but an alert CIA analyst at Headquarters processed the photos through facial recognition software and had three hits a senior Iranian intelligence officer, a senior Iranian military officer, and an Iranian scientist known to be working on the Iranian atomic bomb.

Immediately, an interagency task force was set up to gather more information to determine what was going on.

The Venezuelan president was known to be courting Iran, but seeing these three on Venezuelan soil was a big red flag. The taskforce requested the US intelligence community start collecting more information. High altitude drone flights were sent over Venezuela. Unusual construction was observed in the mountains outside a small port, Puerto Cabello: tunnels going into the mountain, concrete pads, a large warehouse building, what appeared to be military barracks, and the area was surrounded by fencing. At the same time a Syrian-flagged merchant vessel showed up in the port and unloaded outsized containers. They were stored in the port in a heavily guarded area and then trucked to the new facility in the mountains.

The military officer was linked to the Iranian ICBM program. While the Iranians had not exploded a bomb, it was generally believed they had successfully developed one and were producing warheads. The scientist was believed to have set up the warhead storage depots in the Iranian mountains.

The possibility Venezuela was involved in creating an atomic ICBM military threat was a very serious situation. However, before the US could take action, specific proof had to be obtained. As in the case of Cuba in the 60s, U-2 photography was demonstrable proof and was shown to the UN by the then ambassador Adlai Stevenson.

The task force postulated the Iranians were concealing dismantled mobile ICBMs in the containers. The transporters for the ICBMs could easily be taken apart and shipped in other containers or appear to be heavy transport vehicles. The Iranian ICBM was known to have a range of approximately 1800 miles—enough to threaten the Panama Canal or Florida. On-the-ground information was needed.

Apparently the Iranians and Venezuelans had learned from the Cuban history and were hiding the assembly and transportation in a well-thought-out deception operation. An operation to collect more information was requested by the National Intelligence Director. Because of the sensitivity, the mission request went to a special activity, Group 5, to implement. Group 5 had been set up several presidential terms before. Its charter was to perform special operations under the direct control of the President and be completely unattributed to the US or any other country.

It appeared the Venezuelans were trying to maintain a low profile of their activities. The new facility in the mountains near Puerto Cabello was of concern, but the port continued being routinely used for normal cargos, and no enhanced security for tourists or business travelers was observed.

There was one transshipping area in the port subject to military control where the unusual shipping containers were unloaded and moved to the mountain area.

Following their mission in Yemen, Sam's team was assigned to this operation. It was billed as a reward for their team because the threat environment was seen to be minimal. Four of the team would be stationed on a US Navy ship monitoring the operation. The ship had direct communications with a special operations center in the White House. The other two would be sent into Venezuela to place sensors to obtain irrefutable data showing the connection between Iran and Venezuela. The risks were thought to be small.

Sam Dancer and Henrico (Rico) O'Hara were selected to perform the task. Sam had developed a unique ability to infiltrate himself into very difficult situations. Rico's specialty was sensor emplacement—the deployment and setting up of very sensitive data collection devices. He and Sam had worked together with the rest of their team for almost ten years. They were very comfortable with each other's abilities. Their part of the operation was supposed to be the "reward"; they would use a luxury sailboat delivery as their cover.

The US Navy ship cruised in the Caribbean with the support team. The team was in a special operations center on the ship. They launched a Poseidon drone to fly along the Venezuelan coast. The drone could loiter for several days at over 30,000 feet. Virtually undetectable, it resembled an oversized model aircraft.

Its wingspan was over twenty feet; it carried a two-way communications system, a video camera with normal and infra-red and multi-spectral capabilities, a broadband radio receiver, and a relay for the sensors Sam and Rico would put in place.

The ship had several of these drones and could launch a new one and recover the other when its fuel was exhausted. This way, Sam and Rico were in constant communication with their support team and police and military activity could be monitored. All of this data was also relayed to a special operations facility in the White House.

The suite of special sensors to prove or disprove the existence of ICBMs and/or nuclear material was similar to one Sam and Rico had placed in Iran where they had a similar operation.

The two of them were darker-skinned and spoke fluent Castilian Spanish. Rico was a second generation immigrant from Mexico who had grown up in Arizona. Sam's features looked Mediterranean. Sam and Rico often traveled as Spaniards. Spain was a good cover because it was often perceived to be neutral to many of the Western European political concerns. A Vagabond 47 sailboat was their cover. They were two sail captains delivering the sailboat to an owner in Panama. They picked up the boat in Grenada and were sailing to Panama to go through the canal to the delivery point. They were stopping in Venezuela for extra provisions and waiting for some engine parts.

"Land, Ho!" Rico exclaimed as the Venezuelan coast came into view. They had been at sea for several days.

"Wow, look at the mountains, would you Rico?" Sam asked from the helm as they sailed toward the Venezuelan port city of Puerto Cabello.

The weather from Grenada had been beautiful. There were steady winds, and they had sailed most of the way. The Vagabond 47 was an ideal cruising boat, and they had almost believed they were on a vacation as they sailed toward their destination.

Group 5 had bought it in the Dominican Republic and outfitted it for their needs there. Another set of Group 5 had delivered it to Grenada where Sam and Rico took it over.

Rico looked up from a chart he was rolling up in the small cockpit. They were using the GPS on board to navigate, but they both agreed they liked to use traditional charts and celestial navigation just to keep in practice. They often joked they would wear a belt, suspenders, and pins to keep their trousers up. They liked to back up their backups. "I guess we did get a reward mission. I feel more like we're on a vacation than an operation." He smiled. "Maybe we can get a decent meal in the city. We are supposed to act like tourists."

"Yeah, I feel a little sad we might have to scuttle "My Way". She has been a good boat," Sam replied. Part of the retrofitting involved placing two explosive packages in the boat's bilge. When detonated, they would cause the boat to sink almost immediately. Part of the mission planning had the boat disappear at sea if Sam and Rico were discovered by the Venezuelans.

"I'll start the engine and take in the sails now." Sam began pulling the lines to roll up the two jibs and mainsail. The boat had been rigged to allow one person to basically sail the boat from the cockpit. The Vagabond was a ketch rig and only the smaller mizzen sail behind Sam wasn't self-furling. It dropped into a set of lazy jacks when he released the halyard.

"Okay," Rico said as he went aft to shake out the mizzen and tie the sail to its boom. "I'll get the sail covers." He went down into the cabin and came out with the covers for the main and mizzen, and jib staysail.

As Rico tidied up the lines and sails, Sam continued steering the boat toward the harbor, watching for navigation buoys. The entry was beautiful and idyllic; the green of the mountains against the deep blue of the Caribbean was breathtaking. It was hard to imagine someone would want to cause turmoil by bringing ballistic missiles and atomic weaponry to this paradise.

# Chapter 2

It was closing time on Monday and the late July Arizona summer sun was sinking slowly behind the western mountains. The evening cool-down was beginning. Roger Dancer sat on the couch in his studio lobby in Sedona Arizona reflecting on his Monday, his tall, muscular form relaxed with his cowboy boots on the rustic wood table in front of him.

He watched the red colors on the mountains change in hue through his front window. The last of the summer tourists had left his studio. It had been a good day. He had sold several high-priced photographic art pieces.

He looked around his store; actually he thought of it as his studio. The lobby opened into a set of rooms with varying sizes of landscape photographs.

Most popular were scenes of the Grand Canyon and the red rocks around Sedona. His photographs were shot with a high-resolution camera and printed on special photographic paper giving the impression of a painting. Some were as large as six feet by three feet, giving the illusion of looking through a window. They were expensive, some in the thousands of dollars, but they were very popular. His business extended around the world through the Internet. Roger was feeling very good about things.

A police cruiser pulled up in front and parked. This was strange; usually cars that parked in front of his store were tourists interested in buying his outdoor photographs. Deputy Police Chief Jim Rostof, a friend from Rotary, got out. *Must be some Rotary business*, Roger surmised.

Rostof opened the door and walked in and removed his hat, "Evening, Roger," he greeted, but not with a smile. Rostof looked rather grim.

Roger was puzzled by this; normally Rostof was a man with a smile and a joke. He was a large man and a little overweight, but rarely, in Roger's experience, serious. Of course Roger had known him only in social situations. "Gosh, Jim, you look serious. Is there a major crime spree in town?" Roger joked as he sat forward in the couch.

"I'm afraid I have some bad news. We just received a phone call from a police department in Pennsylvania: Haverford Township. I don't know what to say. They told me your parents were murdered in their house Saturday night. They weren't found until this morning when the housekeeper arrived. He's been trying to get you at home, but all he got was your answering machine."

Roger looked at him, stunned. "Janie and the kids are up in Flagstaff at a soccer camp. I've been staying here working. What happened?" He remained seated, trying to make sense of what Jim had told him.

"From what the lieutenant told me your parents came home from dinner Saturday night in the evening and were the victims of a home invasion.

"The robbers tied them up and ransacked the house. They killed your mom and dad. The police told me they didn't have any significant leads as yet, but they and the state police were investigating the crime. I talked to a Lieutenant Jacobsen in the Haverford Police Department. He suggested you get in contact with him."

Roger and Jim chatted for a few minutes and Roger took the phone number from Jim. Jim apologized for bringing such bad news. "If there is anything I can do to help, let me know. I can also talk to the police there to give them any information to help in their investigation, but it sounds like you probably wouldn't have any knowledge that would be helpful."

Roger thanked him, and Jim left. Roger called his wife, Janie, and told her the news. He suggested she not tell the kids until they got home. He was going to call the police in Haverford to see what they might say. Roger sat for a while digesting what he had learned.

He realized he needed to contact his brother Sam, a career Navy SEAL. He was thirty-nine and Roger's older brother by two years. Roger was never sure where Sam might be. He was often off on a classified mission or "operation." Sam had given him a number to call in case of an emergency. Roger usually heard from Sam every few months. Sam would call and see how things were going, but Roger never knew if Sam was in the US or somewhere else. Sam had occasionally been stationed in the US and made time to see their parents or Roger.

He dialed the number, and got an answer: "Hello, this is Sam's phone, please leave a message."

"This is Roger Dancer, Sam's brother. I have just been notified our parents have been murdered. Sam, please call me as soon as you can." He left his phone number. A minute later the phone rang, "Hello, this is Roger Dancer."

"Roger, this is Sam's Commanding Officer. Sam is unavailable for a week or two. I'll have him get back to you as soon as possible. I can't give him the news while he is working, but I will let him know as soon as I can. Is there anything I can do?

"No…thanks. I'll probably be travelling to Pennsylvania where our parents lived. I'll give you my cell phone number. Also, Sam can send me email. I'm not sure he will have to do anything. It sounds like by the time he gets back, I may have buried our parents. I'll send him an email with any details I can find out."

Roger hung up. He needed to go home and break the news to his kids when they returned: Jenny, fourteen and Chris, twelve. But first, he called the Pennsylvania number and asked for Lieutenant Jacobsen and explained what he needed to talk to him about. Lieutenant Jacobsen was home by this time, but the duty officer said he would have the Lieutenant call him.

He was driving home when his cell phone rang. It was the Lieutenant. "Mr. Dancer, this is Bill Jacobsen. I'm sorry to have to talk to you like this. This is a very unhappy situation for you, I know. We, here, are shocked by the crime. We have not had any home invasions here for many years, certainly not of this sort."

Roger continued talking with Jacobsen and got some more details. The activity made no sense. His parents didn't keep any large amount of cash or jewelry in the house.

"Mr. Dancer, can you give me any reason why your parents might have been a target for such a crime?"

Roger racked his brain. His dad was a very cautious man. He had a security service monitoring the house alarm. He was a prominent surgeon, but was not a high-profile person. His mother did a few charities. They were in their early sixties and beginning to think about retiring and moving to a smaller house.

"Lieutenant Jacobsen, I remember my father showing me his coin collection once. I don't remember if they were extremely valuable. I do remember there were some gold coins though."

"We will follow up on that. Your parent's maid identified the bodies. They should be available to move to a funeral home by the end of the week. Because this was a murder, there has to be an autopsy. "Jacobsen replied.

"Thank you Lieutenant. I'll keep in touch. I'll be coming back to arrange my parent's funeral and settle their estate." Roger and Janie had just been back with the kids in June to visit his and her parents in Pennsylvania. They had spent a week with her parents and a week with his parents, and then gone to the Jersey shore for two weeks. Both sets of parents had come over to their rented beach house for short visits. It had been a really nice time. Trying to explain to his kids what had happened would be a terrible thing, but he had to do it.

That night after telling his kids what had happened, Janie and Roger discussed what needed to be done next. They decided Roger should fly back to Pennsylvania to get his parent's funeral arranged and to try to settle the estate and she and the kids follow when the funeral arrangements were made.

Roger arrived at the Philadelphia Airport on Wednesday evening and drove to Ardmore, where he had booked a room at the Marriott. Then next day he called Bill Jacobsen and arranged to meet him at his parent's house in the afternoon. As he drove along the streets shaded by old trees, he reflected how fortunate he and his brother were to grow up in such a beautiful area. They had good parents, good educations, and positive lives. He turned into the driveway leading to the Georgian style brick house. It was a very comforting house, looking as if it had been there during the Revolution. It had been raining, and the humidity was high.

It was strange to drive up the driveway, realizing his father would never again be there to meet him, his mother never again coming out of the kitchen to hug him. His feelings alternated between anger and great sadness. A plain-clothes police car was parked in the drive in front of the courtyard gate. A slightly overweight, middle-aged man stood in front of the gate to the garage parking area. He was dressed in a rumpled dark suit, his necktie untied. He looked uncomfortable in the late July heat. Roger assumed it was Bill Jacobsen, the police lieutenant he had talked to on the phone. There was another police car with a uniformed officer inside parked in the street in front of the house. After greeting each other, Jacobsen explained to him what they had learned so far.

"We think the burglars came through the forest behind the house. Unfortunately, it rained shortly after the crime and there isn't any trace of footprints anymore. They wouldn't have been much help anyway. The burglars waited until your parents came home and then overpowered them as they entered the house.

"Why they killed them, we don't know. It appears your father may have been assaulted in front of the downstairs safe and then dragged to the dining room where your mother was tied up. It was there they were killed.

"We have one lead. A man out for a run Saturday evening noticed a white van pulled into a parking area on the other side of the woods. There's a small park there. He said it was a Dodge utility van, and he thought he remembered two or three letters from the plate. We ran the numbers and came up with one registered to an individual who did time for armed robbery. However, we also came up with 452 other vans. We intend to question the individual tomorrow." Jacobsen summarized with a grim expression on his face. "Let's go through the house and see if you can find anything that might be helpful."

As they walked through the house, Roger could see there was little evidence the thieves had stolen anything except what was in the safes. Things were overturned and drawers were opened, but it looked haphazard.

"Lieutenant, it looks like they just threw things around. There doesn't seem to be much stolen." Roger observed.

Jacobsen replied, "We noticed this, too. I wanted to see if you saw anything else missing that was valuable. There was a silver coffee and tea set on a table in the dining room thrown on the floor, but not taken. It looks to us as if it were a targeted robbery instead of a real home invasion."

Roger had thought about what the reason for the burglary might be. "You know, Lieutenant, the last time I saw my Dad and Mom, he brought me in here and had several gold coins on his desk. He showed them to me and said here was his grandchildren's education. I told him not to worry. I had savings. He was obviously very proud of the coins and said he had shown them recently at a local coin convention. He said several people came up to him and showed interest in buying them. He then took them into the other room and put them away in the wall safe."

Jacobsen looked thoughtful. "That's valuable information. If we know what we're looking for, we might find something if someone tries to sell them."

"I'd like to look through my father's desk. He might have kept a list of his coins. I know he was very proud of his collection. If we can find a list, we might know if there was anything particularly valuable. My mother had some valuable diamonds she kept in the upstairs safe, but I don't know if there's an inventory."

They walked into his father's office. Jacobsen stood next to Roger as he went through the desk. Roger pulled out a folder labeled coins. In it was a newspaper clipping with a picture of his father showing some coins at a recent coin convention in Philadelphia.

The article gave his father's name and the fact he had a coin collection. The folder contained several sheets of paper listing the coins, each with a photograph. Next to each coin was an estimate of its value. There were several US gold coins, each worth over $20,000 apiece. Several other coins were listed: four over $300,000 and there was one, apparently very rare, with an estimate of $1,000,000.

Roger took a deep breath, "Lieutenant, I had no idea he had coins worth this much. He had been collecting since he was a teenager, but he must have added significantly after he became an adult. If he showed these coins at that coin convention, he might have become a target."

Jacobsen nodded. "We'll check into that. It could explain why the robbers didn't go after anything else. This is a good lead." Jacobsen took the coin file. "Roger you can have access to the house on Friday. We should be finished by then."

"Thanks. I'll be going to my in-laws who live in Valley Forge until then."

"I'll let you know if we find out anything more." Jacobsen replied.

Roger drove to Valley Forge and pulled up in the drive of his in-laws' house. They lived a little farther out from Philadelphia in a newer area. They were solemn and saddened, as he was. Roger was very close with Janie's parents; they were almost a second set of parents. He told them about the meeting with Jacobsen and that he would arrange a funeral, perhaps the following week. He told them he would sell as much of the furniture and belongings as possible and give the rest to charity.

In his parent's will they named him the executor. He also needed to meet with his father's lawyer and tax man to determine what else he had to do to settle the estate. The house would be put up for sale, too.

He decided would stay in the house once the police were through. His mother-in-law was concerned about him staying there, but he said it would be more convenient. There was no way for these tasks to be anything but sad. He would just have to face it.

On Friday Roger walked into the house and wandered through his childhood home. He went up the stairs to the second floor and walked into his old room. His parents had used it as a guest room, but kept some of his childhood pictures and awards. He walked into his brother's room, which was decorated the same, except there were no college memories; his brother had left home after graduating from high school and joined the Navy with the hope he could become a SEAL. Sam had powered his way through SEAL school and impressed everyone with his attitude, leadership, and physical abilities. He had been offered a path to become a commissioned officer, but never seemed to have the time to follow it up. After he was in the SEALs for ten years, Sam seemed to have some sort of career change, but still was in secret work.

Roger stood in his parent's room and suddenly was overcome with the fact of his loss. He sat on their bed and sobbed. He sat there for several minutes, thinking about the whole situation. *What kind of people would attack an older couple and slit their throats?*

He could not imagine anyone could do such a thing. He could understand in war soldiers fought each other to the death, but murdering his parents was beyond anything he could conceive of.

He then went to a funeral home to arrange for his parents burial. There was a family plot where his grandfather and grandmother were buried.

**********

The next week Roger met Janie and his children at the airport and took them to her parents. She and he began planning the funeral. He knew there needed to be a viewing. His parents were prominent in their church, community, their golf club, and had a lot of friends and associates from his father's business and interests. Roger decided to have a wake in the golf club. He was impressed by the number of close friends both his parents had. They were involved in several charities for children Roger hadn't known about. The funeral was held in St. George's Episcopal Church, a very beautiful old church. The service was crowded, and Roger and several other men gave eulogies. His family flew back to Arizona afterward.

Within two weeks, Roger had settled most of the estate and kept a few private effects either for himself or Sam, sold some, and given the rest to charity. The house had been professionally cleaned and was up for sale.

He was surprised by the value of the estate his parents had left to him and Sam. Sam and he were now independently wealthy. The coin collection had not been insured except when his father took it to a coin show. His mother's diamonds were, and were quite valuable. His father apparently was a very shrewd stock investor and had made a great deal of money trading during the dot com bubble and stock market collapse. His dad and some of his friends were also investors in several very successful venture capital companies. None of this made Roger's grief any less.

As he was getting ready to leave, Roger checked in with Jacobsen at the police station in Haverford. It was late in the day and Jacobsen looked weary. "Roger, I'm sorry to say we haven't really come up with any strong leads. We checked several van owners, especially the one who had a record. He has a supported alibi as to where he was the night of the murders, but I think that guy is the culprit, or one of them. He lives with two other ex-cons, and I just have a feeling about them. His alibi put him in South Philly in a local bar, but the bartender wasn't real sure."

"The other two could have been in on it with him. We know there had to be more than one person involved. The other two said they were at home. We had the local police search the place where the three live, but nothing was found. A white van has been seen at the scene of two other burglaries, but we can't link a specific van to them. We have a tire print from one other burglary, but the van belongs to the one we have the partial license plate number from has new tires. We'll keep an eye on them." Jacobsen ended his recount with a sigh, clearly frustrated.

"We also checked out the coin lead. Your father did show some of his more valuable coins at that show in the paper. We talked to several other exhibitors who were there, but they didn't have any ideas about who might have had an interest in stealing the coins. One person we talked to said he had some stolen from his coin shop after a local coin show. The thieves had broken into his shop and actually stole a small safe with some valuable coins in it. He said the coins never appeared on any market he was aware of."

"I want to tell you unofficially, I am pretty certain these three are the perpetrators of this crime. There are too many coincidences: the van, the fact the three are ex-cons, their attitude when we questioned them. In fact they called their lawyer in when we questioned them. You know, you get a feeling after dealing with this sort of thing for your entire career. It really pisses me off."

Roger nodded sympathetically, "I understand. Is there any other information you might have? My brother is in the service overseas, and I haven't been able to tell him about this situation yet."

"Oh, what branch is he in? I was in the Army during Desert Storm," Jacobsen answered.

"He's a SEAL. That's why I haven't been able to contact him. Apparently he's on a special mission somewhere."

Jacobsen thought for a while, "Roger, I hate to tell you this, but I am afraid we won't be solving this crime unless we catch the perps in some other crime. I'm retiring at the end of September, and we have enough stuff to do. I think this will fall to the bottom of the list. Unless you get a real tight lead within a week or so, most crimes go unsolved. This one is already getting low on our priorities."

Roger looked at him in consternation, and shook his head. "I don't know what to tell my brother when he surfaces. Do you have any write-up or anything I could give him?"

"I'm not supposed to release anything official, but I would like to do something that might help you. I'll make a copy of our file and let you have it. Maybe your brother can think of something that could give us a lead. At least he'll know what we know." Jacobsen said in a low voice.

Roger thanked him. Jacobsen said he would give it to him the following day. Roger could meet him down the street at a coffee shop.

The following day Roger got the copy of the file, thanked Jacobsen, and left. He went back to his in-laws for the night and left for Phoenix the next day. He sat on the plane looking out the window the whole trip from his first class seat. He could not make any sense out of the whole thing.

# Chapter 3

Shamika Johnson had a small stack of papers on her desk; on the top was a classified document form with several colors on its border. She wasn't smiling, but she welcomed a short, pudgy young man into her office. "Burton, come on in and sit down. I've just received notice you have been cleared for access to a special project, and you have been assigned as my Deputy Director for Special Programs. I need you to sign these papers. Tomorrow morning when you come in you will get a briefing on exactly what this is all about."

As Burton walked out to his car he reflected on how he had managed to put Shamika in her place.

Clifton Burton Jamesway III smiled smugly. He had been assigned to the African-American woman after applying for a job in the White House. She had treated him as a nonentity since he arrived two months ago. She was a special assistant to the President for some sort of secret stuff.

He had asked her many times to be allowed to have more responsibilities, but she had always diverted him to what he considered menial duties: checking a press release, passing paperwork to the various offices in the White House, nothing befitting a person of his background.

After all, his father was a close friend of the President, a major donor to the party—a million dollars! Besides he, Burton, had just graduated from a prestigious Ivy League college. He was a member of Bally Back, the most secret Ivy League society, more secret than "Bones".

This woman had blocked him from any sort of advancement. Just because he was a recent graduate didn't mean he couldn't be trusted with serious matters. His family background should count for something more.

Burton had tried to befriend the woman, but she resisted his charm. He finally had to go to his father and tell him about the circumstances. He really didn't like to use his family connections, but after all, he was a Jamesway, a member of a much respected, old New England moneyed family. He explained to Shamika who he was and his family background. That should have told the woman something, but she couldn't be reasoned with. His father came through and made something happen. He wouldn't disappoint the old man.

Shamika waited while Burton signed the papers. The program was code-named BREAKDOWN. Burton thought this a little melodramatic, but said nothing. Shamika tried to smile, and said "Welcome, Burton, you will have a complete briefing tomorrow morning. Come to the Situation Room at 9:00. There will be a briefing and then a tour of a special facility here in the White House."

Burton grinned at her, "Shamika, thanks for your help in getting me this. I'm sure we will make a great team." He left the office

**********

Shamika took a deep breath and let it out. She didn't know whether to scream or throw up. A career intelligence professional for twenty-five years, chosen by the Director of National Intelligence for this assignment; she had a master's degree in International Studies from Georgetown, and ten years of overseas assignments fighting terrorists. She still had scars from being shot in a car ambush in Greece, and now she had to deal with this politically connected twit.

Burton had bothered her from the moment the President's Chief of Staff told her he was assigned to her area. During her initial interview with him, he came across as a pompous idiot. He spent the entire interview trying to impress her with who his family was and how he needed to have an important job. When she attempted to ask him questions regarding his knowledge of national affairs, his answers were shallow. She could see he was not interested in learning anything from her; he already knew it all. Allowing Burton access to this program was wrong, but she had been told by the Chief of Staff this was going to happen—period.

**********

The next morning Burton showed up in the Situation Room. A man he had seen around the White House was standing in front. The man introduced himself as the Chief of Operations for Group 5 activities. Burton had no idea what Group 5 activities meant. The man began a briefing using a projector with a Power Point presentation.

Apparently, several years before, a special activity called Group 5 had been set up. It was basically a special operations group reporting directly to the President: authorized to conduct assassinations, bombings, and whatever else was needed to assure US interests under the President's direction. It was small, only 50-100 people, mostly former special operations types: SEALS, Delta, CIA, etc. Its headquarters were on an Air Force base in Florida. Burton was impressed. This was awesome stuff.

The man finished the briefing and then asked him to follow him. They walked down several corridors and down some stairs. Finally they arrived at a door with a special device on the wall. The man placed his face against the device and the door clicked. They entered and walked by a few offices and into an area evidently some sort of control center. The man introduced him to another woman sitting on a platform at a console with video screens in front of her. Below, in front of her, were four other positions with video screens; two had women doing something with their keyboards. The other two had men studiously looking at their video screens. There were video displays on the wall, too.

My God, Burton thought, how can they trust all these women to do this kind of sensitive work? Then he reflected, maybe it's not that big a deal anyway. If it were really important they would have men soldiers in uniform. Burton had never been in the military, but his father had. His father had impressed upon him: soldiers were important people who did important work.

The woman began to explain there was a very sensitive operation going on code-named DAWN TRADER. They were in constant communication with a Navy ship.

Two men were going into Venezuela on a sailboat, posing as sailboat delivery men. They were supposed to find out if the Iranians were working with the Venezuelans to introduce ICBMs into the country. Burton nodded and oohed and aahed at the appropriate times. Following his introduction to all this, Burton went back to his office and pondered what he had learned.

*What nonsense*, he thought. *If we want to find out what the Iranians are doing in Venezuela, why don't we just send in the army and find out? Especially silly is the use of two guys on a sailboat. What a secret operation*! He almost laughed out loud. He shook his head. He would have to have a chat with his father about what he had seen. The activity had all the marks of a rogue operation. He bet if the President really knew what was going on, there would be hell to pay. He did feel good, though, about now being someone important. He was now a Deputy Director.

# Chapter 4

Sam and Rico anchored in the harbor entrance and flew their quarantine flag and called the Captain of the Port. The customs boat came out to meet them. The customs and immigration inspectors went through the boat. Their electronic devices were passed off as navigation and radio parts. Their weapons were hidden in special compartments in the cabin headliner. Their cover was accepted. After a bit of harassment and some surreptitious cash transfers, they were given clearance to enter. They tied up at the Puerto Cabello marina, paid for boat protection with the local police, and began to settle in. They were good for a month. There were only two other sailboats in the marina. The rest of the boats were mainly sport fishermen.

The first few days they spent establishing themselves as a no interest activity. They used their scuba gear to clean and inspect the bottom. They swam a few miles a day down the coast to keep in shape. They observed the activity at the industrial part of the port. There were a few large container ships that came and went. As they walked around the city, they appeared to be normal tourists. They wore Bluetooth earpieces, but the cell transmitted to the drone.

Wherever they went they were in constant communication with their teammates. The cell phones were not necessary, but were a good device for when they were around people.

Communications gear was also cleverly hidden in shirts they could wear. There was cell phone circuitry, a battery, and a high-gain antenna imprinted in their shirts. A microphone was in the lapel of the shirt and an earpiece that looked like a hearing aid could be placed in their ear. If they got into a situation where they needed to move fast, this means of communication was a good back-up. All the controls were in the sleeves of the shirt, disguised as buttons. An added plus was their location could be seen on their support team's display screens.

A few days after they arrived, a Syrian-registered ship entered and tied up at one of the container off-loading cranes. This ship had been followed by intelligence sources from the time containers were loaded in the port of Bushehr, Iran. Attempts had been made to trace them from their beginnings in Iran, but the Iranians were clever in their operational security. The containers came from different areas in Iran as best could be determined. Once they came together at the port, the ship was tracked.

Sam and Rico were able to find a spot to observe the unloading activity without causing any interest. The sizes of the containers were unusual. They were larger in width and length, and there were only ten of them. The rest on the ship were normal-sized. Because of the size of the ten containers, special handling gear was fitted. There was also unusual military activity around the ship. No one was allowed near the ship while the containers were unloaded. Only the ten were loaded on special truck transports and taken to a separate area in the port. Every move was guarded by army troops.

Sam and Rico decided to make their move the following evening after the containers were put in the guarded area. Their team on the ship, using the imagery from the drone, reported to them regarding where there were guards and what their movements were. Sam and Rico got their equipment together and put it in a waterproof bag. They would have to swim underwater for about three miles and pull the bag with them. This was not a big deal; they had done much more difficult operations.

They slipped into the water about 11:00 p.m. and quickly dove to thirty feet. They were using a special inertial reference system allowing them to navigate to their target in the dark. After two hours they approached the concrete pier where the containers were stored. The pier was approximately eight feet above them and well lighted. A special grapnel and rope system allowed them to climb up to the pier surface. The grapnel was lined with rubber to prevent a large noise when it was thrown up on the pier. They removed their scuba gear and hung it on the bottom of the grapnel rope. Then they hauled themselves up the rope and peered over the edge of the pier. Using their night-vision goggles, they searched the area. No one was visible. Their teammates' information indicated the guards patrolled the fence perimeter, but did not come near the water side of the pier. The containers were lined up perpendicular to the water. The sensors they had to install went onto the tops of the containers. They crawled over the edge of the pier.

A small "Hummingbird" would be used to place the sensors. The Hummingbird was a micro-flying device about twelve inches long and wide. Rico controlled it like a model airplane and the sensors were RFAID (radio frequency identification devices): very small radio transmitters about the size of a postage stamp with special sensors to detect atomic radiation and the chemicals associated with ballistic missiles. The Hummingbird could carry fifty of these devices. Each RFAID had a special epoxy adhesive that would adhere to the container once the temperature reached ninety degrees.

While Sam searched for any sign of activity, Rico flew the small aircraft over each container and dropped a sensor on the top of it. Once he was finished, he flew the Hummingbird back to them. Sam picked it out of the air. Rico then flew a second Hummingbird with a special receiver and transmitter over the containers and dropped it. It was the size of a cigar and collected the transmitted information and provided the necessary signal strength to forward it to the overhead drone. The devices were all powered with solar cells and batteries enabling them to last for several months. This technology was some of the most secret the US possessed.

Rico flew the second Hummingbird back to Sam who picked it out of the air and slipped it into the bag. They lowered themselves into the water, retrieved the grapnel, and placed it into the bag.

As they swam back to their boat, they released the bag in the center of the channel which was about seventy feet deep. It fell to the bottom, and they returned to their boat. As they pulled themselves onto the boat, the very first light of dawn was beginning.

They slid into the cockpit and quickly put their gear down into the cabin. The sport fishermen were beginning to get ready to go out. They were just in time to be unobserved.

Sam sat in a seat in front of the navigation station in the cabin on the boat. To any observer it appeared to be a normal set-up: GPS, navigation display, VHF and single-side band radio, laptop computer. This was normal equipment for a well-outfitted cruising sailboat. The major difference was their radio transmissions were all VLPI (Very Low Probability of Interception). Anyone with a radio would only hear static when they were transmitting. They could also communicate directly with their ship using an encrypted cell phone. The drone acted as a cell tower relaying their communications back and forth.

Sam tuned the VHF to a special channel and began typing on the laptop. "Initial sensors in place. Please verify." Shortly on the laptop a message appeared, "Receiving data from 10 sensors. Chemical analysis in process. No apparent radiation. Will advise. Over." Sam then connected a small video camera specially configured for low light levels. They had videoed all of the operation also. He downloaded it to the laptop and then transmitted the video to the ship. All of their communications relied on commercially available software. The only difference was it was all VLPI and encrypted.

Sam turned to Rico, "The sensors are working. The chems are in analysis, no rad."

Rico smiled, "Well, we need to take a little camping trip into the mountains to relax for a while."

Sam nodded, "Let's get our stuff together. I'll look into a rental four-wheel drive." Sam hit the ESC button on the laptop which erased both messages.

They planned to drive the highway to San Esteban, just south of the city in the mountains. There were areas for tourists to camp and explore. The Venezuelans had created the new facility about ten miles south of San Esteban. They would pull their vehicle into the jungle and then go by foot to the facility. Before going on their trip, Sam was going to talk to the local tourist bureau to see if he could find out whether there were military checkpoints in that area. He would go in as a camper needing directions. The CIA had sent campers to the area about a year before when routine satellite surveillance had noticed large ground scars in the area. Sam and Rico received a complete briefing from the Agency on the area before leaving the Navy ship to pick up the Vagabond, but Sam wanted to make sure there was no new information.

Sam walked into the city looking for the tourist information center. The day was clear and warm. He strolled toward the tourist center, which was in the Plaza Bolivar near the marina. He entered the tourist center and walked up to a desk where an attractive young woman was organizing some brochures. She looked up and asked in Spanish, "Hello, may I help you?"

Sam replied in Spanish, "Yes, my friend and I are thinking about going camping in the mountains near San Esteban. Do you have any information about that area?"

The woman's expression went from pleasant to serious, "Yes, but you have to be careful there. There are some government facilities under construction and parts of the area are prohibited. However, there are some very nice areas for campers."

Sam pretended to be puzzled by her cautious reply. "I did not know that. I had a friend who camped there several years ago, and he told me it was a very pretty place to explore."

She nodded and said, "Well, there have been some changes. There are oil and mineral explorations going on there, and the government has made some areas prohibited due to the dangerous equipment being used. But you don't have to worry, there are many areas you can camp and explore. I have a map of them and you may have it. Would you like to see it?"

Sam smiled, "I would indeed. My friend and I only have a few days, and it will be very helpful if we have such assistance."

The woman opened a topographic map of the area and began to show him where the best camping area would be. She also indicated where the prohibited area started. She suggested staying well away from those areas.

Sam asked, "We will be driving a vehicle up to the area. Is there a safe area to leave it while we go into the camping places?"

She thought for a while. "I have a friend who lives in the town. He would probably watch your vehicle for a slight fee."

Sam nodded in agreement. "If you would contact him and let me know what he would require, I think that would work very well. I have a cell phone you can call me on." The woman wrote down his number and gave him the map.

Sam walked down the street to a car rental agency. He asked the agent behind the counter if the agency had any four-wheel-drive vehicles. The man asked where he would be going. Roger explained what he and Rico wanted to do.

The agent replied, "The roads to San Esteban are not that difficult and the government is upgrading them. I have a Subaru that would fit your needs. I will have to have it brought from Caracas this evening, but you can pick it up tomorrow morning."

Sam agreed to his suggestion and filled out the rental papers. He had a Spanish driving license and an international license, which the agent readily accepted. His credit card had been issued in Barcelona. All of his papers were in order.

As he returned to the boat, he stopped by the marina office and explained to the manager about their plans. He made sure the manager would keep an eye on their boat. He boarded the boat and went down into the cabin where Rico had been getting their equipment packed.

"It's all arranged, Rico," he said.

Rico nodded. "I've packed our equipment and the two things from the overhead."

He meant the silenced Walther PPKs. They didn't think they would need them, and there was the risk they might be stopped.

It was a close call, but they both felt naked without some sort of protection. Not only against a military or police stoppage, but also any local who might think they could rip off two rich tourists.

That evening they received a message from their ship; the shipping containers had been loaded on trucks and appeared to be ready to leave in the morning. Things were getting interesting.

The next morning they picked up the vehicle, loaded their camping equipment and set off. It would not be a long drive, only about eight miles from the city, but there was a bit of traffic, and the streets were narrow at times where construction was going on. They came up behind the convoy of the shipping containers and had to stop at an intersection. There was a military policeman controlling traffic. After about a half hour, they were allowed to proceed. Rico was driving. "I don't think we'll have any problem knowing where they're going."

Sam smiled in return. "It'll make it a lot easier to see what's going on if we can see them unloading."

As they drove along, there was a bit of work going on the road, widening it and improving the paving. There was obviously some need to do this as they could see where the large trucks had broken down some of the sides of the street. "There must be some pressure to get something going. They didn't get the road in order before bringing whatever is in those containers on this," Sam observed. Rico replied, "I think we'll be getting there just in time for some interesting activities."

Their pre-operational planning on the Navy ship had included development of a visual fly-around using computer-generated graphics and the most recent drone imagery. For a campsite they had settled on a ridge looking across a valley into the new facility. They brought a high-resolution camera and lens to take any pictures of the activity in the compound.

They found the house of the man who had agreed to watch their car. The man came out in front and pointed to a spot next to the house. The man told them he was the cousin of the woman in the tourist agency. After they had chatted for a while, the man told them with some seriousness, "Be sure not to go too near where the map shows the prohibited area. There are military there who will not hesitate to rough you up or maybe even shoot. One of the men in town accidently went into the area, and they arrested him and accused him of being a spy. He was lucky they only knocked him around a little."

Sam and Rico thanked him for the advice and began their hike. They figured they had about five miles to go along the highway before they would go into the jungle. It was late morning and the sun was high, the temperature in the high eighties. It had been hotter nearer the port, but cooled down a bit as they climbed into the mountains. Still, with their backpacks it was going to be a warm hike.

Staying off the road, they managed to reach a point where they knew they had to get back into the jungle to stay unobserved. Their GPS allowed them to navigate through the jungle, and they tried to stay along a ridge going south as they ascended the mountain.

The jungle consisted of high trees and some undergrowth. The going was not difficult, but required pushing through the underbrush at some points and climbing up steep slopes. Birds called to each other as they hiked.

At one point they came out onto a ledge and could see across the valley to the new facility about three miles away. The Venezuelans had leveled a portion of the mountainside and established a large area capable of storing the containers outside. A very large warehouse had been built with a large sliding door at one side, capable of allowing one of the containers to be moved inside completely. They could see the line of trucks with the containers wending their way up the mountainside toward the facility.

The entire facility appeared to be about a half mile square on each side. The mountainside facing them had been cut into and there appeared to be three tunnels running into it. They would have to go on about another two miles south in order to be in the best place for observation. They continued their hike. The terrain was difficult because there were many small streams going down the mountainside, ravines and heavy vegetation.

Rico observed, "It's good this is so difficult. No one would think anyone would come this way."

"I agree. I think we have about another hour, and then we need to set up camp," Sam answered.

Rico nodded and they continued on their way. About 4:00 they entered a clearing, a large rock area about 100 feet across. No trees or underbrush could grow there. They backed off into the jungle in order to not be visible to the facility. They took off their backpacks and began to organize their equipment.

Rico contacted the ship and told them where they were and what they were planning. He walked into the clearing, and the ship reported they had them in view. They settled down for a quick meal and talked about how best to perform their activities. As dusk fell, a small rainstorm passed through. They covered their equipment with tarps and waited, hoping it would pass. The ship told them the cloud was moving eastward and would leave them shortly. As predicted, the rain stopped and the stars came out. The night was clear.

They both slept until about 2:00 a.m. Rico uncovered the small aircraft, which would fly across the valley and end up as a covert camera and sensor. The aircraft, Vulture, looked very much like a large bird. It had an electric motor to assure silence and wings long enough to carry it the distance to the facility. The propeller was mounted on a pod on the top of the wing.

Rico set up a low-light video camera on a tripod. The camera was connected to a set of what appeared to be eyeglasses, but which was really a video screen projector. Sam would monitor the facility with this.

Rico put on another set of glasses, which was connected to two small low-light-level cameras on the Vulture. This would enable him to fly the aircraft as if he were in it. His altitude above the ground and speed, as well as what was in front of him was also displayed to him. On the belly of the Vulture was the payload camera and sensor system.

Rico started the engine on the craft, checked out that it was working properly, and launched it. Using the small control-box joystick, he flew it in ever-higher circles until he was satisfied it was working properly. He steered it toward the facility.

Sam, using the camera on the tripod, said to him, "Rico, there is minimal activity at the facility. I see one guard at the entrance in a shack. It looks like the best place to set up the Vulture is on that light tower toward the mountain."

Rico answered, "I see it. I think I can fly up to it and hover. Then I can go vertical and attach it." The Vulture was capable of hovering vertically with its propeller acting as a helicopter blade. Rico was flying around the tower looking for a good surface, either vertical or horizontal.

Finally he saw a small flat plate on the side of the tower. He maneuvered the Vulture so it was vertical with the propeller away from the plate. He sent its belly right at the plate. There was a very sticky substance on the payload. It stuck to the plate. The Vulture hung there for a moment, and then Rico released the payload, allowing the Vulture to fly away.

"It's on." He said. He then flew the craft around the tower and looked at the payload. "I think it's set." He looked at a display in the eyepiece. "The transmitter is on and working. Check with the ship to see if they are receiving."

Rico then flew the craft around the facility, keeping it out of the lighted area. The video images were being transmitted to a relay to the overhead drone. Finally, Rico said, "It's getting low on power. I'll bring it back now."

"Roger," answered Sam. "I don't see any evidence anyone noticed anything. The ship is receiving."

Rico brought the Vulture back to the clearing, stood it on its nose, and brought it down until he could grab the tail. He then shut of the motor and retrieved the craft. "Mission accomplished," he said with some relief.

Sam nodded. "Let's get packed up and get out of here." They would take all their surveillance gear and bury it on their way back. They wanted nothing left to indicate they had any intelligence mission going on. The only anomaly would be their guns if they were stopped. They figured they would ditch them, too, if they saw anything unusual. So far there was no indication anyone had any interest in what they were doing. This was good. Their cover was working.

# Chapter 5

Clifton Burton Jamesway III floated out of White House. Not only was the evening cool for a Washington summer, but also he had just had his access briefing to the most secret activity in the White House

The day had gone well and that was why Burton was floating as he walked to his car in the White House parking lot. Not only was he now somebody, and on his way for a career in high-level politics, but also he had a date with Carlita. He had met Carlita in a Georgetown bar. She told him she was in the US as a student at George Washington University. She was beautiful, sensuous, fun, and best of all she thought he was really neat. Burton had to admit he was not the best looking guy—only 5'7", a little overweight and his ears stuck out a bit too much, but on the whole he was a good catch. He had thick hair and kept himself well-groomed. He was a good conversationalist. Not that Carlita was marriage material: perhaps a long-term mistress. His father had a mistress, and Burton understood. His father explained it to him: men had more sexual drive than a lot of the women in their circle; you needed someone to fill those needs. Marriage was for a family and continuing the line.

As he drove out of the parking lot, a man in another car followed him. When Shamika was forced to sign up Burton, she had checked the box: CLOSE WATCH. This meant Burton would be scrutinized regarding his activities for the next month by a special section of the Secret Service. White House employees were routinely watched at random, but when someone was given special access to something as sensitive as BREAKDOWN, there was a special review. There had been an extensive background investigation before he was allowed into the White House staff, and he had a polygraph, but too often things slipped through the cracks. There were not going to be any cracks if Shamika had anything to do with it. She had serious concerns about Burton.

Burton actually met Carlita only recently and did not put her name down on the security forms as someone he knew. He had already submitted them, and thought it a bit silly to have to add someone he just met. By the time everything came through, he was having regular sex with her. But it was not serious, so why make any waves?

He drove home to his townhouse in Georgetown his father had purchased for him as a graduation present. Furnished by a decorator his mother knew, it was a great place for impressing people. He was supposed to meet Carlita at a restaurant in Georgetown, and then they were going bar crawling. He showered and changed into something less formal than his tailored suit he wore to work. Burton was eager to see Carlita. He felt like James Bond.

He arrived at the restaurant in his BMW and let the boy park the car. Carlita was waiting for him in the entrance. Her small trim figure turned him on immediately. She had large breasts and luscious hips. Her long dark hair fell over her shoulders, and she had a way of flipping it and looking at him sideways taking his breath away. She came up to him and gave him a deep kiss. He could see other men in the restaurant looking at him and her. They could wish all they wanted. He was her man.

They ordered drinks and dinner. After a desert of flan and coffee, they decided to go down the street for an after-dinner drink. Burton ordered a Lafroigh. Carlita ordered a Black Russian and sipped it. "Burton, you are such an attractive man. I am so proud to be with you. How did your day go? Were you successful in getting your new appointment?"

Burton wiggled on his bar stool; he was so excited to tell her of his new job. "Not only did I get the job; I was promoted to a Deputy Director. And, I learned about some really secret stuff. I'm on my way. I showed that black bitch who was who. My father is too important for her to stand in my way."

Carlita's eyes grew wide. "That is great news. You are too much a man for any woman to hold you back." She sat for a while looking up at him with admiration. "I tell you what, Burton; we need to go back to your place so I can give you a reward for your news."

Burton grinned. "I think I know what kind of reward I need, too." They left, and Burton gave the valet the ticket. Carlita was all over him as they drove to his townhouse.

The couple who had been sitting near them left as they covertly watched them. The man asked the woman. "Did we get the entire conversation?"

"Yes, and I got pictures of her. I'll send them to the Center over the Net. I also put the RFAID (Radio Frequency Identification Device) on her dress when I went to the Ladies. It'll also transmit whatever they say. The Center can copy and track her."

They followed Burton and Carlita to the after-dinner bar and waited until they left. "I'll let Fred know they're going back to his place," the man said. "I think we can head on home for the evening."

Depending on the device design, an RFAID, the latest in surveillance technology, was basically a micro-computer and transmitter of limited range (1-2 miles) with a one-week battery. It could be programmed for whatever a mission needed and was approximately the size of a thick postage stamp.

The next morning a black couple sat in a Lincoln Navigator down from Burton's townhouse. A police car came slowly up the block. The officer looked curiously at the couple. The man in the Navigator raised his left hand and signaled 5, 5, and 2: the daily code notifying the officer they were a law enforcement activity. It changed each day. The officer nodded and drove on.

James and Helitia were Secret Service agents assigned to observe Burton's activities. There was already a great deal of concern in the Secret Service based on Burton's meeting with Carlita the night before, especially since they had no idea who she was.

Burton's garage door opened and his BMW drove out with Burton and Carlita. She was dressed in the same dress as the previous evening. He was dressed for work. The couple followed him as he drove her to an apartment house near George Washington University. Carlita got out of the BMW and walked into the apartment house.

"Let's see if she stays." James said to Helitia.

"She'll probably shower and go see someone," Helitia replied.

They waited for about an hour. Carlita came out and walked down the street toward the Foggy Bottom Metro station. "I'll follow her." Helitia said. "It looks like she's going to the Metro. I'll let you know where she's going. You can drive there. We'll rejoin when we can."

He nodded. "I'll drive slowly and let you off at the Metro."

They followed Carlita, and it became obvious she was going to the Metro station. Helitia got out and began following Carlita.

James found a place to park the SUV temporarily. Ten minutes later he looked at a display on the dash; he received a text mail, "Orange (Line)."

About twenty minutes later the display read, "At MC (Metro Center), RL (Red Line) to SG (Shady Grove)." He now knew where to head: Connecticut Avenue. He drove slowly up Connecticut waiting for the next text. In a half hour the display read, "Cleveland Park". He knew where to wait and drove quickly there.

He saw his partner coming out of the station with Carlita behind her. A good tailing trick was not to always be behind. His partner got into the car, and they began tailing Carlita.

Carlita walked to a Starbucks and went inside to the counter. She ordered a coffee. The two in the Navigator parked down the street and casually walked to the Starbucks. They held hands as they walked in. Carlita had taken a seat at a table outside in front of the coffee shop. The surveillance couple bought coffees and sat inside where they could see what developed. Carlita was texting as she sat. Within ten minutes a man walked into the store and bought a coffee and went outside and sat with Carlita.

Carlita and the man chatted for a while, and paid no attention as they were photographed with a pen-sized camera. They began talking intensely. The surveillance couple got up and walked out of the shop. Carlita and the man didn't notice James had stuck something looking like chewing gum under the railing next to their table.

James and Helitia went across the street as Helitia began listening on her phone. "Okay?" James asked her. She nodded. They stood in a doorway for the next half-hour listening.

Carlita and the man stood up, and left in separate directions. The couple across the street went to their car and began following Carlita's contact as he walked down the street. The contact seemed unconcerned about any possibility of surveillance. He walked for two blocks and went into an apartment house.

The couple sat in the Navigator. "What did you hear?" James asked Helitia.

She shook her head slowly, "It's not good. Carlita told him Burton just got a new job in the White House as a Deputy Director of some secret program. Also Burton was briefed on an operation going on in Venezuela to find ICBMs: there were two guys on a sailboat sneaking in there. She said he told her all kinds of details. Carlita said Burton is a pompous idiot and she was finding it hard to deal with him. The man reminded her of their deal—I got no details about that—but Carlita said 'I know.' He told her she needed to continue her relationship with Burton for a while until they knew where it might go. About then they left."

James shook his head slowly. "What a fuck-up this is. We need to find out who Carlita's contact is. Send the pictures to Center and let's see if there are any recognition matches."

The woman inserted the pen video camera into the dashboard. She pressed several buttons on the dash. "It's sent," she said. She dialed a number and began talking to someone. "Yeah, can you look for any match on the guy? It looks like he lives in an apartment house on Connecticut, 3726." She listened for a while and turned to her partner. "They can give us a list of everyone who lives there." She listened again. "They have a facial match from Homeland Security. He lives at the address we gave them. The guy is an employee of the Iranian Interests Section at the Pakistan Embassy. He's not a protected diplomat, supposedly works in the kitchen—Jabir Sharzad, supposedly from Pakistan. He's here on a work permit. They want us to stick with him. See if he comes out, where he goes."

Her partner nodded, "We need to type up what you just told me and send it in."

She began typing on an iPad. "I think I'll give Burton a code name. How about Dickhead?"

He looked at her with a wry smile. "It fits."

**********

At the Secret Service control center in the White House basement, the senior watch officer was calling his superior. "Sir, we have a real problem. Could you come down right away? Yes sir, it's a real problem. I need you to decide what to do."

Ten minutes later his superior came into the center. "What's up, William?"

"Well, Jack, here it is." The senior watch officer explained what information they had collected over the previous twenty-four hours.

His superior shook his head in disbelief. "We've got to tell Shamika immediately. I don't know anything about what mission they may be working on, but this is serious. I'll call her."

Shamika responded by telling Jack to come down to her office. Jack had limited access to the Group center. He knew of its existence and generally what its mission was, but was not allowed access to its on-going operations.

This was necessary compartmentation for security reasons. Jack pressed a button on the wall next to the face recognition device. Shamika opened the door and brought him into her office. She closed the door, "What's up, Jack? It must be serious for you to be this concerned."

Jack looked at her grimly. "Shamika, do you have a mission in Venezuela going on?"

Shamika looked stunned. "How do you know about that?"

Jack explained to her the results of their Close Watch operation.

Shamika shook her head. "I knew that snotty son-of-a-bitch was an idiot, but I had no idea how stupid he is. What should I do about him?" She was concerned if they acted too fast, they might not have enough information to arrest him or prosecute him. Next, was what to do for her people, Sam and Rico, in-country.

Jack asked, "Where is Jamesway now?"

Shamika thought for a minute. "He took the afternoon off. Said something about going over to Annapolis to eat crabs."

Jack considered this. "Don't worry about the legal situation. We need to get him under control. I'll have the police pick him up." Burton's car was registered with the White House parking lot. It wouldn't be hard to find him.

Shamika thanked Jack as he left, and turned to go into the Control Room. She had a lot of work to do. Two of her people were in immediate danger.

**********

Burton and Carlita were returning on Route 50 from Annapolis after a crab-eating feast. They were both enjoying their day, Burton because of Carlita's adoration, and Carlita because she was coming nearer to getting her fake documents that would let her go from an illegal immigrant to one appearing to be legal.

She knew Jabir could get her something to keep the police off her. All she had to do was keep Burton happy and get him to keep telling her what he was doing in the White House. She really didn't understand much of what he told her, but she had no problem remembering what he told her and telling it to Jabir. She also was beginning to work on Jabir. It wouldn't be long before she got him to have sex with her. Then she could get him to do whatever she wanted.

The BMW M5 roared down the road. Burton had set his cruise control because he knew how easy it was to exceed the speed limit, and the cops patrolled Route 50 regularly looking for speeders. A cop car came up in his rearview mirror and began flashing its lights. Burton was puzzled; he hadn't been speeding. He slowed down and moved off the highway to the roadside.

Carlita was in a panic, "What do you think he wants? You weren't speeding were you?"

"No Carlita, maybe I have something wrong with the car, a tail light out or something." Burton was very confident that when the cop found out who he was, he would get an apology.

The policeman walked up, and Burton opened his window. The policeman asked, "Please give me your license and registration, sir."

Burton reached in his wallet and handed the license. "My registration is in the glove compartment. Just a moment, officer." Carlita sat still, tense as a stone figure.

The officer looked at Burton's license, "Are you Clifton Burton Jamesway?" he asked.

"Yes officer." Burton was getting annoyed. What was this about? He handed the officer his registration. As he did so, another patrol car pulled up behind the first. Two more officers joined the first. One went to Carlita's side.

The first turned to the other two and said, "This is Jamesway." He turned back to Burton and said, "Sir, I have to ask you to step out of the vehicle."

Burton looked in disbelief. "What? What is this about?"

The officer repeated his request. Burton sighed and opened the door and stepped out.

"Sir, do you have any weapons on you, knife or gun?"

Burton frowned, "Weapons? No!" This was becoming crazy.

"Sir, you will have to come with me. Your lady friend must come too."

"Am I under arrest?" Burton asked.

The officer looked at him seriously. "Yes, please turn and put your hands behind you."

The officer looked through the BMW window and said to Carlita, "Miss, you must get out of the car, too. Please show the officer some identification."

Carlita trembled as she opened the door. She fumbled in her purse and produced a driver's license.

The other officer looked at it and her. "Are you Carlita Meraz?" She nodded. "You are under arrest. Please put your hands behind you." She began to cry.

, "What are the charges?" Burton raged. "What am I being arrested for?"

The first officer looked at him with a flinty expression. "Sir, it is a national security matter. You will be taken to our station down the road. You will be turned over to the FBI there. I cannot tell you anything further. You will have to take up your concerns with them."

Burton blanched. National security? He *was* national security. He was one of the most senior men in national security. This was all nonsense. The officers put him in one car and Carlita into the other. The third officer got into Burton's BMW. They all drove off.

**********

Shamika went into the Group control room to the Mission Director. "Jennifer, where are Sam and Rico now?"

The Mission Director looked at her. "Just returning from the facility near Puerto Cabello. They should be on the boat in about a half hour."

"Where is the drone now? Can we see the boat?" Shamika asked.

The MD looked at a display showing where the drone was. Its position was overlaid on a map similar to Google Maps. "It was over the area they were operating in. I can move it to take a close look at the boat." She entered some commands on her console and moved a joystick. On the display a circle appeared showing what area the video camera was covering. On a large high-resolution screen in front of them they could see the boat and the marina.

"Any sign of interest in the boat?" Shamika asked. There were four other people sitting at consoles in the room. The MD was on a higher platform, the other four below her. On each position below her were small signs: Video, Communications, Threat, and Technical Status.

The MD spoke into a headset microphone, "Any sign of unusual interest in the boat, the guys, anything? Police activity, military?" Each of the positions began scanning their consoles.

One-by-one they answered, "Negative."

Shamika put on a headset. "I need to contact Sam and Rico."

The MD nodded, and spoke into her headset as she touched her screen. . "You're on."

# Chapter 6

Sam and Rico were driving into Puerto Cabello when they both received a beep in their headphone signaling a priority communication. It was the mission director in the White House. This was very unusual. Their communications had been only with their team on the Navy ship.

"Sam, Rico, this is Shamika. We have just learned your operation may be blown. You need to get out of there immediately. We don't see any signs of activity with the police or military, but we are concerned. Get the boat going and head out to sea. We will arrange a pick-up at sea. You are authorized to scuttle the boat when you get far enough out. Any questions?"

Sam and Rico looked at each other in amazement. They had never had any communication like this in the ten years they had been assigned to the Group.

Sam answered, "This is Sam, no questions now. We're a few minutes from the marina. We'll get the boat ready and leave. We'll tell the marina manager we're going out for a few hours. It's getting near dusk and he might think it odd. At any rate we will get going. We'll stay in contact and see if we have anything else. Sam out."

Sam turned to Rico as they pulled into the marina parking lot. "I'll go tell the marina manager we're going out for a few hours. You get the boat ready."

Rico nodded. "Right."

Sam walked into the manager's office. "Hello, Emilio. We came back a little early. We're going to take the boat out for an evening sail. I'm going to leave my rental SUV in the lot overnight. Is that okay?"

Emilio looked up from his desk where he had been getting ready to leave for the day, "Hello. How did your camping trip go?"

Sam winced. "We got a little too much rain. So we decided to come back and take the boat out. At least if it rains, we can keep dry." He smiled.

Emilio nodded. "I agree. You can leave the SUV here overnight. Have a good sail."

Sam thanked him. He had looked closely at Emilio and saw no indication he was nervous or edgy.

Sam went quickly back to the boat where Rico had gotten the motor started and was coiling lines and getting ready to cast off.

Rico looked up from the bow of the boat. "We're ready to go. Any sign of trouble?"

"I didn't see anything unusual. Let's go." Sam jumped on the boat with the stern line in his hand and went to the cockpit. He put the boat in gear and began to move slowly out of the slip.

Rico came to the rear and looked at the shore as they motored out to sea. "I don't see anything going on."

Sam said over his shoulder, "Let's hope it stays that way. I think we should get our scuba gear ready. We can be ready to go over the side if there is any trouble. Set the charges to be ready with the trigger in the cockpit here." He indicated a place next to the wheel.

Rico was looking at the GPS display in the cockpit. "We make about seven to eight knots. If we can get about four hours out, we should be well outside of the Venezuela territorial limits. I'll contact our team and let them know what we're planning."

"Good, get your gear on and relieve me and I'll get mine on."

Rico went down into the cabin and radioed the Navy ship. Their team responded, and said they were proceeding immediately to just outside the territorial limits. They would arrive there in about two hours. They were going to put a large inflatable dinghy overboard to pick them up in. The dinghy, called a RIB, was about thirty feet long, had a hard bottom and two large outboard motors, and was capable of speeds in excess of forty knots. It was a standard special operations piece of equipment. Rico signed out and got his wetsuit on. He lifted the two sets of tanks through the hatch leading to the cockpit and put them to the side. The sea was calm and quiet. They were making good time, their wake phosphorescent behind them.

Rico said to Sam, "If we weren't in the shit we are, it would be a nice night for a cruise."

Sam nodded glumly, "I sure would like to know what the hell is going on." Sam handed the wheel to Rico.

Rico looked at the GPS display. "We're making about eight knots. We should be at the limit in about ninety minutes."

Sam went down into the cabin and put his wetsuit on. Their plan was to initiate the charges to sink the boat, giving them five minutes to get off the boat and well away. Once the charges went off, the boat would sink in minutes. They would swim for about a mile and then surface. By then their team should be in place to pick them up. Assuming the Venezuelans hadn't gotten onto them yet, there would be no sign they had ever existed.

Every fifteen minutes Sam went down into the cabin and contacted their team with their progress. The team was following their progress using a VLPI transponder on the boat. The drone was using its low-light-level and IR cameras to monitor the port area.

They were about ten miles from the coast when they received an emergency communication from the team. A Venezuelan naval patrol boat had left its dock in Puerto Cabello and there were what appeared to be military vehicles at the marina. The patrol boat could be on them in less than twenty minutes.

Rico pushed the throttle to its maximum. Sam had set up the switch for the charges.

Sam put on his scuba tanks. "Rico put your tanks on. I'll handle the boat."

Rico gave Sam the wheel and began to put on his tanks. He took out some night-vision goggles attached to a set of binoculars. "Shit, I can see a boat out there and it's coming fast." He turned to the GPS display.

"We're almost at the territorial limit." He picked up a hand microphone attached to the console at the helm. "HQ, we can see their boat. How close are you?"

The immediate answer came, "We are a half hour away, but we put the RIB out and they should be there in less than that. You should be very near the territorial limits. Do what you have to do. We can monitor you once you are in the water."

Rico turned to Sam, "We need to get out of here, ASAP."

"Right," Sam answered. The Venezuelan boat was now about 500 yards away. Suddenly a stream of tracers was fired across the bow of the Vagabond. "Shit, they mean business," Sam yelled. "Let's get overboard."

"I'll set the charge once you're over," Rico yelled.

More tracers shot across the bow as the ship drew nearer. Sam set the boat on autopilot, and sat on the side of the boat and prepared to fall backward into the water. Rico leaned down to switch on the charge timer. Sam fell backward, and as Rico straightened up to follow him, the Venezuelan boat raked the Vagabond from bow to stern. Chunks of fiberglass were ripped off and the mast was hit and began to fall. Sam was in the water looking for Rico, but Rico had not gotten to the rail yet. He was trying to duck the bullets.

There was a tremendous explosion. One of the tracers had hit Rico's tank. Rico's body was blown into pieces, over the side and into the water. He hit next to Sam and his body began to sink into the deep. His head was a bloody pulp. Rico was dead.

Sam realized he had to leave his partner of ten years. He had never left anyone, but he had no choice if he wanted to live. He put his regulator in his mouth and dove deeply.

He swam for about five minutes when he felt the scuttling charges go off in the Vagabond. He kept swimming. He didn't know if they realized there was anyone in the water or not, but he wasn't going to risk finding out. His underwater inertial guide kept him going north toward the territorial limit.

As he swam he thought about Rico, the friend he had the longest while in the Group. Because of the variety of missions they performed, teams were formed and dissolved, but Rico and Sam had been different. Because of their skill combination, they had been on several missions together. Sam got to know Rico well. He was married to a beautiful woman, Connie, and had two children. They lived in a nice house in Panama City. Sam had often visited the family and thought of himself as part of them. He couldn't imagine telling Connie about Rico's death. He swam on with mixed feelings. After about an hour, he slowly came to the surface. He didn't think the Venezuelans had figured out he was in the water.

He looked around. In his ear he heard, "I see you Sam, I'll be there in a minute." Sam heard the sound of a muted outboard, and within seconds the RIB pulled up beside him. Two sets of arms pulled him into the boat.

"Rico's dead. They hit his tank with a tracer and blew him to pieces," Sam told the two holding him. The RIB turned and sped away. Sam sat on the side of the boat, stunned.

---

This was the worst operation he had ever been on. In ten years they had never lost a man. They had all been shot, stabbed, or had broken bones, but never had an operation been blown and someone killed. *Someone should pay*, Sam thought.

# Chapter 7

Two days later Sam was back in Florida at Hurlburt sitting on the sofa with his feet on the coffee table in his room with the door open. He was still stunned by the failure of the operation. No one had said very much once he was back on the ship. They had returned to the Florida coast, and he and the team were flown by helicopter back to the base. The Group 5 commander, Heck Knowling told him to get a night's sleep, and he would debrief him in the morning.

As Sam sat running the events through his head, Heck knocked on the door frame. "Mind if I come in?" he asked.

Sam looked up, "Hey, how's it going Heck?" Sam liked Heck a lot. Heck had recruited him for the Group, and they had formed a friendship over ten years.

Heck closed the door and sat in a chair opposite Sam.

Sam sat up. "Heck, I have racked my brain to figure out what Rico and I did to blow the mission. I can't believe we did anything."

Heck looked at Sam, "No, no, no Sam. You guys didn't do anything. The mission was blown in Washington. We had a guy who leaked the mission to the Iranians. You guys pulled off a perfect mission.

" In fact the sensors you emplaced haven't been discovered yet. We've gotten confirmation there are ballistic missiles in the compound. "

"You were screwed by a guy who couldn't disconnect his dick from his mouth. He blabbed to a girlfriend who was working for Iranian security."

Sam's mouth fell open. He shook his head. "What? What the fuck? You mean we had a spy?"

"Not quite a spy—a guy who got cleared through political connections, who never should have been given access. Don't worry about him. He's in jail and probably will be there for the rest of his life."

Actually Burton was in a special jail where he could not contact anyone. The FBI was trying to figure out what to do with him. His knowledge of Group 5 made him very dangerous, plus they were afraid to put him on trial because of the possibility of exposure of the Group 5 operations. Nevertheless, Burton wasn't going anywhere for a long while.

"But Sam, I need to talk to you about something else," Heck went on. Sam looked at him with a frown. "Sam, I got a call from your brother while you were in Venezuela. I don't know how else to tell you this, but your mother and father were murdered in a home invasion in late July. You need to call your brother. He has all the details. I'm very sorry I have to tell you this on top of everything else. It makes me sick. I know how you must feel. Call your brother. I'll talk to you later."

Sam was in shock. He looked at Heck. "Okay, Heck. Thanks, I don't know what else to say." Heck walked out to give Sam some privacy. Sam pulled out his cell phone and called Roger.

Roger answered and, after greeting him, told him what he knew and that their parents were buried and the estate settled. Sam and Roger talked for about an hour as Sam got up to speed. Roger told Sam about the police file, and that he had scanned it in and would send an email to him with a PDF file attached. They agreed there wasn't anything for Sam to do. Roger suggested when Sam got settled, he might want to visit Roger and his family in Arizona. Sam said he would have to decide what he would be doing, and they hung up.

Sam sat on the couch and tried to digest what he had learned. He didn't know what he thought or what to do. All his training had not prepared him for such a terrible thing. Losing Rico was bad enough. While the team had never lost anyone, everyone on the team knew their operations always had the potential for grave events.

Later that day Sam logged onto his laptop and downloaded the police file. The file had mug shots of the three individuals who were suspects and detailed background information. Sam didn't know what to do with the file.

If the police couldn't arrest them, maybe they didn't really do the crime. He wasn't sure how capable the police were. He really hadn't been in the US for any length of time for the last twenty years.

He didn't know what the US culture was or what kind of society it was. If his parents, who lived a quiet life in a nice area, could be attacked like this, what the hell was going on?

Sam wasn't sure what he was going to do. He didn't want to go see his brother yet. He thought he might like to visit his parent's old house and see their graves. He was used to having something to do—a mission, an operation. He had nothing facing him. He really didn't have a home or base. He had lived the last twenty years overseas, either on a ship or on an operation. He had few personal possessions. What he had was in a storage locker in Panama City, and it wasn't much.

His brother told him his parents had left the two of them a great deal of money. This really didn't affect him; he had his own independent source of money. He also had his Navy paycheck. Money was not on his mind. He went for a ten-mile run hoping it would help him think. When he returned, he sat and read and reread the police file. Something bothered him; who were these guys?

He decided he had to call Rico's wife Connie. She had been visited by Heck and another member of the team, but Sam knew he had to see her and provide whatever comfort he could. After contacting her he borrowed a car and drove to Panama City to see Connie and her kids. Her sister from Texas was there along with several friends. Sam couldn't say much to her because of the security restrictions, but he did manage to tell her Rico hadn't suffered and what he was doing was very important. After a few hours he returned to the base.

At dinner time he decided to walk over to the chow hall. As he walked, he turned the problem of his parent's murders over and over in his mind. He stood in line next to another member of Group 5, Aloysius (Allo) Franklin. No one who compared Allo to the usual Group 5 teams would have included him. He was tall, gangly, and not very muscular. Allo was a member of the Group, but usually didn't go out on operations. He was a highly skilled research analyst and was used by the teams for obtaining information helping them in their operational plans. One of his main sources was the Internet. He was a master hacker and often was used to cause the targets a great deal of consternation. Sam thought for a moment as he filled a cup with ice. Allo was standing next to him with a tray and filling his cup with tea. "Allo, how are you doing these days?" Sam asked.

Allo looked at Sam sympathetically. "I'm doing fine. I'm sorry to hear about Rico. He was a good guy."

"Yeah, he was. Losing him that way was completely unnecessary. Say, Allo, I have something else going on. I'd like your opinion. Would you like to sit with me?"

Allo nodded. Not sure what was going on with Sam. He didn't know how Sam was reacting to Rico's death. They sat down, and after Sam told Allo about his parent's murder, he said, "I've got this police file, but I don't know what to do with it. I was wondering if you could look at it and see if you could dig up any more information about these three guys."

Allo nodded eagerly. "If I can help in any way, I will. Let me have the file and I'll take a look at what's there and see what else I might dig up."

They finished their meal and walked back to Sam's room. Allo lived off base in an apartment, but spent a lot of his time in the Group 5 area. He took the file from Sam and said he would go to his office in one of the other buildings and see what he could do.

**********

Allo entered the Group 5 headquarters and walked down to the secure part of the building in the complex. That portion was guarded and required a special clearance to enter. There was an operations center which brought in all sources of information, classified and unclassified. There were several large conference rooms, but most of the building consisted of office space for analysts. Depending on what mission was being planned, a team could be assembled to create the entire activity, from the skill set of the operatives, to the equipment and logistical support, to the intelligence data required. Sophisticated computer systems provided support for timeline development. There were links to the entire Internet and means to hack into any computer system in the world.

Once in his office Allo sat down in front of his computer and logged on. What he was about to do was against the rules, but he didn't care. Using the Group 5 computer system for personal use was forbidden, but Allo wanted to help Sam, who had been a good friend.

Many of the special ops types looked at Allo as a nerdy, non "guy." Allo was not a manly man. He dated and was straight, but appeared different to many of the operators.

Sam had always treated him well and often asked for his advice on how a mission could be accomplished. In fact on one operation, Sam had taken Allo along so he could do some mischief to a laptop.

Allo began to surf. His first task was to see what unclassified information he could find out about the three men in the file. Next, he would dig deeper and deeper. Where he went in cyberspace depended on what he found as he explored. This was something he excelled at. It was like a giant puzzle, and he was good at puzzles.

Allo spent about an hour looking at various government files containing personal information on individuals who had criminal, terrorist, or other connections putting them on a watch list. When he was satisfied he had downloaded all the information he could from the official sites, he stood up and walked out of the compound.

It was Friday afternoon and time to go home. He needed to use his personal computer equipment. Allo had one of the most extensive personal computer set-ups he was aware of. He had built all the equipment himself, and he was connected to an ultra-high-speed Internet service. He could sign onto the Internet and be completely untraceable. Much of what he learned personally he was able to bring into the Group 5 planning operations.

He worked over the weekend. As he delved into the backgrounds and information sources of the three individuals in the police report, he became more and more convinced the police weren't wrong about them.

He prepared a file of information for Sam and a summary of what he found.

********

Monday morning when he arrived at the compound, he went to Sam's room. Sam wasn't there, so he went to the headquarters building. The Marine NCO at the reception desk greeted him, "Hey, Allo, how's the week going so far?"

Allo smiled at her. "So far so good, Marylynn. Have you seen Sam Dancer this morning? I need to talk to him."

She smiled back. "Yeah, he's in with Heck. I think they're debriefing him on the mission."

"Do me a favor, please. Tell him I need to see him if he comes by. I'll be in my office," Allo answered.

"Will, do. Say, I have a problem with my computer at home. Could you maybe give me some help with it?" She was a bit taken with Allo and never gave up trying to get him to show some interest in her.

Allo had no problems with computers, but girls were a different thing. He wanted to help her, but wasn't sure how to deal with Marylynn. She was nice enough looking; maybe all she needed was some help. "Sure, I'll talk to you later about it." He quickly walked down the hall to the secure area.

An hour later Sam knocked on the door jamb of Allo's office. Allo looked up. "Come on in Sam. I've got some interesting stuff for you." As Sam came in, Allo looked at him seriously. "Shut the door."

Allo pulled a file folder out of a drawer in his desk. "Turns out there's a lot of stuff on those guys the police thought were the killers. They just don't have the access to information the way I do. The three guys, James William Burns, Lamont Mason, and Rafael Jesus Martinez, have a lot of baggage. I won't go into the backgrounds in the police file. As you know they are all career criminals, but currently they're living together and posing as former convicts who are trying to be normal citizens. What I found makes me a little skeptical." Allo paused for a minute as he took out some sheets of paper. "I also found a link to another guy.

"It took me a while, but I enjoy puzzles. First, I think they're part of a criminal enterprise directed by this man, Robert Kidd, also known as 'Doc'." He pointed to the picture of a man sitting at a desk. The man was obese and was smiling at the camera. "I got this picture off his website.

"Here's what I think is going on: Doc runs a company in South Philly called Collectables, Inc. He has a legitimate website. Ostensibly he buys and sells collectables. In fact I think he actually does have a legitimate business, but there is another side to what he does. If someone indicates to him they really want something badly, he finds out how badly they want it. He sends them to another site.

"This site is anonymous. It can't be traced to any owner. The server is somewhere overseas and maintained by someone I can't find. It is very well done, but I think Doc owns the site."

Sam was frowning in puzzlement. "Hang in there with me, Sam." Allo said.

"I'm not that Internet literate. Understand Allo, I've been living in a different world for the last twenty years. I know about the Internet, but some of its more intricate aspects lose me," Sam said with a rueful smile.

"No problem. I won't get too much into the geek stuff, but this is a really interesting activity going on here. I got on to Doc by first finding out if any of the three had an Internet account. One of them, Burns, does. Burns communicates a lot with Doc via email. Anyway, Doc uses this special site to serve very special customers. If someone wants an extremely valuable collectable—by extremely I mean over a half million and up—they put their order in with this special site. There are people who collect things and don't care where they come from, whether the item is obtained legally or illegally."

Allo paused for a moment. "Let's say you saw a coin at a coin show you really wanted, but it wasn't for sale. You might talk to the exhibitor and see if he was interested in selling it. You might try to develop a friendship or acquaintance.

"You might try to find out where they keep their collection. Many collectors of small things like coins either keep them in a safety deposit box or a safe at home. So, you identify what you want and maybe who has it on the special site. You indicate what you might be willing to pay for your collectable.

"There are at least two hundred individual accounts on the special site. I hacked into each one. Some have orders unfilled; some have orders filled. Once an order is filled, they are notified. They transfer money to an account in the Cayman Islands. When the money is deposited, the item is delivered to them. Delivery is done in many ways: normal mail, in person, or they pick it up somewhere, or whatever. It's all very circumspect and discrete.

"Let's say the item is in the Philadelphia area. Doc sends an email to Burns and tells him the rent is due—the three rent the house from Doc. Doc sends back: Let me know how you want it paid. Then the emails are encrypted. But I broke their code; it wasn't very complex. Doc gives Burns a name and address and what is wanted. Apparently, after that Burns goes out and figures out how to do the theft with his two buddies. One interesting one they did was steal a bunch of Mayan artifacts from Central America. The artifacts themselves were illegally imported into the US. Doc found out where they were stored and had the Burns bunch steal them for his customer. Of course the guy that imported them couldn't report the theft. That little caper was worth $1.5 million. Neat huh?

"I first searched police records in the Philadelphia area for any break-in crimes that seemed to just target something particular. Things like coins, artwork, collectables, manuscripts, you know, that kind of stuff. I then looked at the communications between Burns and Doc.

"I also went to the special site and looked for Philadelphia area requests. There were interesting correlations. Take a look at these."

Allo laid out several sheets of paper. On one sheet were emails from Doc to Burns, on another Burns to Doc. There was a list of wants, and a fourth sheet listed dates, burglaries, and any information relating to the crime. It was obviously from police reports.

Allo pointed to a request for a 1915-S Panama-Pacific $50 Gold coin. "These usually go for well over $100,000. There were only about 400 minted. Your father had four of them. They are rarely sold, and the ones your father had were in better condition than any that had been for sale in years. The individual said he would be willing to pay $1 million for them. Your father had just exhibited them at a Philadelphia coin show."

Sam stared at Allo and shuddered.

"There was an exchange of messages between Doc and Burns, which basically ended in an agreement. Burns would case your father's house and determine if it could be burgled. Doc determined somehow your dad stored his coins at home in a safe.

"Doc made clear there should no violence. Later there was a message from Burns who said he had cased the house, but he had no one who knew how to crack a safe. He suggested his team could capture the man and wife and terrorize them into opening the safe. They wouldn't hurt anyone, but Burns felt confident he could do the job. Doc agreed after a few more emails."

Sam looked at Allo. "You have proved they murdered my parents."

Allo shrugged. "Yeah, but I got all this illegally, and I'm sure the police couldn't use it. Most of it couldn't be recreated without all kinds of legal action, and by the time they got the authorization, the sites would disappear. I got some of this data from my government computer and some from my home. I could face prosecution. I just wanted to help you, Sam. At least it gives you closure. You know who did it. Maybe you could help the police.

"Another thing, it looks like this guy Doc has two other guys who do some of this work for him. I'm trying to find out about them and what is going on there."

Sam looked grim. "Allo, thanks for what you've done. I'll have to think about it. I won't let anyone know you were involved. I'll just have to see if there is a way the police could get to these guys. It looks like this guy Doc and his guys will continue their operation unless the police could run a sting or something."

Allo nodded. "There's something else I found." He pulled out another sheaf of papers. "The three guys seem to have their own criminal enterprise. They belong to another website dealing in porn sales, but porn sales of a particularly nasty type—snuff videos. I found they were advertising on a website saying they have unique videos. I hacked into one of their samples. It shows some girl being raped and strangled as she is raped. I don't think it's a fake. I think they really killed the girl.

"Again, Sam, I don't think I can use this as proof of anything. It's on an untraceable Internet site somewhere overseas. Any money they make is deposited in another account in the Caymans. I'm just telling you this to let you know what kind of people they are. I wish I could think of something to do, but so far I haven't come up with anything."

"Okay Allo, I understand. Look, I really appreciate what you've done. I realize the risks you've taken. If you want, I'll take the stuff and look at it and see if I can think of anything."

Allo handed him the file. "I'll poke around and see if I come up with anything else. Good luck."

Sam collected the file and returned to his room. His head was reeling with Allo's information.

Sam spent the next week coming up to speed on Group 5 activities. Heck had suggested Sam might want to spend some time in the headquarters and help them improve their mission planning and operations. Sam decided to make an appointment to have a talk with Heck.

Heck's admin assistant ushered him into Heck's office. "Would you like a coffee or water," she asked.

"No thanks, I'm good."

Heck gestured to a sofa for Sam to sit. Heck sat in one opposite him. There was a coffee table between them. Heck propped his feet on the table. "Well Sam, you've had an opportunity to see what we're doing. I hope you've found a place you'd like to help us in."

Sam considered what he was going to tell Heck and how to tell him. "Heck, I appreciate your interest in me and concern, but I've decided I'm going to retire from the Navy. I think it would be good for me to take some time off and just think about where I want to go with the rest of my life." Heck looked at him in surprise and started to speak.

"No, Heck let me continue. It's nothing about you or the organization. I've realized I've been in a different world since I joined the Navy when I was nineteen and the Group ten years ago. I'd like to see what the civilian world is like. I think I'd like to get my college degree my parents were always so eager for me to have. I also think I might like to try a different line of work, an EMT or maybe even a doctor." Sam took a deep breath and sat back and looked at Heck.

Heck pursed his lips and looked at Sam for a while. "You know, I understand what you're saying. I was prepared to do anything you wanted, and still am. I thought you might want to transfer to a civilian status, maybe with the Agency or Homeland Security. But, I can see you're in a different mind. That's okay. I will support you in whatever you want. Have you considered the money side of things? I know you'll get a pension from the Navy, but it's not much and the US economy is expensive."

Sam smiled at Heck. "I don't want to appear smug, but I have some personal investments that have ended up making me quite wealthy, and on top of them, my parents have left me independently wealthy.

"It's not the way I wanted to have them pass on their legacy, but I'm okay from a money situation. I guess, once I realized that, I began to think about what I wanted to do with the rest of my life. Rico's death only made me realize I could go on some mission and lose my life, and I haven't really experienced all life can provide. I don't even own a house, car, or much of anything. I've never really had time to have any long-term relationship. I think you know about Felicia. We never really had a close relationship, although we both thought we might. On top of everything else, I lose my parents before I could even say goodbye."

"I value your dedication and efforts to the Group," Heck said. "You have a lot of friends here who will be sad to see you leave, but I know everyone will understand the direction you wish to go in. If you ever want to come back in any capacity, you're welcome."

They chatted for a few more minutes, and got up and shook hands. Sam decided to go down to the personnel office to see what he had to do to put in his papers. As he walked down the corridor, he felt both sad and excited. This was going to be a new adventure unlike any he had in his life. He would be going into the America he really didn't know. It was almost like going overseas for the first time.

**********

Before he signed out there was a ceremony and large party to wish him well. Allo came up to him and suggested they get together the next day. Sam gave him a wry grin. "If I'm in any shape to talk to anyone, I will."

Allo said, "I'll make it later in the day. Let's make it in the NCO club about 3:00."

Sam nodded in agreement.

The next afternoon Allo was sitting at a table in the rear of the bar sipping a beer, his long legs sticking out from his chair. He had tied his hair back with a rubber band. For him this was dressing up. Sam came and ordered a soda water from the bar and walked to Allo's table. His usual bounce was subdued, and his face was pale. He had obviously had a good time the night before. "Hey, Sam, it looks like you enjoyed your goodbye party."

Sam pulled a chair back, set his drink down gingerly, and said quietly, "You don't have to yell, Allo."

Allo smiled. "I'll try to be quieter. I've been thinking about what we could do with the information we got. I might be able to give the police an anonymous tip about one of these events Doc plans with the Burns team."

Sam thought for a minute. "I would like to do something, but I also would like to go up to Philadelphia and check out things for myself. You know, see what the situation is like there and then I could suggest something to you, and we could be more effective."

Allo nodded. "Good idea. What sort of time frame are you thinking?"

"Well, I wanted to spend a few days in Fort Myers to see an old friend, and then I thought I'd go up to Philadelphia. I don't think there's any rush on this. Those goons seem to be operating as normal. I'd like to think through it before we do anything. If we act too quickly, they might be able to hide any trace of what they're doing. In the meantime you might want to check into their bank accounts. Can they be hacked?"

Allo thought on this for a minute. "Okay, I'll try to monitor what they're doing and keep you informed. The bank account angle might be fun. If I come up with anything, I'll let you know. What would be good is to be able to catch them in the middle of something."

They chatted for a while, finished their drinks, and then shook hands and left. Sam went out into the Florida fall sunshine, blinking as he went. He put on a baseball cap and sunglasses and walked to his rental car. He had never owned a car in his twenty-year career.

He wasn't sure what kind he wanted or exactly what he was going to do in the next month, but his first step was to go to Fort Meyers and begin thinking about a mission, a mission Allo didn't need to know about.

# Chapter 8

Sam was tired. He was tired of the whole overseas world. He had lived there, out of a sea bag, for almost twenty years. On top of everything the long drive from Panama City was made difficult because Hurricane Evelyn was heading up parallel to the Florida coast toward New Orleans and the entire drive from I-10 to I-75 south was nothing but pouring rain. He had driven it in one leg. It should have taken about eight hours, but ended up taking fourteen. A semi had jackknifed just outside of Sarasota. He decided to take 41 south, but that didn't improve things much. Everyone else took it too. Reflecting on his decision to do the drive with a hangover, he decided he needed some recuperating time. The reason he had decided on going to Fort Myers was he could sort of disappear from his previous life, and Fort Myers had stores with the equipment he would need.

He checked into the Holiday Inn at Ft. Myers Beach. He needed to get something to eat, shower, and tune out for a while. By the time he could lie down in bed it was 11:00 p.m. He lay in the bed and began to relax.

Half asleep, he reflected on his life. How did I get here? He remembered talking to his father about the world when he was in high school and taking a history course. The Desert Storm war was fresh in everyone's mind and people were speculating about the future of warfare and international relations.

He remembered a conversation with his father. "There just seems to be a lot of evil people in the world," Sam had said to his father. In school he was studying World War II and the rise of the Nazis. He was thinking about Saddam Hussein.

"You're right," his father replied. "There always has been and always will be. It's the way of the world. Each of us has to decide how we would like to live our lives and do it in a positive, constructive way."

Sam considered this. "I just think if we could eliminate some of them, the world might work a little better."

"Well, that's a hard thing to do. Figuring out who they are, where they are, and then being able to deal with them in a legal manner leaves you either a policeman or in the military," his father replied.

"I guess I'll just keep my options open. Being a policeman or soldier doesn't really appeal to me. I still want to go college and maybe study medicine like you."

His father, nodded. "Right now it's important to keep your grades up and be thinking about the future. You don't have to make any decisions for a while."

He began reviewing the last assignment in South America which ended with the death of his best friend, Rico. That had really hit him hard. He had worked with Rico for ten years. It was time to retire. The team had spent a month preparing, inserting, and then trying to get out. It hadn't worked out according to their plan. It worked out very poorly. Maybe things in the US had changed or were different from what he thought the US was. How could a traitor be allowed to have access to Group activities?

As usual on a mission, he could not be contacted. And then to return and be told his parents had been murdered—what was going on in the US? He had participated in dozens of missions where they killed really bad people. There was nothing about "bringing them to justice." The team *was* justice. The President had decided unilaterally the cockroaches they were after should be eliminated, and that was that. Now, he knew pretty certainly who had killed his parents, but was almost powerless to do something using the law. In fact, if he used the law, the scum might get off. At the least, they might live in a prison taking up space for the rest of their lives. When he talked to his brother, Roger had suggested he visit him and Sue in Sedona when Sam returned. He was not ready to face Roger.

Sam was stunned when he heard the news of his parents. He had not been home in two years, but was intending to surprise his parents for Christmas. They were not old or infirm; they were always there in his old home. How could this be? They were the only stability in his life.

While Heck was supportive of his decision to leave the service, Sam didn't think anyone knew where his mind was. Twenty years of the life was usually enough, especially all operational. Many former SEAL or Group operators segued into training or ops planning or even shore duty. This was especially true for a lot of the guys who got married and had families. Even so, many continued in operations. He wasn't sure he was as dedicated to the life as before. Things seemed to have gotten all turned around. Here, the US was wandering around the world, fixing the world when things were crazy at home.

Allo's computer data had triggered something in his head. Sam had years of training to takeout bad people. He had killed...he had to think for a minute...maybe fifty or more people, some in close combat.

As he lay in his motel bed, he thought back to the event that changed his life. He was in his senior high school year. It was Christmas. His father was telling him about a medical case he had worked on at the Philadelphia VA Medical Center. A young man had lost his left arm during a military operation somewhere. His father had invited the man to come to their home for Christmas. Sam and his brother, two years younger, were fascinated to meet this individual. Neither of them had any experience with the military.

The young man arrived in a cab, and the family welcomed him into their Christmas celebration. Sam and Roger questioned the young man, Dave, about his military experience. Dave told them he had grown up in a foster home and when he was eighteen had joined the Navy.

Dave had learned about a branch of the Navy, the SEALS. He decided to apply. He explained it was the toughest, most elite part of all the military services. He had been able to pass all their tests and became a SEAL. Sam and Roger asked him how he had lost his arm. "Just unlucky," Dave had answered. He said his team was on a mission, and one of the people they were working against had fired a shot shattering his arm and made the amputation to near his shoulder necessary. He said their father was helping to attach a prosthetic arm. They questioned him about what he was doing, and he explained most of the missions they were on were classified. He said the main thing the SEALs did was prevent bad things from happening. Often only a few people knew what they did. "Sometimes only the President and a few others," Dave said. "We try to prevent bad people from doing bad things." They questioned him about what tests he had to take. "We have to be very good swimmers. We learn how to handle lots of different guns and explosives. We learn to scuba dive, parachute, just about any skill the military needs."

Sam and Roger were entranced. They both were good swimmers and had competed in summer leagues. They were black belts in Tae Kwan Do. They wondered if they could do something like this. Dave told them they should concentrate on getting their college education. After they graduated, they could see if they could get into the SEALs. He explained while he was an enlisted man, being an officer got better pay and a little better lifestyle. He told them they would be good candidates.

The next day Sam and Roger talked about what they had heard. Their father listened as they talked. "The military can be a good career, but you should get your college behind you before doing anything," he advised. The boys decided they would just try to learn as much as they could.

They figured they were big enough and in good enough condition to be able to pass any SEAL test. Roger was a wrestler in high school, and Sam was on a power lifting team at the local gym. In fact they were both Sea Scouts. He and Roger had never played team sports; they liked individual sports where they could excel. Sam had always been exceptionally strong.

They had just never heard of the SEALs and had not even considered a career in the Navy. This was exciting. They had no doubts that after college, they could do this.

At this point their mother chimed in and said, "Just be careful, it sounds like these SEALs do a lot of dangerous things."

They could see she was supportive, but had misgivings. No one in either their father's or mother's family had ever had a military career. Their great grandfathers had worked on the home front in the Second World War, one as a steamfitter in a factory and the other as a fireman. Both had critical position deferments. One of their grandfathers had been in the Navy during the Viet Nam war; the other had been in college.

Sam liked the idea there was a part of the military dealing with correcting wrongs. The family attended the local Episcopal Church, but was not extremely religious.

Sam had always been concerned about the way people treated each other. If people were Christians, why did he see so much bullying and nasty behavior in high school? Because of his size and strength he was often able to step into a situation and calm people down. He just didn't like the way people acted. His father and mother explained a lot of people didn't have the environment he grew up in. They both agreed with him that many people didn't really behave as Christians. "They are Sunday Christians," his father summarized.

The whole remainder of the Christmas holiday Sam thought and rethought what he had learned. He researched the SEALs. He read several books. He became obsessed with the idea of being one. As the school year wound down, he began training to try to meet the physical requirements he had found on line. He told his father he needed to see if he could join up when he was eighteen. He could join without his parent's permission, but he wanted their blessing. He could see his father was not pleased, but after a long set of discussions, his father agreed to go with him to the recruiter when he graduated from high school. The rest was history. He joined up, passed every test the SEALs could throw at him, and he was a "made man".

His brother had followed the rigorous training Sam had to go through. Being two years younger than Sam, Roger decided he wasn't sure he wanted to follow Sam's career decision. Once Roger entered college, he had decided he wanted a different path in life.

Sam had spent most of his time overseas. After ten years in the service, he was invited to join the Group. Those next ten years turned out to be more confusing, dangerous, and demanding than he could ever have imagined.

He turned on his side in the motel bed and fell asleep. Enough history, he had to think about his next mission.

# Chapter 9

Sam's career with the SEALS had taken him into many situations where guns would be a disadvantage, either because of their noise or because of their bulk. Each mission was different. After about five years and several missions, he had become known as a specialist in "close-in ops". For whatever reason, he had a capability to observe and quietly infiltrate himself into places without alerting the enemy. His teammates began calling him Ghost Dancer. When a sentry needed to be taken out, he was selected. He had once killed a sentry and four men sleeping in a room, who were guarding a terrorist chief. None of them ever knew what hit them. The terrorist chief was so stunned he offered no resistance when the team spirited him away.

As the years went by, he removed many evil persons. His view of evil he figured he derived from his Protestant upbringing. He was not religious, but had accepted somewhere along the line there were certain things people should not do to other people: killing women and children, maiming people, killing in the name of a religion.

As far as he was concerned, the killing he had participated in was justified on the basis of what he knew the individual or terrorists had done to others. He never considered what he was doing as evil, more retribution for what evil men had done to others.

He sometimes wondered if he had lost a sense of moral value. The evil things he had witnessed committed by hundreds of enemies kept his head straight by focusing on the fact these missions were ordered by the United States in pursuing a national goal. He was trained to kill in many violent ways. He believed the US usually exhausts every possibility of peaceful resolution before it resorts to military or violent action. He thought: this fact is not often understood by US media.

Sam had just finished a mission in Somalia, when he had been in the SEALS for ten years. He and his team were relaxing in their special quarter's area on the amphibious assault ship *Bataan*. The mission was an especially rewarding one: terrorists were murdering refugees and the UN doctors and nurses trying to help the refugees. His team had been able to get the UN team out and settled and then return to the area where the terrorists were camped. They had wiped out the entire camp and been able to rescue some children who were being trained to be terrorists.

The SEAL team Commanding Officer requested he come to a room on the ship. The CO told Sam to sit down. There was an opportunity he would like Sam to consider. There was another man in the room

The man spoke, "I have a serious need for someone with your skills."

The speaker was a tall black man, wearing a golf shirt showing a very muscular torso. Sam had only met a few men with the "leadership demeanor" the man possessed. This man had been there and back.

"In order to find someone with your skills, I used several sources. I have talked to some of your previous CO's. I have reviewed your Navy file. You fit my needs."

The man continued, "I am the leader of a team of special operatives. We answer directly to the President of the United States. Every mission we perform is specifically authorized by the President. Our operations are all "denial missions." We are not traceable to the military, the US, or any country. I would like to know if you are interested in joining us."

Sam looked at the CO, who nodded as if to say "tell him what you think."

"Well," Sam began, "it certainly sounds interesting." He turned to the CO. "I don't want to leave the SEALS. I like belonging to the brotherhood."

The CO pursed his lips in thought. "I understand. I also know this unit is the most elite of all Special Forces this country has. Only a very few people know of its existence, and fewer are asked to join. Their operations are the most sensitive the country has. I was never asked, but I would have joined."

Sam thought for a moment. "Tell me more. What happens if I say yes?"

"You will be transferred out of the Navy on special assignment. They will carry you on a list of very few individuals kept in a safe in the Pentagon. As far as the official Navy and your friends know, you will have resigned from the Navy. You will retain your current rank.

If you are performing acceptably, you will be promoted with your peers or ahead of them, but no official record will be published. You will effectively disappear from the military. You cannot tell your family about this organization. You can tell them you have joined a company supplying special services to US armed forces. You aren't married, so that's not a problem. If at any time you wish to leave the organization, you will be returned to the Navy. They would then decide what to do with you. We have never had anyone leave.

"I'll tell you the reason I'm asking you. Our team is quite small and we select individuals based on their personalities, their experience base, and any unique skills they possess. We are in the planning stages of a mission requiring your skills of surveillance and close-in operations. The individual we usually rely on is not able to work with us anymore. Our time limit is short and the mission is one of the most critical facing the US today. We need you badly."

Sam considered what he had heard and made a snap decision. "I'll do it. The fact we work for the President directly is very intriguing. My personal commitment to my career is to do what the country wants me to do to ensure its survival. If this organization works to do this, and it needs me, I'm in."

The CO turned to Sam and said, "You will immediately be transferred. I will tell your team you have been put on special assignment. They will understand. You can go say goodbyes and get your things when you're finished here."

The CO left. The man opened a briefcase and pulled out a sheaf of papers. "I need you to read these and sign them. They will explain some of what we've talked about. I can't tell you a lot more right now. We're not in the right spaces."

Sam read the forms. They were standard classified access forms. If he disclosed anything to unauthorized personnel, he would be subject to severe legal actions. He had signed many forms similar to these. He signed them.

The man shook his hand. "Sam, my name is Hector Knowling. Call me Heck. Welcome aboard."

Sam shook his hand, bemused by the whole thing. He was also surprised. A special operations activity as secret as this appeared, and he had never run across it during the past ten years? That was impressive.

Sam had never collected many personal items. He had a footlocker of stuff on the ship, and a small storage locker in Norfolk, but that was it. After getting off the carrier via a helicopter to an airbase in Somalia with Heck, Sam found himself on a C-130 headed for somewhere else. He wasn't sure where.

Stopping in Israel for a change to a C-17, the next stop was Hurlburt Field in Florida. Sam wasn't surprised. He had been on several missions where they trained with Air Force people. There was a place on the base no one talked about. He was now to find out what that place was. They got off the plane; a Humvee was waiting for them. A driver welcomed them, and said to Heck, "Looks like you got your fish."

Heck nodded to him and said, "Let's get him some chow and a room."

They drove through one of the forests on the base to a compound surrounded by a chain link fence. They were stopped by a guard and required to show ID's. The guard examined a list and waved them through.

They ate in a small cafeteria and chatted about various topics. Heck put him in a room and told him to shower and get some rest. The next day Heck explained he was from the CIA; however the team was not a CIA operation and his status was similar to Sam's. The section was run by a senior government official direct from the White House. They were designated as Group 5. The designation meant nothing; they had to be called something. There were about 100 people assigned to the Group. They were selected from a variety of sources in the government. Seventy-five were support: intelligence, logistics, training, etc. The remaining twenty-five were operatives. Most were from the military, but there were some from the CIA and other government organizations. Where he was now, Group 5 Base or GFB was only one of their staging areas, but GFB was their headquarters and where much of their training went on.

"Sam, we're right in the planning phase of a very special mission, and I lost the man who had your special talents. When I say lost, he resigned due to a family problem. I completely understood, and he left with a Presidential Citation.

"You will meet the rest of the team this afternoon. We're in the planning phase of an operation to kidnap an Iranian nuclear scientist. We need someone to pose as a Spaniard for cover reasons. The man is in Argentina on vacation. We have a team posing as a business development team surveying some business opportunities. We plan to grab him and take him to a location where we can interrogate him. We believe the Iranians may be planning to create in South America either a missile base or a base nuclear-armed terrorists can operate from against the United States. One advantage you have is your darker skin. We also need a Spanish speaker. I know you're Defense Language Proficiency Test Level 3 in Spanish. You are a perfect fit for the mission."

Sam considered all this. "How long do we have to prepare?"

Heck answered, "We know the man will be in Argentina for a month. He just arrived. We figure two weeks. It will be close, but the team has been training for a month. You can catch up. I know you will."

"Let's begin," said Sam.

For the next ten years Sam became so enmeshed in such a variety of operations he barely had time to create a personal life. The Group's operations were very different from most SEAL operations. He felt he was more like a James Bond spy. Teams were formed for an activity and then disbanded.

Each operation was different and needed special talents. Because of this you came to know quite a few people who could do unique things.

Sam's talent was infiltrating places and eliminating individuals who were in the way of US interests. He also acted as the weapon-carrying member of the team. Often the operation required a specialized computer technician or electronic specialist. Sam was the sheepherder for these individuals. He was an expert at protecting and getting his team into a situation requiring a low profile, but where violent action might happen. He was the one who took care of that part of the operation.

# Chapter 10

Sam slept twelve hours and awoke to the sound of waves on the beach at Ft. Myers. He stretched and looked out the Holiday Inn window to the Gulf. As he closed up his life at the Group, he had begun a plan in his mind. After all, he was trained to fix difficult situations using violent means. He had twenty years to perfect that skill. Why not create his own operation?

He realized he needed some exercise and food. He put on his swim trunks and walked down to the beach. He swam out a few hundred yards, swam north for two miles, and back to the beach. He ran down the beach back to the hotel. The water had been cool, refreshing.

He had been lazy at the Group and had not followed a demanding enough regimen. This was good; he needed to stay in shape. He needed to be at a peak level of physical conditioning to complete his next mission. He toweled off and walked up to his room. After a hot shower he went down to the coffee shop and ate a massive breakfast: three eggs, whole grain pancakes, bacon, orange juice and coffee.

He was feeling better. He found a local dojo and began working out with the local master. He was getting back to mission readiness. His financial picture was excellent. He really didn't need the retirement pay.

On one of his SEAL missions they had rescued the American ambassador to Brazil and his entourage kidnapped by terrorists protesting something the Brazilian government was doing. Sam didn't care what their complaint was. His team happened to be in Brazil training some Brazilian special forces and was hastily relocated with some Brazilian army personnel to perform the rescue. The team eliminated the terrorists and rescued everyone without any harm coming to anyone except the terrorists. The man was effusive in his thanks and formed a relationship with Sam as the team took them back to safety. The official told Sam to invest as much money as he had in a Brazilian petroleum company. Sam was always frugal and had amassed $50,000 through savings and investments. He put the whole amount into what the man suggested. Within a year, the stock had appreciated over 2000 percent. He kept in contact with the man who periodically gave him more tips. His wealth gave him a great deal of latitude. He arranged for his USAA bank to wire transfer funds to a local bank. He was going to operate on a cash basis as much as possible.

When he went to the local bank, they were surprised he wanted the $20,000 in cash. They explained he would have to sign a special government form. He said it was no problem; he was going to buy a car from Craig's list and the seller wanted cash. The bank manager said he understood, and counted out the money. Sam realized carrying that amount of cash would be risky. He opened an account at another bank and rented a safe deposit box. The important thing was his movements and activities not be traceable with credit card charges.

He had been stationed in Florida for a short time several years ago and had gotten a Florida driver's license and a concealed weapons permit. He went online and found a five-year-old Chevy hybrid for $15,000. He met the guy and bought the car. It was in decent shape and had been well-maintained. He was looking for a good portable tablet computer for his mission planning and went to a local Best Buy. Sony had just come out with a new version of their iTab. He followed his routine for the next several weeks.

**********

Lorraine Clarkson got up early and decided to take a run on the beach. She had been staying at the Holiday Inn in Fort Myers for two days, but had been sightseeing each day. The Everglades City tour the previous day was enough Florida, she decided: wild pigs, bears, alligators, and swamps. She was trying to clear her head from work and personal stuff and needed some exercise. She ran a mile down the beach and back. As she returned, she noticed a man jogging toward the water in front of the hotel. He swam out several hundred yards until she could barely see him and then it looked like he turned and swam north. She decided to see what he was doing. Eventually she lost sight of him. She sat down and thought, *Should I tell someone? Was he trying to commit suicide? Maybe he was an Extreme Triathlon guy. Maybe I'll wait a bit.*

About forty-five minutes later she saw him running down the beach toward her. He looks a little like that guy I saw in some movie. The Rock or something. Whoever he is, he's really fit.

Sam had been in the Holiday Inn for three weeks. As part of his new mission he had grown a short beard and let his hair grow long. One morning after his swimming routine, as he returned down the beach, he saw a young woman standing near his towel and beach gear. She was barefoot in Bermuda shorts and a T-shirt. As he ran up, she greeted him. She was about 5' 8" tall, slender but somewhat muscular, longish light-brown hair ponytailed in a baseball cap, attractive. The most striking feature was her eyes. They were gray, but crystalline, almost transparent. He could lose himself in them.

"Hi," she said, "I saw you go out so far and then disappear. I didn't know what to think. I guess I just didn't know anyone could swim that far, and I was wondering if I should tell someone."

"Hi, no worries, I'm just a workout freak. I like to swim in cold water. It gets my blood moving in the morning. I'm sorry if you were worried." He looked at her more closely. She was really pretty. She reminded him of a movie star he had seen. Gwyneth something. He had not talked to a woman in months.

"It's okay. I run and work out at a gym, but probably not as intensely as you do. I won't bother you anymore."

"Look, I'm going to get some breakfast. Would you like to join me?" He had checked out her ring finger and saw none. He had not really talked to anyone since he returned. An attractive woman might be a welcome change.

"I don't want to bother you, but I haven't had breakfast either. I'm staying here, and I'd be happy to have some company since I'm here alone. It'll be Dutch treat, okay?"

"Fine, I'm staying here, too. Let me towel off and we'll go in." He pulled on his T-shirt and slipped on his flip-flops. They walked on the sand toward the entrance to the coffee shop together, chatting.

She offered her hand. "I'm Lorraine." She was from a suburb of Chicago. She was a surgical nurse, and was continuing her schooling to become a more advanced nurse. He guessed she was about thirty-one or thirty-two. She had never been married, she said.

"But, I'm just talking about myself, what about you. You just hang out at Holiday Inns on the beach and swim?" she joked.

"No, I just retired from the Navy. I'm taking some time off while I decide what I want to do. I'm not married, never been. I was just bouncing around the world too much. I had a few relationships, but nothing took."

"What did you do in the Navy?" she asked.

"I was on a variety of ships. I was a radarman. I worked in a shipboard control center. It was interesting work, but I wanted to get back to the US and start a new career." He could not tell her about his actual career. It was something he wasn't sure he could ever share with another person who had not lived in the shadow world of violence he had for his adult life.

They ate breakfast and continued chatting. He was enjoying the company of a young woman for the first time since Felecia. He quickly cleared that memory—another world destroyed.

As the waitress cleared their dishes, Sam had a thought. "I'm enjoying your company, Lorraine. I have some business to do today, but would you like to go to dinner? You pick, and I'll call you later. I'll treat. And make it a nice place. Don't worry about money. I'm a rich ex-swabbie."

She laughed and said, "I'd be happy to share another meal with you. It's not necessary for you to pay, but I will find a nice place for us to eat. Do you have transportation?"

"I do. I just bought it. It's second-hand and not much to look at, but we can go to Miami if necessary."

"I won't make you drive that far. I'll see what I can find."

They went back to their rooms and agreed he would call her when he returned.


The Florida sun was in for a while as torrential rain fell. Sam stepped out of the Holiday Inn entrance and ran for his car. He was out to scout some stores and also picked up some cash from his safe deposit box. He went by the dojo and worked out for two hours, looking forward to his date. He was amused by his anticipation. He had not really felt anything toward a woman for a long time. His encounters were more for sexual release. The women he was with understood this and were pretty much of the same mind. This was different. He had enjoyed their brief meeting. There was a maturity and humor in her that appealed to him, and the fact she was very attractive was a decided plus.

# Chapter 11

By the time he returned to the motel, the rain had passed and the sky was clear. The evening promised to be clear and cool. After showering and cleaning up, he called Lorraine. "How are you doing?"

"Great. I found a nice place to eat. It's on the water and supposedly has a great view. I am into ambiance."

"Ambiance is always a good idea. What time do you want to meet?"

"How about half an hour—6:00 in the lobby?" she answered.

"I'll be there. Looking forward to it."

They met in the lobby. He didn't want to react to her, but he did. She was really pretty. She had on a light pink dress with showing off her slim figure. Her light brown hair was up in some sort of bun. He was impressed.

He had not really been close to a woman for several years. He had had several short-time affairs since Felecia: an embedded news reporter, a USAID worker, but nothing serious. His desire for any long-term relationship had dwindled to nothing. He had purposely chosen to concentrate on operations at the expense of a personal life. He believed he was not destined for a serious, long-term relationship.

As they approached his car, Sam was feeling very happy. He liked Lorraine and couldn't believe he was going with such a pretty girl to dinner. "Where are we going?" he asked.

"Naples," she answered. "Do you know where that is?"

"Sort of," he replied. "Do you have an idea how to get there?"

"Yep, I looked it up on Google Maps. Get on 45 and go south."

"I can do that."

He opened the car door for her. She looked at him in surprise. "What's the matter?" he asked.

"Nothing, it's just I'm not used to gentlemanly touches like opening my car door."

He looked at her cynically. "My mother performed some pretty rigorous training on my brother and me when we were younger."

"She should write a training manual."

As he walked around the car, Sam suddenly was quiet. He had almost forgotten about his loss. It was still hard to realize his parents were gone.

As he drove down toward Naples, he realized he was enjoying this. She was a very pleasant companion. She kept the conversation going with observations about the ride, some current events, and even discussed a movie she had seen that appeared to be interesting. It was not the typical chick flick or shoot'em-up. She was obviously educated and had traveled overseas.

She had chosen a restaurant in Naples in an upscale shopping center on the water. They had seats on a deck overlooking the water. The color of the water was a deep blue and the setting sun turned the clouds into iridescent reds and blues. Their waiter took their drink orders and left them the menus. She suggested they have the stone crabs.

He had never heard of them. "Stoned crabs?" he joked.

"No silly, they're a real Florida delicacy." She suggested a Caesar salad and a Pinot Grigio wine. He liked the fact she had chosen the menu.

"How did you learn about stone crabs?" he asked.

"My parents used to come down to Florida for vacations. We stayed here in Naples. There's a crab shack we used to go to, but I didn't want to suggest it to you for tonight. It's pretty raw."

"This is great. I can stand raw, but I was ready for something a little more upscale. My parents used to go to Florida, but on the East Coast."

"I think it depends on what Interstate you come down on. If you're in the Midwest, you come down I-75. I guess your parents came down I-95."

"Right, when I was a kid we would go to the Jersey shore, but after we left home—I have a brother—they started going to Florida."

She looked at him seriously, "I don't want to pry, but you said used to, are they still living."

"No, they lost their lives in an accident last year." He didn't want to go into the horror of their murders.

"I'm sorry. My parents are still alive. They live outside Chicago. He's a doctor, an anesthesiologist. My mother's a high school English teacher. I have a sister who is married and lives near them. I was the youngest, and my parents were not happy when I went overseas."

She began explaining her background, "When I graduated from nursing school, I decided I wanted to do something positive, not just go to a local hospital and tend patients. I worked in a hospital for three years and got tired of it. I wanted to see something of the world. I found a position with a company that had a contract with the UN. I went to Africa, where I spent almost five years. My experience there was very good until the end."

"What do you mean by 'the end'?" he asked.

"Well... I had developed a close relationship with one of the doctors, but he was killed when our clinic was being hassled by some Muslim extremists. They didn't like us treating the local women. They told us to leave. There were ten of us. My friend was the senior doctor. He decided he would ignore them. They continued to threaten us, and then one day they swept into our compound. My friend confronted the leader. The man pulled out a gun, and shot him. He then rounded all of us up. The next day the UN troops came and got us out. That was a little over a year ago."

Sam was thunderstruck. He had lived through a similar experience with Felecia, the only woman he had ever truly loved. She was French.

He was in the Group and had just finished an operation in Northern Africa. He had met her while on leave in Morocco. He had a bout with the touristas and went to a local clinic for an antibiotic. Their meeting developed into an intense and passionate affair. They continued to meet on and off as their schedules permitted. There was an unspoken agreement, sometime when they were finished with this phase of their life, they would marry. Their relationship was such they needed no ring, no paper, nothing, only the knowledge that someday they would be together.

Felecia was killed by a terrorist bomb in a marketplace. He didn't find out until a month later when he tried to set up a time together on the French Rivera. Her phone was not answered; so he called her clinic. The nurse there told him the news. Sam had never cried in his life. He not only cried—he fell apart. He was on shore leave in Abu Dhabi with some teammates. They couldn't console him. He was lost. This was after the second mission he had gone on with the Group. Heck was concerned about his ability to continue. He went on an extended bender until his teammates recovered him.

Heck wanted to know if he could continue. Sam thought it over, and said, "I need to continue. I'll be okay if I can get back into our work. Get me on a mission so I can lose myself. I'll be all right." Heck nodded. He was concerned, but understood Sam's desire. The next mission was unusually complicated, but Sam and his teammates pulled it off with plaudits from the President.

Sam looked at Lorraine with disbelief.

She stared at him. "I'm sorry if I upset you. I'm over it pretty much. I came back to the States and decided to try to do some good here. Because I was a surgical nurse I was able to get on a special team dealing with children who have heart problems."

Sam was sympathetic. "I'm not so much upset, just struck by a similar thing that happened to me. I had a very close relationship with a French nurse who was killed by a terrorist bombing in Morocco. We were thinking seriously of marriage when I retired. That was about three years ago. I guess we both know how dangerous a place this world is."

She nodded with a serious expression on her face. "Let's have a nice dessert and lose ourselves with an after dinner drink."

He quickly agreed.

As they drove up the coast back to the motel, they continued their casual conversation. They talked and laughed as if they had known each other for years. He told her about his parents, but not about their deaths. He couldn't talk about that yet, but he did want tell her about his growing up and how he joined the SEALS. He wasn't sure how to do that. Some people really didn't understand the need for violence. He wanted to open up to her more, but the task ahead of him was in his mind. He wanted to see her more. His mission was still on his mind, but he wanted this to go someplace. It was a combination of her underlying seriousness with a cynical view of the world. She had been around. She had seen things the average American woman would never see, but she could still find humor in life.

They walked into the lobby. "Would you like to come up to my room," she asked, both of them knowing what she was asking.

He considered this. Was he ready for a serious relationship? He didn't know, but he needed to be with her. "Yes I would."

*********

Their lovemaking started tenderly and became more passionate with each time. They fell asleep. The next morning they were lying in each other's arms. She drew back a bit and looked at him. "I want you to know. I like you a lot, but I don't want you to feel like we have to go anywhere with this."

"I'm certain I want to go somewhere with this. I'm sure you're questioning the quickness of this. We seem to have something. I really feel it. Look, let's just let it happen."

She nodded. "My plane is the day after tomorrow. I only came down here because I wanted to see some warm weather and the Gulf. I wasn't looking for anyone. I didn't think I'd ever find anyone who could fit into my life again."

"I have some business I have to attend to for the next month or so. I then was planning on driving out to see my brother and his wife. They live in Sedona Arizona. He's a landscape photographer. He's quite famous. Has several stores in upscale malls where he sells his stuff. I could take a detour through Chicago on the way. By then we might sort out what we really want."

She reacted as if he were trying to extricate himself. "I understand," she replied coolly.

"No, no," he replied, "I really am saying I desperately want to try to include you in my life, but I just have something I must attend to before I can move on."

She seemed to relax with this. "All right, I'll have to trust you, but there is one thing I want to tell you." He looked at her with a quizzical expression.

She traced a scar on his arm. "You have two scars that are definitely bullet wounds. Believe me, I know bullet wounds. You also have what look like knife wounds. I know you were not some shipboard swabby. I met your type in Africa."

"My type?"

"You were a SEAL. I got to know one well when our compound was overrun once. They came in and beat back the local bad boys until the government troops could reestablish control. You guys just have something about yourselves. It doesn't fuss me. In fact I like it. I feel safe with you."

He closed his eyes and took a deep breath. This was not what he expected. It confused him. He could tell her he had been a SEAL. That wasn't classified. It was the Group time that was. As far as his records went, he was a retired SEAL. "You're right. I just retired, and it's new to me to talk about it. Your reaction is cool with me. I'm glad you feel safe. I'd like to provide you that feeling for a long time."

She leaned over and kissed him. They made love again. This time it was very overpowering. This was new to him. She said, "That was the most intense feeling I have ever had."

"Ditto," he said. "There are no words for what we just shared."

They lay together for a while. Sam turned toward her. "There's something about your body that puzzles me."

Lorraine looked at him with a cynical smile. "I've never heard that line before."

"No, I'm serious. You're very strong and athletic. You have muscles many women don't have. You said you work out, but you have more muscle than just working out."

"Well, if you must know, I do martial arts—Tae Kwan Do. I also do weight lifting for strength. I used to do wall climbing, but I don't have the time now."

"That's neat. There aren't many women who are in the condition you are. Look, I'm kind of bewildered by you. No, that's not right. You're so beautiful to me, it takes my breath away. I look at you, and I'm almost dizzy. I've never even thought about a woman like this."

She looked at him intently. "You have some good lines, mister." She didn't want to tell him, but he turned her on like no one had before. He was so good looking, and she liked his intensity. His skin was an olive color, but not dark. She asked him, "Talking about looks. You have slightly dark skin, but I thought you said your dad's family was from Germany."

"They were, but my mother's family is Greek. I look like her; my brother looks like my dad. My brother is actually a little taller than me. You wouldn't know we were brothers. In fact my sister-in-law accused us of trying to trick her when we first met."

"Well, my sister and I look very much alike, but she's a bit older than me. She has always acted very motherly toward me. We both are athletic, though. That's due to my dad. He made sure my sister and I could do a lot of things. He's a workout guy, and he started us at it early. Our mother keeps in shape, but not as much as he does. He also made sure we had exposure to many things. My sister and I learned to pilot a plane, skydive, swim well, sail a boat, and one of the most fun things we did together was fully restore a 1964 Pontiac Grand Am."

Sam got up on an elbow. This was fascinating. "You know how to do things most men don't."

"My dad believes in women's equality. He beat it into our heads. My sister took a slightly different track from me—the marriage and kids thing. She still keeps in shape and works out, but she's a lot more intellectual than I am. I'm good at academics, but she was always interested in school and learning. I'm a little more interested in physical activities, although I'm still going to school.

"My sister is five years older than me. She went to college and became an academician. She got her PhD in child psychology. I was impatient to get on with my life. My dad wanted me to become a doctor like him, but I didn't want to go to school that long, so I became a nurse, a surgical nurse. I found my surgical background helped a lot in Africa."

Sam digested this information. There was a lot more to Lorraine than he had learned so far. She was a fascinating person. "I don't want this to end. I really want to learn about you. I want to have time to do that."

As she got sat up in the bed, she looked at him and said, "I want to learn who you are, too."

He watched her as she walked toward the bathroom. She was unselfconscious about her nudity. She moved lithely and smoothly. *Wow, how could I have been so lucky to meet such a beautiful woman?* He asked himself.

They agreed to meet in the lobby and go out for breakfast and then a drive. He got up and went to his room to shower while she showered in hers. When they met, she was dressed in a skirt and top. He was impressed by her look.

"You look fabulous." She always looked like she stepped out of a fashion show, but casual and relaxed.

"Well, my mother was concerned my father was going too far in his program, so she made sure my sister and I knew how to dress and look good."

"She succeeded," he told her.

They drove to a quaint small town north of Fort Myers, Punta Gorda, where they bought a lunch on the pier overlooking the harbor. Driving back, she said, "When I go back home, I'll wait for you. We can keep in touch by phone, email, texting, anyway you want, or not. But if you change your mind at any time, let me know. I'll understand."

"I have to tell you I'm not much of a texter. I will try to let you know how I'm doing, but I may be unavailable for a while. Don't read anything into that. I also want to assure you, it's not about any other woman. I just have some business I need to straighten out before I can go on with my life."

She looked at him as he drove, leaned over and kissed his cheek. "I'll trust you. I understand whatever it is, it's very important to you. If ever you want to share it with me, okay. If not, okay."

When they returned to the motel, she told him she needed to pack. They decided to meet in the motel bar about 5:30. They could have some snacks and drinks. Their meeting was tense, but both of them were obviously happy to be with each other. They went back to her room again and made love. He left about 12:00 and told her he would take her to the airport in the morning.

When they met in the lobby, he looked at her one-bag carry-on, and said, "Wow, a woman who manages to look beautiful and chic, but does it out of one bag. You are a potential keeper."

She smiled. "It's something I learned overseas. Don't bring more than you can afford to lose."

They arrived early enough to have coffee at the Starbucks kiosk in the airport. He tried to reassure her he would see her again. She tried to convince herself this was true, but the situation was so iffy she couldn't keep the thought without feeling very blue.

They went to the security entrance, kissed goodbye, and she walked down the corridor toward the gate. He turned and went out to his car in the airport parking lot. He had a lot to do.

# Chapter 12

Lorraine Clarkson relaxed in her aisle seat on her flight back to Chicago. What was she doing? Falling in love with someone she had no idea who he was. The scars told her a story, but who was Sam Dancer? How could she get to know who he was? He was certainly attractive, ruggedly handsome, even with his beard and long brown hair. She was often almost as tall as the men she had dated. Sam fit the mold of a great guy. This in itself was worrisome. Why had he not married? Maybe the SEAL life was too disjointed to settle down. He did say he had a serious relationship. This was complicated. She would need to get to know him better.

He had some mysterious business to attend to. He wouldn't even hint at what it was. It seemed very serious to him. Their lovemaking was truly sweet—she even felt a flush thinking about it. But, that was lovemaking. What was it to him? Would he ever want to be just with her, and where? She took out her Sony iTab and looked up Sam's brother. He had a website showing several of his landscape photographic portraits. They were truly beautiful. He looked successful. She searched for the name Dancer and Philadelphia; Sam had said something about Philadelphia. Two items came up:

***Philadelphia Enquirer, City and Local, May 6****: (Picture)
Local doctor an avid coin collector. Dr. William Dancer shows his
extensive coin collection of early US coins at the US Coin Show at
the Philadelphia Sheraton Convention Center this week.*

***PHILADELPHIA – July 28 (PVI)*** *– William Dancer, a
prominent surgeon in Havertown, and his wife Angela were found
dead in their home on Monday morning, apparent victims of a home
invasion. Police said the bodies were found by their maid. Police
have asked for anyone having information regarding this crime to
call the Police Hotline.*

*Oh my God!* She thought. *What do I make of this?* No
wonder he didn't go into his parent's death. She took a deep breath
and sat back in her seat. Why didn't he share this with me? But, of
course, we really don't know each other. It must have been very
distressing to him. She looked at the dates—just this summer. He
said he had just retired. It must have happened about the time he was
retiring. She didn't know what she should think. If he hadn't told her,
it was probably not up to her to talk to him about it until he wanted
to. He probably had to settle the estate. She thought. *That could be
very distressing.* She closed her eyes and just tried to process this
new information.

She couldn't relax, so she opened up her email. Her sister had sent one telling her she could meet her at the airport. There weren't many others. Her mother wanted to know if she was all right. Her mother and father had left on a one month cruise to the Mediterranean. She had confided in her sister the reason she wanted to go to Florida. She had to get away. The events in Africa were still very raw on her mind. She had considered working with children with special needs, but wasn't sure. Surgical nursing was interesting, and she was good at it. She was concerned, she was burnt out. Africa had been a frustrating place. There was so much to be done and so many conflicting parties. The ever-present violence was nerve-wracking. She took a deep breath and exhaled. Five days in Florida was supposed to clear her mind a bit. Now, she was even more confused than before. Was Sam Dancer someone who might be in her future? Would he come see her? Was he ready for something long-term? She sank back in the seat and tried to tune out.

Her sister met her at the gate. Sarah was happy to see her. She knew Lorraine was in a difficult state. Lorraine was younger than Sarah, and Sarah had always been protective of her and given her advice. "How was the break?" she asked.

Lorraine didn't know where to begin or how to reply.

"What's wrong? Weren't you able to get a little relaxing time away?"

As they walked toward the car, Lorraine wasn't sure how to reply. She shook her head. "I met a man. I am really confused."

Her sister stopped as they got to the car and looked at her disbelief. "You met a man? What do you mean? Did you get married? Engaged? Oh no, I know, you had sex. Well you really know how to relax." Her sister tried to hastily react in a lighter vein.

Lorraine looked at her. "I am... I did... I mean, no, not... Oh heck, I have to start at the beginning." They got into the car, and Lorraine told her about what had happened.

By the time they had arrived at Lorraine's condo in Chicago, the story had been pretty well laid out. Sarah shook her head, "Wow that's some relationship. You meet a guy who appears to be an ideal catch. You have great love-making. You both really hit it off, and you leave with no idea who he is or where he's going or what he's going to do."

"That's about it, sister," Lorraine said. "I have a cell phone number and an email address, and I can use it, but I don't want to hit him with a barrage of communications."

Sarah looked at her, "You shouldn't. Let him make the first contact. If he doesn't, then you had a nice vacation, some good sex, and now move on."

"Yes, but there was something very sincere about him. I think he needs someone. He almost appeared lost, but very focused."

"Okay, but you need to protect yourself. Don't invest too much in this yet. I know you. You are the lost-kitten, poor-doggie, hurt-child rescuer. You put a lot of yourself into needy others, or who you think are needy. You have always been about correcting evil in this world. There is probably too much evil for one person to correct."

"I know, Sarah. I almost lost myself in Africa. But I don't want to think I'm such a bad judge of people I let myself be seduced, literally, by some charlatan. Sam is a good man. I know it."

Lorraine put her bag in her condo. Sarah invited her over for dinner with Mike and their two kids, Michael Junior and Lilly. The children were in their early teens and Aunt Lori was their favorite. Mike was an attorney in Milwaukee specializing in business law. Sarah was a teacher, but had taken off ten years to home school her children. When they reached high school, she put them into a local charter high school. She wanted them to be socialized with their peers and she thought they had developed good enough study skills to succeed in a more public school.

Because of her experience in home schooling, she began to research gifted programs for schools. She became an expert on these and opened a consulting program for parents for gifted students. Her business had become quite successful. Her decision to send her kids back to the local high school was right; the two kids were doing very well and were in the gifted program. Lorraine had a nice dinner; they discussed the children, latest news, how nice Florida was this time of the year. Then after dinner, Lorraine went home.

She showered and went to bed; she was tired. The next morning there was an email on her iTab from Sam:

<Hi, hope you got home okay. I'm trying to sort out my activities. I'll keep in touch.> Sam.

She thought, At least it's something. He probably isn't used to a lot of communication with anyone. She sent back a short message.

\*\*\*\*\*\*\*\*\*\*

A week went by. He sent her occasional emails and called once. She began thinking about how she could find out something more about the enigmatic Sam Dancer. When her compound was rescued by the SEALS, she had met their leader, Lieutenant Commander Jason Cloud. She and Jason had become good friends. When they came into the compound, he had been hit by a stray shot. She patched him up. He had a wife and three kids in California. He was very proud of his family and showed her pictures of them. They kept in contact with Christmas cards, but she had not spoken to him in over a year. His last card had said he was living in California and training SEALS in Coronado. She decided to contact him and see if Sam were really a SEAL. Who was he really?

"Jason, this is Lorraine," she began.

"Gee Lorraine; are you coming out her to visit? I've told Sally all about you. She would love to meet you. Are you still single? I've got a lot of guys I'd like you to meet."

"I'm not coming out, not right now Jason. I have something to ask you. It's a little odd, and if you can't help me, I'll understand."

He was silent for a while. "Sounds serious. I'll help you any way I can."

"I met a man while I was on a short vacation to Florida. He seems to be a really nice guy. He told me he was a retired SEAL. Actually, I pried the admission out of him just based on what he told me. We had a nice time together. We agreed to meet in about a month, but I need to know if I'm talking to a real person."

"It sounds like you would like to be serious about this man. Let me make a few inquiries to see what I can find out. Don't be afraid you're asking a lot of me. We have guys claiming to be SEALS all the time. I'll get back to you as soon as I can."

"Jason, you are a good friend. Anything you can find out will be really helpful. I want to believe what he said, and I want to trust myself." She told him what she knew about Sam, and they chatted about Jason's family and how he liked being back on shore and then they ended the conversation.

**********

A few days later Jason phoned her. "I have some good news. Your Sam Dancer is a real ex-SEAL. Have you checked your email lately?"

She admitted she hadn't. She logged on and opened his email. There was a photo attached to the email. Even though he now had a beard and longer hair, it was Sam. Tears blurred her eyes. He was at least who he said he was. She told Jason, "That's the guy I met."

"Well you picked a real hero. He has a Silver Star and two Bronze Stars with V's for valor. Two of the medals' particulars are classified. There is one odd thing about him—a lengthy period of his career is classified. It could mean he was involved in some very special work. He's a real unique guy.

"He's never been married. He retired in September. He has a brother who lives in Arizona. He has had a real tragedy; his parents were killed this year in a home invasion.

"There're a few guys here who remember him. They worked with him about ten years ago. He was a real leader for any team he was in. I hope it works out for you. Where is he now?"

"I don't know. He only told me he had some business he had to attend to, and it would take about a month. He said he'd keep in touch, and he has sent me a few emails. We also talked on the phone once."

"Well from what I have found out, you should rely on his word. I'm sure he has some things to work out regarding his family. He's known as a very tidy person. Very organized and pays a lot of attention to details. He is also extremely loyal. He was known as someone who if he gave his word, he would go to hell to satisfy it. If I find out anything else, I'll let you know."

They chatted a while and hung up.

Jason had provided the same information in the email. The picture of Sam was from a military photograph, probably his personnel file. She liked him better without the hippy look. His short brown hair gave his face a more angular look. There were some physical particulars: 6' 1", 210 pounds, hazel eyes. Yes, that was Sam. He looked very serious, but there was a bit of fun in the slight smile on his lips. He looked like he was laughing at the whole photo process. She shrugged. She would let her sister know what she had learned, and then just get on with her studies and job. She would have to wait and trust Sam to come to her.

Over the next several days she thought seriously about what she expected in a man. She went to school at night and also worked with several young women in their late teens and early twenties. She listened as they chatted about their boyfriends. It was obvious they had little idea of what they were looking for: abs and butts were a great topic and after that what the boy did for a living, also what kind of car they drove. She never heard a great deal of depth in their discussions. Maybe it was because they didn't want to appear odd to their friends, but Lorraine thought it was because they didn't have any real idea of what they should be looking for. Also, maybe it was because of the age of the boys they were dating or in a relationship with. Many of the boys had had no real life experiences.

A few of their boyfriends were in or had been in the military. They seemed to be a bit more mature, but the girls had had no real life experiences either. Lorraine thought for a while on that.

In order to have a real understanding of who you needed in your life, you needed to really get out and see the real world. And, she realized, most people do not want to do that. Hiding in TV and movies and bar life, a world of unreal, was a safe way to not force any deep thought.

Her first overseas assignment was in a village in Liberia. They were setting up a clinic for the local population. The village they were working in was overrun by guerrillas. The Liberian government asked the US to help rescue the village.

Jason was the leader of the team that came in and saved them. The guerillas were preparing to rape the native women when suddenly the SEAL team appeared as if by magic and killed every one of the guerillas.

Lorraine was at first appalled by this, but then realized; there was no choice. The guerillas were prepared to fight to the last man and kill all the villagers and probably the UN workers in the process. The UN pulled her out of there and sent her to the Sudan.

She thought about the first time she met Paul Vanderhill in Khartoum. The UN had authority to send a medical team to the south to work with the refugees who were finally getting settled, and the new government seemed to be supporting their efforts.

Paul was the most spiritual man she had ever met. He was Lutheran like she was, but neither of them practiced their religion. He had just taken the Christian ethic and implemented it. He was also a brilliant doctor and surgeon. She was taken immediately by his sense of mission. They formed an immediate bond; they were going to make this work.

There were thirty of them. Some worked directly for the Sudanese government, some the UN and the rest for a contractor who provided services to the UN. There was no rivalry within the team. They were flown to Nyala and then drove about sixty miles out into the countryside where there was a medical compound.

There, she and Paul worked to set up an organized practice supporting women, children and some of the men. The men were difficult. They were often too proud or suspicious of the medics' motives to ask for help, and they certainly didn't want a woman touching them.

But, as the months and a year went by, the local populace began to trust them. This led to trouble with a local government chief. He was convinced they were trying to undermine his authority.

He had a son who was his heir who began coming into the compound demanding the local women leave. He was a Muslim and was infuriated that a man, even a doctor' would look at a woman. Paul had confronted him several times.

Paul believed if he showed a peaceful and non-aggressive manner, the young man would eventually realize they were doing good for the people. The young man just got more and more angry. Paul could speak Arabic and tried to talk to the young man and explain that what they were doing was according to the Koran. This just seemed to set him off even more, and he stormed off.

Finally, one day the young man marched into the compound with armed men and threatened to burn it to the ground. Paul walked out to him, and told him they were there in peace. The young man pulled out a handgun and shot him in the chest. Lorraine rushed to him, but it was too late. He was shot through the heart. She knelt with Paul and turned to the young man. He strutted around and stalked out. The next day the UN sent some troops in to calm things down, but the medical team was withdrawn.

Afterward, she began to have deep thoughts about how one should deal with evil. Christianity says to "turn the other cheek." But if the Allies in World War II had just tried to talk and negotiate with Hitler, nothing would have been accomplished. The Nazis were like cockroaches. They had to be exterminated.

If the Allies had waited, the Jews would have been completely exterminated. Who needed to be exterminated more? She decided goodness must be the moral compass, but evil had to be excised.

It could not be wished away or discussed away. She had seen evil at its worst. Without the use of brutal force, she would have been raped and left for dead.

She realized a man like Sam might be someone who understood her feelings. She had loved Paul, but his refusal to defend himself had led to his death, and could have led to hers also. She was far from a violent person, actually to the contrary, but defending herself was something she began to realize was something she stood for. Perhaps she was no longer a good Christian.

She still had compassion for the less fortunate and the sick and poor, but she was angry with Paul for what he had done. She had never realized that before. By confronting the young man, he had challenged his masculinity. This was a part of the world where a challenge like that couldn't go unanswered. The only answer was physical. Paul had told her he believed you could change the world through Christian reason. Lorraine had listened to him, but had doubts. Young, violent men in the world with little to lose were everywhere. Lorraine often thought about this as she went about her day and watched the interplay of men and women in this different culture. American and European cultures had moved beyond some of this. It was still there, but their societies controlled it to some degree and were certainly less violent.

As the weeks went by she heard infrequently from Sam. He used email mostly, but occasionally called. His calls were brief, but they were warm and reassuring. *He is, after all, a man,* she laughed to herself.

He told her his business was going well and he hoped to finish it soon. She began to hope they might find each other. She had despaired of someone else being in her life. She had been asked out by several men since she returned, but they seemed a bit shallow and bland. She didn't need excitement from a man; she wanted something else—someone who knew the world and how to deal with it, but had a moral compass of right and wrong.

# Chapter 13

Cherie Lapham was walking home from school. She had stayed late studying in the library and doing her homework. It was about 4:00 and there was a chilly wind in mid-October. Fall was here and winter would be coming soon. She hadn't put on a sweater that morning and only wore a light windbreaker. Cherie was a junior at Henderson High School. She liked the school because she could avoid being home, plus there was a teacher who was nice to her. She didn't like being at home since her mother had come home with a new boyfriend. A few years ago her mother had a boyfriend who had raped her. Luckily someone in the apartment heard her cries and called the police. Her mother was really mad with Cherie. She was sure Cherie had done something to cause the boyfriend to lose his control.

Cherie, a slight, blonde girl was attractive, but unkempt. Her ability to look nice was hampered by her home environment. Her mother either ignored her or yelled at her because she was "in the way".

Cherie knew that to mean that she was anywhere near her mother. She tried to keep out of her mother's way, but she felt she had nowhere to turn. Her mother lurched from boyfriend to boyfriend.

When her mother had a new boyfriend, Cherie was often relegated to the living room couch to sleep in their one-bedroom apartment. This latest one had stayed for several weeks. He worked at a local garage. His main claim to fame as far as Cherie was concerned was he bought some groceries and beer.

Her mother's latest boyfriend acted all straight around her mother, but Cherie didn't like the way he looked at her when her mother wasn't looking. One time he had tried to put his arm around her when her mother had gone to the store for groceries, but Cherie had left the apartment and waited until her mother returned. She was pretty sure the boyfriend wouldn't be there at the apartment. It was too early for him to be off his work. Her mother would be home soon, and Cherie would be okay. Cherie had been sleeping in the only bedroom with her mother in one of the double beds until the boyfriend moved in. Now she was sleeping in the living room on the couch. Her mother told her the boyfriend, Lonnie, was planning to get them a bigger apartment.

Cherie put her key in the door and opened it. The apartment was quiet. She went to the kitchen and began washing the breakfast dishes and trying to clean up. She looked in the freezer and found three frozen dinners. Lonnie liked "Hungry Man" dinners, and Cherie and her mother liked Stouffers. Cherie particularly liked the Lasagna, but her mother would only get it once and a while. Her mother liked the macaroni and cheese.

The front door opened and Lonnie came into the living room. "Hey, Cherie how's your day?" he asked.

A shiver went up her spine. Lonnie was home early. Her mother was not home yet and probably wouldn't be for another two hours. Maybe she could put Lonnie off until she got home. "Hi Lonnie, you're home early."

"Yeah, the boss closed up early. He had a meeting of some kind. I guess your mom won't be home for a few hours. That gives us some time to get to know each other."

Cherie shrugged as she set the kitchen table for dinner.

Lonnie went to the refrigerator and took out a beer. "You want one?" he asked casually over his shoulder. He knew Cherie didn't drink. She shook her head. "Aw common, Cherie, you need to learn to relax. You're a good looking girl. How you gonna learn to be with guys if you don't have a beer once and a while?" He turned around and walked over next to her at the sink. Lonnie was tall and very thin, but with a muscular torso. He was dressed in a greasy white T-shirt and greasy jeans from work. He hadn't shaved that day and his black hair was cut in a home-done mullet. He considered himself to be quite attractive to women.

She edged by him and went into the living room and turned on the TV. Cherie was small, barely five feet and only weighed eighty-five pounds. Cherie's father left her mother when Cherie was born. Her mother told Cherie she screwed up her mother's life. Her father was the only man she truly loved. Cherie had thought about her mother's feeling and decided her mother was wrong blaming her. From reading and watching TV, Cherie had decided there weren't very many good men.

Cherie sat down on the couch and spread her homework on the coffee table. She was a straight A student and in all the advanced classes. The guidance counselor had tried to talk to her mother about Cherie getting a scholarship, but her mother told the counselor she was sure Cherie was cheating to get the grades she got. The counselor talked to Cherie about college, but Cherie wasn't sure how she could get into one without money. The counselor told Cherie she should really try to go because she was so smart, and she might get a scholarship. Cherie wasn't sure whether the counselor was just being nice.

As she sat down and began opening one of her books, Lonnie sat next to her. Cherie tried to ignore him, but he put his arm around her. "Now Cherie, you should be nice to me. I know how to make you feel real good." Cherie tried to move away from him, but he pushed her down onto the couch and put his hand over her mouth. She struggled, but he lay on top of her. "Calm down Cherie, you'll like this. I promise." He unzipped his fly and at the same time pulled her jeans down. He began pushing himself around her underpants into her. It hurt, and she tried to scream, but he kept his hand over his mouth. "Oh, boy, you're a tight one," he gasped.

As he was just coming, the front door opened and her mother entered. She had returned early from her job at K-mart. Her mother wasn't looking toward the couch and announced, "The power failed and they sent everyone home early." She turned and let out a screech. "Cherie, what the fuck are you doing? Leave Lonnie alone. Lonnie what's going on here?"

Lonnie pulled himself out of Cherie and jumped up. He immediately began apologizing to her mother, saying, "I couldn't stop myself. She came on to me. You know how easy I'm aroused."

"Cherie, you no good slut. Get your pants on. Why can't you leave my boyfriends alone? You ungrateful bitch. After all I've done for you. You're nothing but a shitfull of trouble." She grabbed Cherie by the back of her neck and propelled her out the door. "Don't come back until you say you are sorry," were her parting words.

Cherie pulled up her pants and stood for a while outside the ground-floor apartment. It was 5:30 p.m. A misty rain was beginning. She shivered. When her mother's other boyfriend had tried to rape her, she told her school about it, but her mother had explained the boyfriend tricked her into allowing him to stay in the apartment. Nothing happened to her mother. Cherie was skeptical anything would happen this time either. Her mother had insisted Cherie take birth control pills. Her mother had gotten pregnant with Cherie when she was seventeen and was convinced Cherie would do the same.

This time, she wasn't sure what to do. It wasn't the first time her mother had thrown her out of the apartment. She thought a school friend she stayed with a few times before might allow her to stay at her house. The girl's parents were very nice and even took her to church with them once. Her friend's house was about three miles away. She thought she should call her, but she suddenly realized she didn't have her purse or any money.

Her cell phone was in the apartment. She began walking along West Chester Pike. It was getting dark, and it felt like it might rain, and it was chilly. She was only dressed in jeans and a T-shirt and running shoes. She needed to get going.

As she walked along the road, she shivered. She was afraid she might get sick. A misty rain began and cars whizzed by in the dark. She was hungry and crying. What had she done to deserve being thrown out? Her mother knew what Lonnie was like. How could she choose him over her? If she ever had kids, she would love them and protect them no matter what.

A van slowed down beside her. A man called to her through the open passenger window.

# Chapter 14

The Dodge utility van drove through the chain link fence to the back of a small strip mall loading dock. The van was several years old with a few dents, rust spots and scrapes. A magnetic sign on the side stated "Ted's TV Service". It backed up to the loading dock. The driver, a tall white man, got out and climbed up a set of concrete steps next to the loading dock. He knocked on a metal door. "Open up Doc, we're here with the stuff."

A grossly obese white man opened the door, eating a large hogie. "You're interrupting my dinner. Hey, Burns, how'd it go?"

"Okay. We got in without a problem. Took only about ten minutes, just like you said. The stuff was all in a closet. No alarm, nothing."

"Good. Was it what I said it would be?"

"Yeah, a couple of wooden crates. We're ready to bring the stuff in, okay?"

"Yeah, I'll open the door."

Two other men, a short, swarthy man and a black man of average height got out of a side door. They unloaded several large wooden boxes into the open warehouse door.

After finishing the unloading, Doc closed the roll-down door and invited them into an office in the back of his store. He offered the three some beers. "How you two guys doin'?"

"Good," the black man answered. "How we doin' with our money accounts?"

Doc smiled at him. "Let me show you on my laptop." He opened a laptop and logged on. He tapped in an Internet address. A bank Web page came up. He entered some log-on information and then a series of numbers. An account page appeared. There were three separate accounts. Each had over $1 million in them. The three hung over Doc's shoulder. "See," he said. "Crime does pay."

"Doc, you're the only guy we would ever trust with our money," Burns said.

Doc nodded. "We have a good thing going. There's no reason to screw it up by acting stupid. My clients ask me to find items they're willing to pay good money for, no questions asked. And I satisfy their needs. This latest stuff is a bunch of Central American relics that just got here. The guy who brought it into the country can't tell anyone he has it or how he got it. So we got it and can sell it to someone else who can't tell anyone they have it. Perfect!"

The three snickered. Doc became solemn. "Just be careful. We don't want any more dead bodies around. When I was at that coin show, the guy told me he kept his coins in his safe. I thought it would be an easy job."

Burns replied, "We know. It was a real fluke, that situation. I couldn't get the goddamn safe open. So I untied him and told him to open it. The guy tried to get smart with me and pulled off my ski mask. We had to waste them then. We much better like no people around."

"Yeah," Doc answered, "but those coins brought us all a cool two million to split. And, you were smart to bring the whole collection and the jewelry. There were some other really valuable coins besides what the buyer wanted. I was able to unload the jewelry too."

"Yeah." Burns nodded. "We're all getting a lot closer to our retirement goal. Costa Rica here we come. Rafi here is looking forward to going home and living the good life."

Rafi was the swarthy man. He smiled, and spoke with a Hispanic accent, "I know exactly where I will land."

"When we met in prison I realized something," Burns reflected. "These two were a minority in the population, but they had special skills. We all decided we would never go back to stir, but we needed to be a lot smarter if we were going to make any money. When you contacted me, Doc, with your proposition, I knew we could make it work. So far the cops have nothing. They've come by our place a couple of times, but there's nothing there for them. We all have jobs. We don't make any trouble. We are being good ex-cons."

"Yeah, what are you guys doing now?" Doc asked.

"I'm working in a bowling alley. Lamont works in a car wash, and Rafi works in a 7-Eleven. Rafi was taken on by the 7-Eleven in an experiment to see if an ex-con could be a good citizen. He has even been in their news rag as a model employee," Burns explained.

Rafi smiled. "I am a model for the community."

"Well we better be goin'," Burns said.

Doc smiled. "I might have something for you in a week or two."

"Well if it doesn't interfere with our day jobs, we may consider it." Burns laughed.

\*\*\*\*\*\*\*\*\*

The Dodge utility van drove along the Pike. A light rain began falling. Burns was driving. Rafi sat beside him. Behind the two Lamont sat on a chair. There was a curtain pulled to the side of the van. Rafi said, "Burns, I got to hand it to you. This gig is really working out."

"I told you we'd do all right. Doc figures out who to hit, takes the loot, and all we do is the job. We get it to him right after the job, and the cops can't connect it to us. That's the problem. Everybody else is sloppy, and they get caught. We've done seven jobs. The cops think they know we have done some, but there is nothing to connect us to them. We're just three ex-cons trying to get our lives together."

Burns partially turned to Lamont. "You know, Lamont, Doc has done us a real favor with those off-shore accounts."

Lamont leaned forward. "I hear you. I just hope we can trust him."

"Doc hasn't stiffed us yet. He got us the house, this van, and he's slipping us enough cash so we can live pretty good. Besides, if he tries to stiff us, he knows we can screw him."

"Yeah, I know. I just don't trust nobody with my money."

Rafi chimed in, "You know what I want is some strange snatch. I'm getting tired of the Roadhouse cunts, and we ain't had a fun time for a while."

Burns laughed. "Jeez Rafi, you can't keep that cock cool for two days." Burns suddenly focused on something ahead. "Hey, look at that. There might be some fun. You two get back behind the curtain." A young girl was walking along the side of the road. The two quickly got in the rear out of sight.

Burns slowed the van and opened the window on the passenger side. He yelled out to the girl, "Hey, you need a ride?" The girl kept on walking. He said, "Look, I'm taking the van back to my TV shop about five miles down the road. It's starting to rain. You're going to get wet. C'mon." He slowed down on the side of the road as the girl began to stop.

"I just need to go about two miles. I guess it's all right." Her hair was wet, and she looked like she had been crying.

"Hop in," Burns said. She climbed in the van and sat close to the door.

"I just need to go a few more miles," she said.

Burns smiled. "Be happy to do that."

Cherie sat against the passenger door. She was disoriented by all that had happened to her. It had started to rain heavily. Suddenly there was a bag over her head; an arm went around her neck, and she was lifted out of the seat and dragged into the rear of the van. "Wrap the cord around her," someone said. She struggled, but there was nothing she could do. She tried to yell, but someone stuffed something through the bag into her mouth. She passed out.

When she woke up later, she couldn't tell how long they had been driving. The van slowed down and stopped. Someone spoke, "Okay, it's dark enough. Let's get her inside quick." She was lifted out of the van. A man put her over his shoulder and walked up some steps. They walked into something—a house? Then down some stairs. Her head bumped against a wall.

He carried her across some space and dumped her on something. The bag was pulled off her head. She looked around in bewilderment. She was lying on a dirty mattress on a metal frame. Three men stood around her. She was in a small room with a shower stall and a toilet on one side. There was a light on the ceiling.

Two held her down and a dark man with greasy hair yelled, "Me first!"

One holding her roughly removed her T-shirt and bra. The other pulled off her sport shoes and socks and her pants and underwear.

A tall white man holding one side of her laughed. "Go to it Rafi."

Rafi entered her and raped her. The other two raped her too. When they were finished, they threw her T-shirt at her. The men walked out, closed a door. The light went off and she was in the dark.

"Oh, God," Cherie prayed, "please save me." She began to cry. She felt sick to her stomach.

Cherie shivered throughout the night. She had not eaten since noon yesterday.

It began to get light. There was a blocked basement window, but some light began to come through.

The ceiling was exposed wood and high above her head. She heard someone walking around upstairs.

Suddenly the light came on. The door opened, and the short man they called Rafi came in with a box of cereal, a carton of milk, a plastic bowl, and a plastic spoon. "Here eat something," he said.

She was hungry, but scared of him.

"Don't worry, I won' do nothin' to you."

She began to eat the cereal.

He squatted down and watched here. "You're kind of cute," he said. "We might keep you for a while."

She didn't know what to say.

"Look, we usually keep our girls for a while. Then we'll take you somewhere and turn you loose. You'll never know where you were or who we were. We just like to have some fun."

She finished eating.

"Take a shower. Clean up. You'll be okay." He smiled reassuringly.

Rafi left and closed the metal door. He slid the bolt shut. Looking to his right he saw several women's clothing items thrown against the wall. He walked up narrow wooden basement steps and opened a door at the top of the stairs. Coming out into a small hallway, he crossed over to a kitchen. Lamont and Burns were in the kitchen sitting at a small table with a porcelain top.

Burns said to Rafi, "She okay? Want some coffee?"

Rafi grinned. "She's doin' fine. She ate the cereal. I told her we'd be letting her go soon."

Burns nodded. "Yeah, yuh got to give them hope."

Rafi looked serious. "I think we got to get rid of the clothing pile. If the cops come again, it wouldn't be good to have that stuff lying there."

"You're right. We got rid of the other girls, but forgot about that. We have another set of buyers for a new snuff video," Burns said.

Lamont looked up from his coffee. "Yuh know Doc doesn't know about our little business. I don't think we need to tell him, but we do need to make sure we're cleanin' up. I think we keep her for only a few more days. The cops could come after us again. Of course our last caper was pretty clean. The guy we stole that stuff from sure won't be reporting it."

"Okay, we play with her for a few days, get some good videos of us doin' her, and then she's done," Burns said with finality.

Lamont finished his coffee and stood up. "I need a little poon right now."

Burns laughed. "Shit, Lamont, I got to finish my breakfast before I do some. You haven't even finished your eggs."

Lamont grinned. "I got's to start the day right." He walked out of the kitchen and opened the door to the basement.

# Chapter 15

Sam drove back to the Holiday Inn. He needed to find a more private motel and organize his equipment and plan the operation in detail. He decided he would get on I-75 and drive north to Ocala and get a room there. He got another $15,000 dollars to carry him and closed out his safe deposit box. He wanted to be very careful and not leave any trail from Ft. Myers. He prepaid his Holiday Inn bill with his debit card, but everything else in cash. He knew even with all the precautions he was taking, a dedicated professional would be able to track him. He was just going to take that risk.

He allowed his beard to continue growing and let his hair get long and scraggily. He wanted to look like a homeless veteran. Where he was going he needed to not look too sharp. He needed to blend in. He had often had to assume the look of local people. He might not look exactly like them, but he wouldn't stand out.

Today was the day he needed to begin acquiring his weapon inventory. He had Bing'ed the Internet looking for the stores he needed to visit in Ft. Myers. He needed to have a hard-to-trace inventory for the operation. He-found several sporting and gun stores that had useful weapons and inventories of knives.

Florida was a great state for weaponry. In fact the latest Supreme Court decisions had made many states much more gun friendly. His first visit was to Guns Florida. Their advertisements seemed to have the widest selection. They also had a range where he could check out what he might buy. He purchased a 9mm SIG P226, 100 target rounds, 100 hollow points, a cleaning kit, and a paddle holster. The latest SIG version was really sweet: very light. He did not want to use a gun for his mission. He just felt undressed without one. The store did their check, and he filled out the registration form. He had no problem leaving this profile; he just wanted to have the gun in case. He took the gun into the store's range and shot the 100 target rounds. It wasn't enough to break in the gun, but he was able to get the feel of it. He would clean it when he got back to the motel.

After buying the SIG, Sam entered a Fort Myers sporting goods store. It had an extensive inventory of weapons. He had his eye on a hunting crossbow.

The proprietor came over. "That baby is great for hunting wild pigs. I've gotten three boars myself with it. Would you like to look at it?"

Sam nodded. "I would need to practice a bit, but it looks lethal enough."

"You bet it is. It will go right through a one inch plank."

As the salesman extolled the virtues of the bow, Sam nodded as if he were entranced. He had used crossbows in several close-in operations.

His requirements were a bow that was very silent, over 300 fps, and would take down into a compact form. The one he picked was similar to the ones he had used. Unfortunately the ones he had used were illegal for public use. Sam bought the crossbow with thirty bolts. He also bought a canvas crossbow carrying bag.

At another gun store, he bought four SOG SEAL Team Elite knives.

The salesman looked at him. "Preparing for a fight?" he joked.

"Just gifts for some hunter friends," Sam replied. He bought a canvas duffle bag to put his equipment into. He stowed the purchases in the bag and put it into the trunk of the car.

Finally, he went to a Harley Davidson store. He thought they might have his final need. The clerk directed him to the clothing area of the store. He bought a pair of Italian lambskin driving gloves. They were very thin and supple. They wouldn't leave any fingerprints, and they wouldn't interfere with the use of his weapons.

When he returned to the motel, he left the bag in the car. *No point in the maid finding this,* he thought. It was now about 4:30 p.m. He went up to his room and showered. He ordered room service and packed the few clothes he had. The next morning he loaded the bags into his car, drove to I-75 and turned north.

The Ocala Quality Inn was off the interstate and tucked back in a grove of trees. Sam chose a ground-level room in the back facing the trees. He brought all of his acquisitions into the room, sat down with his iTab, and opened up Google Earth. He was looking for a specific address.

The police report regarding his parent's murder his brother had sent him provided some detail about the murder. A van was seen parked near a street on the other side of the forest bordering his parent's house. It was a white, non-descript vehicle. The person who had noticed it thought he remembered some of the seven license plate numbers and letters. The van had been pulled off the street onto a lane leading into the forest. The individual was jogging in the early evening and thought it strange it was parked there, but perhaps it was someone just taking a leak or some kids necking.

The police had traced the van to a James William Burns, a convicted burglar and felon, living with two other men, Rafael Jesus Martinez and Lamont Mason, in a house south of Philadelphia. They were all ex-cons. There were mug shots in the report. They were living together with the blessing of the State. Normally associating with known felons would create a problem, but the three had petitioned by saying they felt by living together they would reinforce each others' desire not to go back to crime. They had also been sponsored by a local businessman, Robert Kidd, nicknamed "Doc". The court had bought this arrangement.

The police had gone to the house and told the men they wanted to talk to them. The men didn't object. They did want a lawyer present. Yes, they had a white van with some of the numbers on the plate. No, they had never been in Haverford. Yes the police could search their home, but their lawyer objected. They were ex-cons, yes, but they all held down jobs. They paid their rent. They didn't get into any trouble. Why didn't the police harass some other men? The police walked through their house and found nothing.

The police report left it at that. There were no other leads. Sam's brother had talked to the police at length. They were sure these were the men, but they had no real evidence to use. They promised they would keep an eye on them, but they were sorry. They couldn't do anything else.

Roger's email and phone discussions hadn't offered any better information. Roger didn't know what to do. He told Sam he did what he could and decided to close up their parent's estate and move on. Sam agreed with him. There didn't seem to be anything else to do. It was very unfortunate such a horrible crime could go unpunished. Roger said sooner or later these guys would slip up and get caught for something. They left it at that.

Sam had been in contact with Allo regarding the information Allo had collected. Allo didn't have anything new to provide, but he did say he was getting close to breaking into the bank accounts the three and Doc had in the Caymans. He wasn't sure what he would be able to do, but he was working on it.

The more Sam had thought about murder and the whole situation with the four, the angrier he got. Here he had been roaming the world for the US, removing bad guys for a living. He believed the US would be a better place for his efforts. But his parents, who were good people, contributing to the betterment of the place, were murdered by goons just like those he had been eliminating for years. It just wasn't right!

When he returned from Venezuela, Sam was still depressed about the Venezuela operation. Losing Rico was just too much. In fact, Sam mused, he had lost a lot of people in the last few years: Felecia, his parents, and now Rico.

He had considered just forgetting the whole thing and going on an extended vacation, but something kept nagging at him. Why should bad people go free in his United States when he was sent overseas to remove bad people by the US? He understood the US and the western countries were bound by laws. There was a system protecting people who were accused, but when bad, evil people were known and the system allowed them to escape, there was something wrong. He was aware of OJ Simpson's trial and the gross miscarriage of justice it represented. A double murderer went off unpunished.

He had decided at Hurlburt he was going to do something. The government had spent twenty years training him to be an assassin, and he was good at it. At first he thought he would be satisfied by just finding the men and observing them. Maybe he could find a way to have the police catch them in a robbery. But then, if they did, would they get punished for killing his parents?

It was all too iffy. But then he began to think about eliminating them. If they were erased from the earth, who would miss them? Certainly not him. They were like cockroaches; they bred and infested the world, but didn't add very much, if anything.

*Yes,* he decided, *I will figure out how to eliminate them. However,* he realized, *I do not want to get caught. I'd be ready to accept my punishment, but it seems a bit ironic to be punished for doing what society should have done for itself. The system is screwed up.*

He figured he would proceed as if his activity were an operation. He needed to get as much intelligence as possible, create a means to access the targets, and eliminate them with as little fuss as possible and as little trace of who did it or how it was done.

The first part, intelligence gathering, was already partially in his possession—the police report and Allo's information. From that and discussions with his brother there was no doubt in his mind these were the murderers. He knew who and where the targets were. He needed to get much closer to observe the targets and plan how he would access them. Once he understood that, he would plan his steps to leave as little trail as possible. He was excited; this was what he had been doing for the last twenty years. He didn't need much outside assistance. It was a single-man operation.

Using the address in the police report, he began using various Internet café's computers to access Google Earth and Google Maps to gather overhead intelligence. This was just like using some of the satellite and drone photographs his team had used in planning their missions. The tools to carry out the elimination of the targets were readily available in the US. He was pretty sure what he was going to use and how he would use the tools. Access would come about through close-in surveillance, a skill he had honed for twenty years.

From what he could see on the Google sites, the individuals lived in an area south of Philadelphia that had seen better years. There were several developments of old row houses built close to old factories. Many of these factories either had been torn down or fallen down. Some of the row houses were torn down, but some remained.

He would need to get closer to understand the area, but it looked like he could gain access to the targets' house easily. Few people knew how much could be discerned from overhead photography by a trained interpreter. Sam had a great deal of training and experience in this. It was how he would plan to get into places without alerting guards. If you could visualize the route from actual pictures, it made it a lot easier. When the military and intelligence agencies began using drones, it only increased the ease. He didn't need to use drones. He would be able to walk around the target area.

As Sam sat in his motel room in Ocala, he went over his knowledge of the area—the house, motels, stores, bars. He was getting an overview of what the environment would be like. He called Lorraine on his throw-away cell. They chatted. He told her he was getting a lot done and it wouldn't be long before he could come and see her. His desire to see her was growing more and more each day. "I think we can really have something together," he promised.

He began his drive to Philadelphia. The route from the West Coast of Florida to the East Coast of the US is a long, boring slog. Once he hit I-95, there was nothing but truck traffic and a straight road.

He didn't want to get over-tired by trying to do it in a day; he allowed three days, stopping in Georgia, Washington, DC, and then driving the rest of the way to the Philadelphia area. He was concerned the three thugs might decide to relocate their activities and move elsewhere. He had used an Internet finder service to look up the three names. Burns had appeared at the address Sam input. Sam felt good the address was still valid.

He stayed in a motel off I-95, north of DC, and got started early on the third day. He had determined from Google Maps the exit to get off to get to the area where the house was. He took the exit off I-95, turned right and drove east. The road went over the Metro tracks north of Wilmington. He drove a few miles past the tracks to a main road, turned left going north, and then hit the road leading to the housing area. He turned right onto it, and drove through a forested area for about a quarter of a mile. The road opened up to a decrepit set of row houses. At one time it had been a nice blue-collar area. A pile of bricks and a standing wall with a partially visible painted sign on the wall proclaimed: kin Ball Bear—a ruined ball bearing factory.

The skilled labor supporting the factory had long since been let go and the work sent overseas. Trees and vines grew through the factory floor. The once-neat rows of houses were few and shabby. A few showed signs of being kept up a bit.

He turned right, south, on the target street. The street was about a half-mile long. There were a few houses on each side of the street as he drove down it.

Vacant lots and piles of rubble were broken by intermittent houses in various states of decay, some still occupied. He drove slowly down the street by the house where the three lived. The street ended in an overgrown forest and went left. Sam drove on. The target house was by itself on the block except for a deserted house on its right as he faced the target.

After turning left, the street ended at another pile of bricks and a large concrete apron—what appeared to have been a small warehouse. The entire area was surrounded by trees and overgrowth. A feeling of despair seemed to have overwhelmed the whole area. He turned the car at the dead end and drove out of the complex. What he had seen was pretty much as he had observed from the on-line photography.

He drove back to the main road, passing a 7-Eleven and a car wash. He checked into a cheap motel next to a strip of miscellaneous shops on one side and a bar on the other. Nothing looked very prosperous. The motel was what his buddies used to call a "No-Tell Motel", one where you took the woman you picked up in the bar next door. He didn't care; he wouldn't be there very long. The desk manager barely looked up as he checked in. He wrote a phony name in the register and paid ahead three days in cash. He picked up a hoagie from the 7-Eleven for lunch.

Before he decided on what his takeout plan would be, he had to collect as much information on the activities of the house as possible. He needed to know how many people lived in it, what their daily routine was, and what their vulnerabilities were.

He wanted to use the crossbow because of its quietness. Used properly, it could be deadly accurate over about fifty yards. He practiced with it at a vacant lot in Florida. It could still be deadly at greater ranges, but the accuracy could suffer.

He had used one in several takedowns. Once, he killed four men before they knew what was going on. The bolts dropped people, and anyone around them would take some seconds trying to figure out where the bolt was coming from. By that time they were down.

He was able to reload in about fifteen seconds. This was a disadvantage of the crossbow, but properly configured, a crossbow could be quiet and quick. His initial thought was to take down the men as they came out of the house and down the stairs to the van or as they got out of the van and walked into the house. Walking into the house was preferable. If they were in a line, he would drop the last one first. Generally, then, the second man would turn around. As he tried to figure out what happened, Sam would take him out. The third one would be on the steps looking around for the shooter. He would be down before he could react.

It was about 4:00 p.m. by the time he settled in his room. He put his Dopp kit in the bathroom and washed his face. His beard was coming along nicely, his hair over his ears. He fit into the area quite well, he thought. He watched the weather on the TV. A front was coming through in a few days. He could use rain as a cover, but he didn't want to use that as a primary plan.

He got into his car and decided to see if his surveillance plan would work. It was dark now as he drove back down toward the housing area. He had seen a stand of woods behind the house as he drove in.

Looking at the overhead photo he had seen a dirt track leading into the woods. He found it and drove into the woods. The track was rutted and overgrown. It obviously wasn't used by anyone.

About where the house would be, he stopped the car in a clearing off the track and turned it around. He looked around; the track was probably an old rail siding leading to the ruined warehouse. The rails and ties were long gone. He had brought a machete at one of the sporting goods stores in Fort Myers. He began hacking a trail through the woods toward the rear of the house.

He tried to make sure he kept away from the poison ivy he saw on the bushes and trees as he went along. He had a bad memory of a Sea Scout camp out where he didn't pay attention to the stuff. Most of the leaves had fallen off the trees, but there was still heavy brush. He arrived at a low hill approximately ten feet high behind the housing area. It ran parallel to the street in front of the house. He hacked his way up it. It was about 5:15 p.m. and growing dark.

At the top he could see dimly into the backyard of the target house. The backyard was surrounded by a five-foot-high board fence. He was about ten yards from the fence. The back of the house was another thirty yards away.

The house on the left was obviously deserted. He took out his night vision binoculars and looked around both houses. There was no door on the rear of a shabby addition to the deserted house.

The target house had a set of concrete steps leading to a back door. The sunlight was gone, but looking around the backyard he saw two large dogs lying under a tree at the right of the yard. They appeared to be pit bulls. At 5:30 p.m. a white van came down the street in front of the house. It looked like it may have turned into the driveway in front of the house. He assumed it did since it didn't go past the house.

A few minutes later a light turned on inside the house and shone through the back door window. Another light turned on over the back door. The back door opened and a stocky black man with a shaved head stepped out with two steel bowls. As he walked down the back steps, the dogs ran over to him, wagging their back ends with their stubby tails. The man put the bowls down and the dogs began eating.

He stood there watching them and looking around the yard. He obviously felt very secure where he was. Sam could look into the house through the open door into a corridor that seemed to run to the front of the house. He saw a smaller dark-haired man go from the left side of the corridor, open a door on the right side and disappear through it.

After about ten minutes the dogs finished. The black man picked up a large dog toy and threw it. One of the dogs ran after it and returned it, dropping it at the man's feet. The other dog sat and watched. After a few more throws, the man turned and walked back into the house and closed the door.

Sam continued to watch for another hour. There was no movement in the house that he could see. A light was turned on in an upstairs window. The dogs settled in for the night. A few very late summer mosquitoes were beginning to bite. *No comparison to a South American rain forest,* he thought. But this was early November and getting too cool for them. He decided this would be a good observation point for the next few days. He didn't want to allow anyone to observe him. He had to complete the strike soon. The only worry was the dogs. He would have to mess up their noses for a short time. He thought pepper spray might work. He had seen it used once before. You didn't spray it on the dog, just in the area. It seemed to confuse them and prevent them from discriminating very well. He left his observation point and returned to his car. He stopped at a Denny's for dinner.

He ate breakfast at the same Denny's. The next day he got to his observation point just as the first light of day began. He had checked the weather reports. In two days a front was coming through with heavy rain. He had to get his plan in action before it happened. The black man appeared again with the dogs' food about 7:00 a.m. He stood on the bottom step while they ate, just as he had the night before and then went back into the house. While he was standing there, Sam used his binoculars again to look into the corridor. Again, he saw the short, dark-haired man cross from the left, open a door and disappear. He surmised by looking at the house, the door led to a basement.

The dark-haired man seemed to be carrying a plate with food on in. This was very curious, he thought. *What could be in the basement? Or who? Could it be more dogs?* He put that in a separate thought. He needed to eliminate the dogs and the men he had seen. If he was successful in that effort, he would worry about the basement afterward.

He saw the van leave about 7:30 a.m. with two in it. He assumed the third man was in it too. Sam watched all day. No one came out after that. Nothing much happened in the back. The dogs roamed around the back and slept under the tree. There was a lean-to on the right side of the yard. Sam assumed it was for the dogs if it rained. The van returned about 5:30 p.m. The dogs were fed again by the same man. The dark-haired man went across the corridor with something in his hand. Lights went on as it grew dark. He figured he needed to strike before the weekend in two days and the rain.

The following day was Thursday. At 6:00 a.m., he drove his car into the area and parked on a nearby street. He walked down on the opposite side of the street to the target house. At a point where there were no other houses, he went to the back of that line and went into the overgrowth and through several abandoned backyards. There didn't appear to be a lot of activity anywhere. There were many vacant lots, many of them piles of rubble overgrown with weeds and trees. When he got to the lot opposite the target house, he moved forward to a pile of bricks and rubble from a torn-down house. He had a good view of the target house. He pulled out his binoculars and knelt down behind the pile and waited.

About 7:30 a.m. three men came out of the house and got into the van. He wanted to make sure there were no others in the house. A tall white man got into the driver's side. A short, dark man got into the passenger side of the van followed by a black man. Apparently the short man sat in the rear of the van. They all matched the mug shots in the police report. Sam was satisfied.

He returned to his car and drove to the rear again to make sure he understood their routine. The previous day's activity was repeated. The van returned at 5:30 a.m. The dogs were fed. He knew what to do. Friday evening would be a good time. The guys would have to come home to feed the dogs. They would probably want to go out afterwards, but dogs were dogs.

Sam assessed what he knew about their routine. From his experience it was best to hit in the morning as people were on their way to work. People were in a sort of trance. They had just gotten up, had something to eat, and were on a mental program. The next best was in the evening, but too often they were a little more alert from their day's activities. Based on what he had observed, he decided he would have to attack from the rear of the house in the evening. When the men did not show up for work on Monday, he would be long gone.

When the dogs were going to be fed, their attention would be focused on the man and then the food. He had to get into the house next door in order to be as close as possible. He would have to get in it just before the van returned. He would use the house next door as the place to attack from.

He returned to his room. He would not be coming back after tomorrow. He needed his sleep. He went through his weapons. The crossbow was in its nylon carry-bag; he took four bolts out and snapped them into their carrier on the bag. He took two of the Elite knives out, checked their edges, and made sure they would come out of their sheaths easily. He laid out the driving gloves, a pair of black athletic shoes, jeans, and a black long-sleeve pull-over shirt.

The rest of his gear he packed up and readied it by the door. He would leave early the next morning. He took his iTab out and inserted a pin into a small hole in its side. The iTab was similar to the militarized tablet computers he had used on missions. By inserting the pin into it, the contents would be erased and the whole computer rebooted. He took out his SIG and put it into his holster. The holster was on his left side, the two knives on the right. He did not plan to use the SIG, but he always had a backup just in case. He took a shower and went to bed and fell asleep. He had never had any problem falling asleep before an operation.

# Chapter 16

Burns turned to the bowling alley owner. "Okay if I shove off, Boss?" he asked.

The owner, a short rotund man nodded. "Thanks Burns. It's gonna get hectic here, bein' Friday, but I know you got a life. Jonesie is comin' in to help out. I'll see you on Monday."

Burns smiled. "See you then."

He walked out of the alley. This would be a fun weekend. The girl, Shirley, or whatever, would make a good video. They had not intended to get into the snuff business, but it just happened. The first time was a fluke. Rafi had picked up a prostitute at the Roadhouse and brought her home. She was not half bad looking so Lamont decided to try her. Then Burns did too. The girl began to object and demanded more money.

Burns then had an idea. He grabbed her and told Lamont to help him. They took her down into the basement. There was a room there, a previous owner or someone had used as a storeroom or spare room. It might have been rented out to someone. It had a shower, basin, and toilet. There was an old bed there, too. It also had a bolt lock on the door. The room was built of concrete blocks to the ceiling. It was a good prison. They threw her in there and bolted the door.

Burns went up stairs. "I got an idea. There's a big market for rape videos. I mean real rape. We can get a cheap video camera and fuck the shit out of her and then make a DVD and sell it. We could probably get a few thousand a DVD. I know some guys who can distribute them for us. Wadda ya think?"

They were sitting in the living room and the other two looked at each other. Lamont slowly nodded. "That could give us some extra cash. I don't like Doc havin' all our cash.

Rafi smirked. "I like doin' women when they don't want it."

Lamont nodded. "Especially if you hurt them a bit."

They went to a local Best Buy to buy a video camera. They spent some time with the salesman to make sure they got one that would do the job. The lighting down in the cellar was not great, but the salesman promised them it would do very well in low light. There was a special setting for low light and the resolution would not suffer. They got one that would do HD and sound and had a good zoom lens. They brought their new possession back to the house. They set it up and charged the battery.

The girl downstairs had already been pleading with them to let her go. She was only kidding. She didn't want any more money. The next evening the three of them went down to the room. They had decided Burns and Lamont would hold her down while Rafi screwed her. Burns would hold the camera with one hand. Then it would be Lamont's turn.

Lamont proved to be a little too rough. He slammed into her and she screamed. He then put his hand around her neck and she stopped struggling. He had crushed her larynx. She was dead.

Burns had videoed the entire thing. The three men were wearing ski masks. Burns decided they would make the DVD anyway. They just had to dispose of the body. They took the girl's clothes and threw them out of the room in a corner. They put the body in two large garbage bags and wrapped it with duct tape. The next night they drove to a creek off the Delaware Bay, weighted down the body with cement blocks, and threw it in the creek.

As they were driving back, Burns shared his thoughts with the other two, "Yuh know, I think it was good Lamont killed that girl. There was no way we could have let her go. She knew who we were and would have told the police. I think everything has worked out for the best. If we can sell that video, even better." The other two were silent, but nodded in agreement.

No one missed the girl, and they made an initial $80,000 on the DVD and more orders were coming in. Their distributor asked for more and different ones. Customers would like more fucking and any kinky stuff they could come up with. The demand was really big for this sort of stuff since it was obviously a real death. Following this success, they did it three more times. Each time they got more inventive. They would pick up a girl, bring her back, keep her for a while and then make their video.

Burns picked up Rafi at the 7-Eleven and Lamont at the car wash. They were happy it was Friday. Weekends could be a lot of fun. They stopped for a case of beer and then drove to their house.

The three men were getting their dinner in the kitchen. Burns turned from the stove where he was cooking burgers. "You know, guys, I hate to spoil the fun, but we got to get serious about our roomer downstairs. We shouldn't keep her much longer. I'm worried about cops. Besides, I got an order for a DVD."

"Yeah, Burns, I think you're right. Those snuff DVDs have made us a lot of money." Lamont nodded in agreement. He was standing at a small white table putting dog food into two bowls.

"I know, guys, but she is one sweet fuck," Rafi spoke up from the table chewing potato chips from a bag.

"Well, I say we plan to do it this weekend," Burns said as he turned back to the cooking.

Rafi rose and said, "I'll go give her some dinner. He reached into the refrigerator and took out two pieces of white bread and stuck a piece of American cheese between them and carried the sandwich and the bag of chips with him." He crossed the corridor to the basement door and went down. After ten minutes he returned and sat at the small kitchen table with his back to the corridor. Burns gave him a hamburger and turned to continue his cooking.

Lamont went out the door to the kitchen and turned right and went out the back door. He walked down the steps and watched as the dogs ran to him. They had been sniffing at the fence near the house next door. He thought it was odd, maybe a skunk. He set the dishes down for the dogs. He stood up and looked toward the house next door. He felt a terrible pain in his head.

# Chapter 17

It was dark and cold in the basement room. She wasn't sure how long she had been there. One of the men, Burns, had given her a sweatshirt with the logo Bryn Mawr on it. She thought that was a college outside Philadelphia. She had tried to clean herself in the sink. Rafi had given her some soap and a washcloth and towel. She spent the day lying on the bed. Too much had happened to her. She began to think about her life.

Her mother never had really taken care of her. Cherie had to operate on her own resources since she could remember. Because her mother worked different hours, Cherie had to get herself up, get something to eat, and then get to the school bus. Cherie had loved school since she started in daycare. The ladies and teachers all cared about the kids. At least they cared more than her mother.

One teacher in preschool seemed to like Cherie and worked with her a lot. Cherie learned to read when she was five, and found she loved to read. She could go into a different world.

As she grew older, she would go into the school library and read anything catching her eye. She read magazines and newspapers. There was another world away from the mother who was so bitter and unhappy.

There were happy people. There were people who did many things. They traveled and spoke different languages. There were other countries. Cherie longed to be able to go somewhere. She couldn't figure out how she would, but she would someday go to other places.

She also developed a philosophy. She learned about that from a book. You could have your own way of looking at the world and acting in it. The other girls thought she was weird but would include her because she was somewhat pretty. Boys couldn't deal with her because she was smart. All her grades were A's. She liked school and studied. It came easy to her.

When she got into junior high school, her science teacher asked her if she wanted to go to college. He said she was really smart and should think about going. There were scholarships. Cherie said, she sure would like to go, but when she mentioned it to her mother, her mother went into a rage. She yelled at her about how much money it would cost, and said, "You aren't smart enough to open a closet."

Cherie didn't talk about it anymore.

Her mother brought a new boyfriend home when Cherie was fourteen. Cherie began sleeping on the couch. The new boyfriend started bothering her when her mother wasn't around. Cherie had managed to stay out of the apartment when the boyfriend was there, but one evening, when she thought he was working, he came in and grabbed her and pushed her down on the couch.

He ripped off her pants and panties and raped her. After he finished, he told her if she told her mother, he would kill her mother and her. She was terrified, and realized he would do it again if he could.

The next day she told her school nurse. The nurse took her to a hospital where they took swabs from her. The whole thing became horrible because the police arrested the boyfriend who turned out to be a sex offender. Her mother was called in and Cherie had to live with a foster family for a while. Afterwards, her mother was even more verbally abusive to her. Cherie tried to stay out of the apartment as much as possible.

Her one friend in school tried to help her, but the girl's parents were very strict and weren't sure Cherie was a good influence. They also went to church a lot and that was the time Cherie heard the pastor talk about God. After listening to him, Cherie began reading books about religion and God. She wasn't sure about the various religions, but she thought Christ had some good things that he said.

She formed her own idea of God: he was good; we were here for a reason; there was a lot of evil in the world; you just had to try to be good. She also began building a mental wall whenever bad things happened to her.

She read some books about Buddha and his ideas. She liked the idea of being able to meditate away the bad things around her. Bad things done to her body were not to be considered; what is inside you is what is important.

Cherie was feeling weak. She was very hungry. She slept intermittently during the day. They didn't feed her very much, cereal with milk in the morning. Then they were gone for the day. When they returned, she would get something else. Cherie woke to the sounds of the men walking around the upstairs. She waited because she knew soon Rafi would bring her some food. She thought he liked her. She had hopes he would get the other men to let her go soon. He had told her he would talk to them.

The light came on in the room and the door opened. It was Rafi with a sandwich and some potato chips. She sat up on the bed. He handed her the sandwich. "We'll probably let you go this weekend. I told you we wouldn't hurt you." She finished the sandwich. "Bend over the bed," he told her. She did, knowing what he wanted. He had his sex with her, and then walked out of the room, turned off the light, and bolted the door.

She was feeling very dizzy. She was afraid she was coming down with something. She wasn't sure, but she thought she had been in the basement about two weeks. She felt hopeful Rafi would keep his word. The other two came infrequently, usually before going to bed, and had her. She just turned off her brain when they did. Every night she prayed God would save her. She remembered the pastor at the one church she had gone to was very positive God takes care of people who trust him.

She heard some funny noises from upstairs. Usually after Rafi left, she could tell they all left, she assumed to go to work. These noises were different.

She heard a crash, a yell and a moan. It sounded like Rafi let out a squeal. Then there was a thud on the floor. It was quiet for a while. Then she heard light footsteps across the floor and a thud. Someone had dropped something heavy. This was repeated two more times. Then it was quiet. She was puzzled. What was happening?

The light snapped on. The door opened cautiously. Her eyes were not accustomed to the light. She could see a dark figure at the entrance. It was a tall man with long hair and a beard. He had a knife in his hand. He walked into the room. Cherie shrank back on the bed. All she had on was her light tee. She had tried to wash it in the sink, but it was ripped.

"Please don't hurt me," she pleaded with a shudder. She was sure this man was here to kill her. God had deserted her.

"Who are you?" the man asked. "I won't hurt you."

"Where are the men? Where's Rafi?"

"Don't worry about them. Who are you? What are you doing here?"

"There's three men who took me when I asked for a ride. They took me here, and they raped me. I've been here for a while, a couple weeks, I think. Please let me go. Don't hurt me."

He stood there looking at her, bewildered by this turn of events. "What's your name?"

"Cherie, Cherie Latham."

"Okay, Cherie. Let's get you out of here." He motioned for her to come out of the door. Cherie weakly stood. She almost fell. He took her arm and led her out of the room. "Are any of those your clothes?" He pointed to a pile of women's clothes in a corner.

"Those are my pants and panties and shoes and socks."

"Put them on quickly. We need to get out of here," he said impatiently, but gently. She pulled on her panties and pants and socks and shoes and laced them. "Put on jacket. It's cold out." He motioned to a jacket in a pile of clothes. He pointed her toward the stairs, "Go up them, and go out the back door."

He followed her, bracing her as she went up the stairs. There was a closed door ahead of her. She opened it. He turned her left and she went out the back door. He followed her and closed the back door as she went down the back stairs.

He scooped up a backpack and slung it over one shoulder. Suddenly he picked her up over his shoulder and ran toward the rear of the yard. She couldn't really see where she was going.

He stopped to unbolt a gate, and ran a few steps and then through some underbrush, up a small hill, down the hill and through a wooded area.

She was out of wind. He ended up at a car, opened the passenger door and put her in.

He drove them off through some woods, turned the car onto a road, and kept on going. She had no idea where she was or where they were going. "Are you taking me away from them?"

He looked at her. "Yes, but I don't know what to do with you."

He seemed to be trying to understand what had just happened. He was silent for about a half hour as he drove. Cherie huddled against the passenger side door.

"Hey, are you hungry?"

She nodded.

"How about a MacDonald's?" One was coming up ahead.

She nodded. "They didn't give me much to eat."

He pulled up to the drive through speaker. "You like Big Macs? Fries, Coke?" he asked.

She nodded eagerly.

He ordered for her and himself and pulled into a parking space. As they ate, she began to shake. She was almost sick to her stomach.

He turned to her, concerned. "Eat slowly, if you haven't had much lately."

She put half of the hamburger down. "I'm so scared. I don't know where I am or where we're going." She began to sob.

He was speechless. He took a deep breath. "Look, let's not make any decisions tonight. I need to find out who you are and then figure out what to do. I'll get us a motel room for the night. You need to sleep and be able to eat something. We'll get you some new clothes tomorrow. Don't be afraid of me. I won't hurt you." They drove into the night.

# Chapter 18

The day of the mission Sam got up before dawn and cleaned up the motel. He wiped down every surface he had touched, door knobs, the sink, everything he could think of. There was little probability anyone would ever check out his room—he was just being a little obsessive, he decided. He ate at a Big Boy and drove to the observation point behind the house. He had his crossbow with him and the two knives, his SIG on his left hip. His main concern was the dogs. He sat on the hill watching the house until about 4:45 p.m.

He went down the hill, staying to the left of the deserted house next to the target house. The dogs were resting under the lean-to. He ran to the left side of the deserted house. Taking a pepper spray from his pocket, he crept around toward the steps of the deserted house. He sprayed over the top of the fence as he went up the stairs into an enclosed porch built out from the house. There was a broken out window in the porch parallel to the steps of the target house. He hid back in the darkness. He could see the dogs. Apparently they had not caught his scent. He took out the crossbow and the bolts. He loaded it and it was ready. He waited.

About 5:30 p.m. he began to hear noises next door. Voices came through the walls. He readied himself. The light went on and the back door of the target house opened. The dogs raised their heads expectantly. They ran over to the black man standing there with their dinners. One sniffed at the fence and sneezed, but came right over to the black man as he put the bowls down. He stood up and turned his head toward the fence.

Sam aimed at his head and shot the crossbow. The bolt went into the black man's eye and came out through the other side of his skull. It almost went entirely through. He stood for a second and fell sideways, dead.

One of the dogs looked up curiously, and went back to eating. Sam cocked and loaded the crossbow. He aimed at the closest dog and shot it in the head. It fell heavily. The other dog jumped back and came over and sniffed the dead dog. He shook his head and began eating his food again. Sam reloaded and shot it through the head also. It fell next to the other dog. Sam looped the crossbow sling over his shoulder.

He sprinted down the back steps, vaulted over the fence. It was nothing like the wall at basic SEAL training. He tossed off the crossbow next to the dogs. He jumped over the bodies and leapt to the top of the doorsteps.

Coming through the door he looked left. The dark-haired man was sitting with his back to Sam at a small table at the left of the kitchen. The tall white man was standing at a stove facing away from Sam.

Pulling a knife from his sheath, Sam stepped into the kitchen, grabbed the head of the dark-haired man and plunged the knife into his heart. The man slumped over the table.

Pulling the second knife from its sheath, he quickly stepped to the man at the sink who was just turning. He grabbed his head and savagely rammed the knife into his heart. Sam held him and lowered him to the floor. The man looked at Sam and tried to say something, "Who...?"

Sam whispered, "The son of the coin owner." The man's eyes widened in recognition, and then the dullness of death filled them. Sam turned to the man slumped over the table. He pulled the knife out of him and tossed it into the kitchen sink. He did the same with the other knife.

He dragged the dark-haired man farther into the kitchen. He went to the sink and washed the blood off the knives. He put them back into their sheaths. He went out the back door and dragged the black man into the kitchen.

He pulled the bolt out of his skull and washed it off in the sink. Returning to the back steps, he dragged one of the dogs into the kitchen. He pulled the bolt out of its head and washed it off. He did the same thing with the second dog.

Looking around the kitchen, he checked to make sure he hadn't left any bloody footprints. He made sure he had not gotten any blood on his clothes.

There were two dish towels beside the sink. He picked up the bolts from the sink and the towels and went out the back. He snapped the bolts back in their carrier and put the crossbow in its bag.

He then wiped up any blood off the steps and landing. He continued to wipe it up as he went into the kitchen. Blood was accumulating in the kitchen, but he didn't care. He threw the towel into the kitchen, stepped out of the kitchen and closed its door. He stood there for a second and took a deep breath. He needed to ensure the rest of the house was clear.

Moving to the front of the house, he saw a flight of the stairs to the second floor. Quickly and quietly he went up them and stopped at the landing and looked around. It was a pig pen, but no one else was there.

Returning down the stairs, he went toward the rear to the door on the left leading to what he had surmised were basement stairs. He opened the door. There was a light switch on the wall; he turned it on and cautiously went down the steps.

When he got to the bottom, to his left was a wall with a door in it. There were women's clothes thrown in a pile on the floor to the right of the door. He couldn't make any sense of that. There was a light switch on the wall next to the door.

The door was bolted; he slowly pushed it open and switched on the light with his right hand. He pulled one of the knives out of its sheath. He stepped through the open door. As he entered, he saw a skinny blonde girl sitting on a bed to the right. She only had a dirty and ripped T-shirt on. She sat there and looked at him as he moved into the room.

He looked around the room. There was a shower stall, a sink, and a toilet on the left.

"Please don't hurt me," the girl begged.

He stood there trying to figure out what to do. She was obviously a prisoner of some sort. He had no idea what the three were planning to do with her or had done with her. He needed to leave quickly. He had no choice; she would have to come with him. He would figure out what to do with her later. They needed to get out. Operations always had unexpected twists and turns. The best response was to get into a safe situation and then reason out what to do.

# Chapter 19

By the time they stopped it was close to 11:00 p.m. and it had started raining. Sam found a small motel near Valley Forge, signed in, and paid the night manager. He carried his duffle into the room behind her. "Cherie, can you sleep?" he asked.

"I think so," she replied.

"Do you want to shower, or just lie down? You can shower in the morning if you want."

"I think I just want to lie down."

"We can talk about things in the morning. I want you to know I'm a friend. I'll do whatever I can to help you. You're safe now, okay?"

She looked at him wearily. "Okay. I think you're my guardian angel. God sent you to rescue me. I asked him to and he did." She had always believed God had a good plan for her. Maybe this man was part of that plan. She really thought he could be her guardian angel. Maybe he didn't know it, but she was pretty sure God had sent him. She would just have to see what was next.

Sam looked at her blankly. Whatever it took to make her feel safe was all right with him. "That's great. I'll be your guardian angel."

Sam told her to lie down on the bed away from the door. He didn't want her to leave during the night.

She had to go to the bathroom. "Is it all right if I don't close the door?" she asked. "I don't like to be in a closed room right now."

"It's fine with me. I won't bother you."

She came out and sat down on the bed, lay down and then huddled up into a fetal curl, closed her eyes and began to breathe heavily. She was asleep, but shivering.

Sam covered her with the blanket. Sam kept his clothes on and lay down in the next bed. He would figure out what to do when they got up the next day. He fell asleep. She woke him up twice in the night whimpering and sobbing. He looked over at her, but she was not awake. He woke up at 7:00 a.m. She was still asleep. He decided he would take a quick shower and get himself together. By the time he was out of the shower, dried off, and dressed, she was curled up in her bed with her eyes open.

"Is this real?" she asked. "Am I really okay?"

"Yes, you are okay. You are safe. Do you want to talk about what to do?" He sat on his bed.

"I guess so. I don't want to talk too much about those men, though."

"That's fine. My name is Sam. You told me your name. How old are you? Do you have parents, a mother and father, somewhere? Someone to contact and tell them you're all right?"

"I have a mother. My father left when I was born. She lives in West Chester. She lives with some guy. He was raping me when she came home and then she threw me out. She blamed me for him coming on to me. I just turned sixteen.

I had nowhere to go, so I was just walking to a friend's house when those men grabbed me. I didn't know where they took me because they had a bag over my head. When I got there, they raped me over and over. It was horrible."

"Cherie, do you have any idea how long you were there?"

"I think about ten days. It was hard to know because the room was pretty dark. I didn't know what to do. I just hoped they'd let me go."

"All right Cherie. I understand. Look, how about this as a plan. You take a shower and get cleaned up. I'll take you to a store and we'll buy you some clothes. Then we'll get something to eat. After that we can talk about how to contact your mother. She might be worried about you."

"Okay, but I don't think my mother really cares about me. When she threw me out, I think she was happy to see me go."

Sam pursed his lips. He could not imagine a mother treating a child the way she described. "Cherie, from now on if we meet anyone, I'll tell them you're my daughter and we're going to see your grandparents in Chicago. We don't need people wondering why we're together. Okay? Let's get going."

She nodded. "Okay, Dad." She smiled.

He drove them to a Target store. The clothing she had would not do to be seen in public. He had given her one of his T-shirts to cover her dirty tee. She had no bra, which was not a big deal, but she needed something.

They walked into the store and back to the teenage girls' clothing area. There was a woman clerk standing there. Sam walked up to her, "Ma'am, can you help us. I just picked up my daughter from her mother. Her mother has custody, but she never spends any of my child support on clothes for her. We're going on a vacation to see her grandparents. She needs everything."

The clerk looked at Sam and then at Cherie. "What kind of a budget are you working to?" she asked.

"Don't worry about it. Just make her look like a typical teenager."

The woman nodded. "Okay, I have two girls myself."

Sam turned to Cherie. "Pick out what you want and let this woman help you. Get some warm clothing, too, a jacket, sweater, whatever. Get some underwear, too. Get enough clothes for five days." Cherie blinked in disbelief. "Five days? I don't need that much."

Sam looked at her. "You may need that much, besides you need some new clothes anyway."

The lady took Cherie by the arm and led her off. Sam went to another part of the store and picked out a small suitcase. He was concerned Cherie's mother might not welcome her. He would then have to find someplace else for Cherie to stay, probably a foster home. She would become the state's responsibility. He began to think about that. He also realized he had not talked to Lorraine in several days. As he walked back to the girls' department he dialed her number. "Hi, it's me, your lost and wandering boyfriend-to-be. Where are you?"

"I'm glad you called. I was getting concerned. I'm at work. I can only talk for a minute. Is everything going well with your business stuff?" Lorraine asked.

"Yeah, I've finished what I had to do. I've picked up something else I have to attend to, but I'm on the way to see you. I'm in Valley Forge, Pennsylvania for a few days, but then I should be really on the road to Chicago, or Evanston, I guess that's where your address is."

Lorraine gave a yell of delight, "I'm going to begin to get excited. Drive fast, but carefully. I can't wait to see you so I can believe you're real."

"Oh, I'm real," he said. "I'm excited to see you too. Hey, I've got to be going. I'm in the middle of something. I'll call you again soon."

"All right," she said. "I guess long telephone conversations aren't your strength. Goodbye."

"Goodbye," he replied as he hung up and walked back to the clothing area.

Cherie was standing in front of a mirror with some sort of a top with straps on, some pants, and low shoes. She was admiring herself. She had a big smile on her face.

The woman was talking to her about what she had on, "Now, Cherie, you don't want to look cheap. You want to look nice and wear things that make you look refined. You look just like a teen model." The lady was a real salesperson.

Sam spoke as he walked up, "You do look like another person. Ma'am, you have done a good job.

---

The lady smiled at him. "Cherie is a nice girl and easy to work with. I've gotten her five nice outfits, two pairs of shoes, and underwear. I also got her two sets of pajamas and a nice winter jacket. Do you want to see what we have?"

Sam looked at the pile on the chair the lady gestured to. "It looks good to me," he said. "I don't know much about girl's clothing, but she looks much better. Thanks a lot for your help."

The woman looked at Sam with a frown. "You know this girl is suffering from malnutrition. She is a walking skeleton."

Sam nodded slowly. "Yes ma'am, I know. Her mother is not a very good mother. That's why I'm taking her to her grandparents. We need to decide what to do." The woman didn't look happy, but she shrugged and raised her eyebrow.

They walked to the front of the store to check out. Cherie was quivering with delight. "Dad," she said in a melodramatic voice, "I have never had such nice things in my life." Then she got serious. "I know you can't take care of me forever, but I just want to thank you for what you've done. I can never thank you enough."

Sam looked at her. "Cherie, come what may, I'll do my best to leave you in a good place. And don't think I'll just walk out on you. I'll make sure you're safe."

Something occurred to him. "Cherie, let's get you some toiletries."

She looked at him as if he had spoken in Swahili. "What're they?"

"You know toothbrush, hairbrush, toothpaste. You should have them with you." She looked at him with a funny expression. "I don't think I ever had a new toothbrush."

He paid the bill. They put her clothes and other items into the new suitcase and walked out to the car. It was still raining steadily. "Let's get something to eat and then talk about seeing your mother," he said.

# Chapter 20

They settled into a booth at a Silver Diner. Cherie looked around the room. "I've never been in a nice place like this," she observed.

Sam looked around. "There are nicer places, but this is a pretty good place to get some breakfast."

Cherie had been studying the menu. "I don't know what some of these things are."

"What do you like?" he asked.

She looked up from the menu. "Usually I just get cereal with milk. I had pancakes once at my friend's house. They were really good. I know what eggs are. What's a waffle?"

He realized her life had been pretty meager. "I tell you what, I'll order some things for you, and you decide what you like. Just take a bite of each one and then in the future, you'll know what is good to you."

She nodded eagerly.

Sam ordered himself a large omelet, toast, coffee, and orange juice. For Cherie he ordered an English muffin, bacon, a waffle with strawberries and whipped cream, and a small omelet, orange juice and milk.

When it all came Cherie looked at all the food in bewilderment.

"Here, put some jelly on the English muffin and take a bite of it."

She did and nodded. "That's pretty good."

"Have a bite of the bacon."

"Umm, I like that too."

"Now try the waffle." She wasn't sure how to attack it, and Sam showed her how. "Oh, wow, that's awesome."

"Okay, you have an idea of what you like, eat up."

Cherie proceeded to eat portions of the food in front of her. "I love waffles," she said. "The omelet was really good, too. I'm filled up. I don't want to waste the food, but I can't eat any more."

He looked at her. "Well, I wasn't sure how much you could eat, but you did well. You need to get some meat on your bones. You're a bit too thin."

This caused her to look sad. "I didn't get much to eat, lately."

"I'm sorry, Cherie, I didn't mean to make you sad."

"It's okay. I'm not going to think about that. I've found in my life the best way to live is look ahead and believe things will be better."

Sam cocked his head and looked at her quizzically. "That's a nice way to think. Now, we need to talk about you. You said you have a mother. Where does she live? Do you live with her?"

"She lives in West Chester. She has an apartment there. There's only one bedroom with two beds in it. I usually sleep there, but lately she brought a boyfriend in. I 've been sleeping on the sofa in the living room. I told you she found the guy, Lonnie, on top of me. She was really mad. She grabbed me and pushed me out and told me to come back when I was ready to say I was sorry."

Sam was puzzled by that. "Sorry for what? He was raping you."

"Well she blamed me for making him want to do it. I didn't do anything. He was a lot bigger than me and just got on top of me. He covered my mouth. It was really bad.

"I have a friend from school who sometimes lets me sleep at her house. Her parents are really nice, but their apartment is small, too. They took me to church one time. I liked it because they sang nice songs, and it was peaceful. The minister was really nice and gave a talk. He said God was with us all the time, and we have a guardian angel. I knew I had one because I can feel it near me sometimes."

"I think we need to go and see her. She may be worried about you. She may have called the police."

Cherie looked at him with concern and hurt in her eyes. "I don't think so. She was pretty mad with me. Every time she has kicked me out before, she just waits to see if I turn up. One time I was gone for two weeks. I stayed with a friend. She never tried to find me. I think she would like me to go away. She even told the Child Welfare Services lady she would be glad if they took me. The lady convinced her to keep me. But I'll show you where she is. If she doesn't want me, I can find somewhere to go."

"Cherie, don't worry about where you will go. I'll contact the proper people to make sure you'll be taken care of."

"Sam, I just want to thank you for everything you've done for me. I don't want you to worry about me. I will be okay somehow."

"Cherie, another thing, you must never tell anyone how I got you. Tell people you were captured by those men. Tell them what they did to you. Tell them one time they left the door unlocked, and you waited until they left, and then ran out. Tell people you just ran and ran. Tell them I found you lying beside the road and picked you up. After that tell them what we've done together. Understand, you can't let anyone know I was at that house."

"Okay, Sam. I know something bad happened there. I will tell just what you said."

"Now, we'll go see your mother. I'll go talk to her to see what's going on. You don't have to see her if it doesn't look good to me. Okay?"

"Okay, Sam."

Sam paid the bill, and they walked out to the car. The rain had lightened to a mist. Cherie was very quiet. Sam was pensive. He wasn't sure how to deal with this situation. From what Cherie told him, her mother was not very interested in her daughter. She seemed to consider her an encumbrance, an annoyance. Sam could not even imagine such a person.

His upbringing had been so good and in such a loving environment, he could not believe someone would treat their child like that. He had seen terrible things in other countries: child slaves, sexual perversions on children, starvation, murder and mutilation. But that was in other countries where they didn't have the advantages Americans had. No one in America needed to act like that. He continued to mull over his thoughts as they pulled out of the parking lot. The rain misted on the windshield.

Sam drove to West Chester. Cherie directed him to a set of two-story apartments. They were in a desultory environment—bare dirt spots where there should be grass, paint peeling. There was an air of lost hopes. A sign said "Chester Mews" as if to try to upgrade the whole environment. It failed. He wasn't sure if this was public housing. Some of the place could be. The cars in the parking lot offered no hope: dented ten-year-old cars, some with no hubcaps, a few trucks. It was about 4:00 p.m. Sam asked Cherie, "Do you think your mom is at home?"

"I think so. You said today is Saturday. She has Saturday off and then works Sunday in the evening. Oh, there's her car. She's here. Her boyfriend's here too. That's his truck. His name is Lonnie." A battered Toyota Celica sat in front of a line of the apartments with a beat-up Ford pickup next to it.

Cherie pointed out a ground-floor apartment. The door faced a sidewalk in front of the units.

"Just sit here until I find out what's going on." He got out of the car and walked to the door. He knocked on the door but didn't hear anything. He knocked again.

A woman's voice yelled from the inside, "Keep your pants on, I'm coming." The door was jerked open.

A short, heavyset woman stood before him. Her brown hair was streaked with some gray and a little frizzy. She was wearing what his mother once called a housedress. She looked like she had been sleeping. Her expression was wary. Sam had not really cleaned himself up. He still had a two-inch beard, long hair and a camouflage jacket over his black T-shirt. He had bought the jacket in a surplus store. It had two stripes on one sleeve and a nametag reading "Hudson." He didn't know if it had been really worn by a soldier, or if it was just for show. "Who are you? Waddya want?" she asked.

"My name is Sam Hudson. I found your daughter a few days ago near Philadelphia. She's in my car and all right. I brought her back. She said you two had an argument and she's sorry."

"Shit, she should be sorry. I had the school calling me, askin where the hell she was. I told them I didn't know and didn't care. They threatened to set the welfare people on me and I told them, 'Go ahead, I don't care.' She's more trouble than she's worth. Now you show up with her bein' sorry. Whoopee!" She backed into the living room of the apartment, and Sam took a step inside.

"Well, ma'am, I just wanted to bring her home. I thought you might be worried about her."

"I'm not worried at all. She can do what she wants. There's no room for her here. Did she tell you she tried to fuck my boyfriend?"

Sam was nonplussed by this. "Look, I'm just trying to be helpful to her. No need to cuss at me," Sam said gruffly. He was getting really irked by this woman.

A door opened from the back of a hallway and a tall, heavy man in a wife-beater T-shirt stumbled out buttoning up his jeans. "Janie, what the fuck is going on? Who's this fella?"

Cherie's mother turned to him. "This guy's found Cherie somewhere. He wants to know what to do with her."

"Shit," the man said, "she's the last thing we need here. Did she tell you she tried to seduce me? It's a good thing she's gone. She's nothing but trouble."

Sam stared at the man. He was about two inches taller than Sam and fifty pounds heavier. The man obviously had been drinking and so had Cherie's mother. "Look, I just wanted to figure out what to do with her. Don't you care how she is? What kind of mother are you?" Sam said with disgust.

"Hey, man, don't you go ragging on Jeanie. She's done a lot for that girl." He stumbled over to Sam and put his hand on Sam's chest and began to push him toward the door. "Why don't you just leave now?" he said as he pushed.

Sam didn't move very much. "Don't push me," he said in a low voice.

"I'll throw your fuckin' ass out o' here." He reached for Sam with his other hand.

The man's hand was on Sam's chest. Sam took his hands and held the man's hand against his chest and dropped to his knees, pulling the man down with him. This was a simple defensive move. He didn't want to really hurt the guy. Unfortunately, he was a bit drunk and fell flat and hit his head. He let out a yell and lay quiet.

The next thing Sam knew, Cherie's mother had her arm around Sam's neck and was punching him on his ear. This hurt. Sam hit her chin with his elbow and knocked her out. He laid her on the floor beside the man. He stood up, opened the door and left. He had decided there was nothing to be gained by any further discussion with those two.

He walked back to the car through the light rain. It was getting dark. He got into the car. Cherie looked at him apprehensively. "Was she all right?" she asked.

"She and Lonnie are fine. Your mother doesn't want you back, I'm sorry."

Cherie looked down at her lap. "I have nowhere to go now. You'll have to call Child Welfare. They have places for kids like me. I don't want you to do anything else for me. You've done enough."

"Let's get something to eat. It's late. We'll find a place to stay tonight and then talk about what we can do. I don't like to make any decisions on an empty stomach and no sleep." He drove away from the apartment. It was best to get away from there before her mother and Lonnie woke up.

Sam was flummoxed by the whole turn of events. He smiled to himself. He had never heard of the word until he had done some work with some Aussies in Indonesia. He thought. *That's the word of the day, today.*

His original plan was to eliminate the three men and split. If there had been others in the way, they would have been eliminated too. Operations always had unknown elements in them, but if you planned right, you could handle them.

He realized there was a new element in this mission. He had no team to work out things with; he had no back-up infrastructure to call upon. He was on his own. This was new territory. He needed to think through the situation and define the problem. From that he could define a course of action. But, for now, some food and shelter were needed. The rain had increased.

He saw a Burger Chef. "Burger Chef all right?"

Cherie nodded.

They ate their food in the car. Both were silent. He could sense Cherie was very concerned. "Cherie, I will find us a motel to stay tonight. I'm not going to abandon you. I don't feel good about Child Welfare. Trust me. I got us this far. I'll figure something out."

She tilted her head toward him and sighed, "Okay."

As he cruised along the highway, he realized he needed to get rid of all of the equipment he had bought to use on the mission. They were passing a large shopping center. He drove around it to the back where there were several dumpsters. He stopped and went to the trunk.

He took the knives out and tossed them into several different dumpsters. He drove a little way and took out the crossbow and broke it down. He threw some of the pieces in several dumpsters. The weather was miserable, which was good. No one would be observing them. He drove to the back of another strip mall and found some other dumpsters. He threw the bolts in them, together with the clothes he had worn, his shoes, and the camouflage jacket. The clothes he had put in a bundle the night before with his shoes. He was soaked by now, but glad to get rid of the stuff. He got back into the car.

Cherie looked at him, but said nothing. She was processing what she had seen.

# Chapter 21

Sam found another motel on the road to Exton. They both went in and fell onto the beds. Sam didn't even bother to undress. He just went into the bathroom, went to the toilet, and crashed.

Cherie did the same, but she couldn't fall right to sleep. She lay in the bed on her back trying to make sense of what had happened. She had no one, no place to live, nothing. She took a deep breath and let it out. She began to meditate. Tomorrow would be better. She fell asleep.

Sam awoke the next morning and lay in bed on his back, considering the situation. Turning Cherie over to any state officials could lead to questions about where he found her and what had happened to her. No, that was not a good idea. Besides, he felt responsible for her. A feeling he had never had for anyone else. He always felt responsible for himself and his team, but other people had to fend for themselves. When he went on rescue missions, the people were targets to be collected and saved and then sent on their way or to be eliminated. They were not a long-term commitment. Felecia was a commitment, but he was not responsible for her. He couldn't protect her. She was doing her job; he was doing his.

Cherie was different to him. He had rescued her, but there was something about her he needed for himself. He needed to fix her life. From what he had seen, her life was terrible, and yet she had a pretty positive attitude. She respected little things and was grateful for the minor things he had done for her. She also seemed to have some intelligence and perception. He couldn't just toss her back into the swamp she had lived in to date.

He also wanted to go to Lorraine. She seemed to be so wise and caring. Perhaps, she might have some ideas as to what to do. He got up and turned on his iTab and plotted a course from Exton to Evanston, Illinois. It would take about thirteen hours, two days taking it slow. He wanted to stop anyway and get rid of the car.

He called his bank to talk to someone about buying a car. He wanted a new SUV. He discussed the various models with a man who seemed very knowledgeable and ended up with a Ford SUV hybrid. The man told him he could go to any Ford dealer, have them call him and he would make the deal for Sam. Sam told him he would transfer cash from his savings account. The man said the bank would arrange for the funds to be sent to the dealer. Sam decided he would buy the car in Cleveland the next day. Today, they would get on the road.

He stepped outside the motel room and called Lorraine. Once again he was thrilled by the sound of her voice. He could not wait to see her. "Hello, it's me again. Did I wake you?"

"No, I was up and doing wash. What's new?"

"Well, I'm on the road, or will be soon. I'm in Exton Pennsylvania today, but will probably be in Cleveland tonight. I do have one slight thing to let you know. I'm bringing someone with me." There was silence.

"And?"

"It's a young girl. She needs help and I thought you could help us figure out some things."

"Some things?"

"Yeah, look it's complicated and I trust you to be able to help me deal with the situation. This is a test. You have trusted me to now. You will just have to hang in there. I know I'm a cipher to you, but you'll see it's okay. If you don't like the situation, you can toss me out."

"I will be waiting," she said with a hint of sarcasm. "So far the whole relationship is the most bizarre thing I have ever been involved with. So a little more bizarre will just seem normal. The wash is finishing, and I have to deal with it. Call me when you get to Cleveland."

When Sam stepped back in the room, Cherie was sitting up in her bed. "Did you just talk to someone?"

"Yes, it's a lady I know who lives near Chicago. I was thinking Cherie; maybe the best thing for you is to go with me and see her. She may be able to figure out what we can do. I don't feel right turning you over to the state people. They'll just put you in a foster home or try to get you back with your mother. I don't think either alternative is a very good one."

Cherie's look was perplexed. "I don't want to bother you anymore. I know you have things to do and your own life. Actually, I was thinking... I don't really know who you are or why you're doing anything for me. In my experience people don't do anything without expecting something back."

"I understand what you're worried about. I just got out of the Navy. I worked with people who were sent by the government to fix things for the United States. We often rescued people in trouble. So, you aren't unusual for me. The difference is I'm doing it for you by myself. You don't have to worry about paying me back. I have enough money to take care of you and myself. As far as expecting anything from you, right now, I don't want you to do anything. Later, when we figure out what your situation might be, I may ask something of you, like go to school, do well, have a good life, and be good to others."

Cherie stared at him. "I can do those things. I meant something more."

"In my experience, if you do those things, you will make me very happy and yourself too. Now, let's get ourselves going. I have something I need to do. You take a shower, and I'll shave here." The motel room had a sink outside the bathroom.

Cherie gathered her few things and went into the bathroom and closed the door. Sam took out a pair of scissors from his Dopp kit and began clipping his beard. By the time Cherie finished her shower and was dressed, Sam had shaved off the beard.

"Wow, you sure look different," she said as she opened the bathroom door.

"I needed a change," he said. "Hey, have you ever been to a beauty salon?"

"No. Why, don't you like my hair?"

"No, it's not like that." He smiled at her. "I'm going to find a barber who will cut my hair short. I thought we might find one of those hair cut places that does men and women, and you might like to get your hair cut, too."

"I don't even know what they do in those places." She looked worried. Cherie's hair was long and tangled. She had thick curly hair. Sam thought it might help her self-image to have some attention to it.

"Well, let's see if we can find one and fix us up." They got their belongings packed and went down to the car. He then drove along one of the major highways leading out of Exton. He turned into a salon offering unisex hair cutting. They advertised they were open seven days a week. He went in and asked if they could have an appointment in about an hour and a half. They were going to get breakfast first. The receptionist said they could accommodate them.

They walked into a Village Inn and were ushered to a booth. Cherie was really enjoying looking at all the pictures of the various foods. She queried Sam about what the food tasted like and whether he thought she would like this or that. They ordered their food.

Sam leaned across the table looking serious. "Cherie, I don't want to keep bothering you about what happened in that house. Not what happened to you, but how I got you? Just make sure you remember what the story is. You were trapped by those men, but you escaped after they molested you. You ran and ran and hid from them. You were on the side of the road when I found you. I picked you up and then the rest you can tell."

Cherie looked at him for a long time. She slowly nodded her head. "I understand about the house and the men. I think I know what you did. I'm not worried about that. They were evil, evil men. They should not be on this earth. I used to watch a TV show when my mom worked at night, 'Law and Order Special Victims Unit.' They always helped rape victims. There was a policeman on there who would be real mean to the bad people. He was very frustrated because he couldn't get rid of them. I know if the police get involved they will want to find out who did whatever. I would never tell anyone I was there. I was just picked up and raped, and then I escaped. I ran and ran and you picked me up. I don't even know where you picked me up. How's that?"

Sam studied her intently. She was so smart and intuitive. How could such a person have been subjected to such a life? *God works in strange ways,* he thought, *I'm not sure I like how he works.*

"You are so good. That will help both of us get through this. We'll just leave it at that."

They finished their meal and walked out into the morning. The sun was shooting rays through broken clouds. Sam drove them over to the hair salon. He told Cherie to look at some of the magazines to get an idea of what she might like. He sat in the chair and told the lady he wanted a short haircut. They discussed how he wanted it. They settled on a Number 2 cutter.

Cherie looked at several of the magazines. She settled on a short haircut a teenage celebrity movie star wore. The lady took her to the back of the salon to wash her hair. Cherie was not sure about what was happening. Sam nodded to her and told her it was all right. The lady cut and shaped Cherie's hair to resemble the movie star. She blow dried the result.

Sam was impressed. Cherie was a cute kid. She deserved to know it. "Cherie, you look like the movie star. You're a good looking girl."

Cherie looked at herself in the mirror in disbelief. "I don't believe it's me." She turned her head and looked at herself from several angles. She had a big smile.

Sam paid the ladies and gave them a big tip. They were having fun. They walked out into a blustery fall day. Vapor from puddles of rainwater floated up into the air. They got into the car and began the drive to Cleveland. They settled into a quiet, restful silence, both with their own thoughts. Cherie picked up Sam's iTab and was looking at it. "Is this a computer?" she asked.

"Yes, you can use it."

"I know a lot of kids at school had things like this. I just had what they provided us." She turned it on and began to operate it. "You know there are a lot of kids I know who have Facebook pages. Those are a nice way to see what people are doing. I never had one. There wasn't much I wanted to say."

"Well, maybe someday you will have a page and good things to share."

She smiled at this and continued playing with the iTab. After a while she turned to Sam, "Is it all right if I create an App?"

Sam was focusing on the interstate. "What's an App?"

"It's a little program that runs on the computer."

"Where did you learn to do that?" Sam was not into computers.

"I taught myself in school. I want to make an App, an application program to track of our trip. It's just for fun."

Sam was impressed with what Cherie thought was fun. "I tell you what. You keep that computer. Make all the Apps you want. Have fun. I can get another if I need one. You can always help me if I need to use a computer."

The drive to Cleveland was uneventful. Cherie turned on the radio and selected a station playing popular songs. They got to Cleveland in the early evening. He knew the address of the Ford dealer he was looking for and had stored the directions in the iTab. She loaded the address in the SUV GPS so they could find it in the morning. When they found the dealership, it was closed, but nearby was a Best Western motel. Sam got them a room, and they went next door to a local Italian restaurant.

The restaurant was a little more upscale than a Big Boy. They were greeted by the hostess who took them to a booth. Sam could see Cherie's head was spinning. "This is really a nice place. They have tablecloths and nice knives and forks and stuff. Wow, Sam you really know nice places."

"Well, we need to have a good meal. Have you ever eaten at an Italian restaurant?"

"Actually, I've never eaten at a restaurant. The most like a restaurant I've been in is a MacDonald's. This is like something on a TV show."

"Would you like to try something really good?"

She nodded her head eagerly.

"How about a ... no I won't tell you the name until you taste it." The waitress came up, and he pointed to something in the menu and said," That's what she will have. It's a surprise." He placed his order, and the waitress wrote down their orders and left. "Cherie, I enjoy having you along. I'm having fun showing you the world. I just hope I can figure out how to let you continue on your journey."

She looked at him for a long time. "I've read a lot of books and done a lot of studying on things on the Internet, too. You are letting me see the things I've read about and seen on TV. I always knew there was a world away from my mother that was new and interesting. I want to be a part of that world. I don't know how to go from here."

"We'll take one step at a time. I'll try to be with you to help you."

The meal came. Cherie looked at what the waitress had delivered. It looked like a small brick. "How do I eat this?"

"Take your knife and cut down…here let me show you." He cut a piece out of the pasta and put it on a fork. "Try this," he said as he moved it toward her mouth.

She opened her mouth and began to chew. A look of delight came on her face. "Is this lasagna?"

"Yes. It is a basic Italian dish. There are a lot of different ones, but I thought you'd like it. The Italians use a lot of what's called pasta, noodles, and such. I got a pasta dish called linguini. Sometimes they put a red tomato sauce on their pasta. Sometimes a white sauce made from cream, and sometimes just a sauce from olive oil. There are lots of sauces and spices they use."

She was wolfing down the lasagna. "I saw some of that on a cooking show on TV, but I didn't understand much about what they were doing. I'd like to learn to cook things. My mother only cooked frozen meals in the microwave. I had Stouffer's lasagna once and liked it, but it was nothing like this."

At the end of the meal Sam ordered canoli's for them. The look on her face was pure rapture. He paid the bill, and they walked out to the car. As he got in the car he said, "Tomorrow, we begin a new adventure."

Back in the motel Sam told Cherie to get ready for bed. She went into the bathroom and began to shower. He called Lorraine. "We're in Cleveland. We'll see you tomorrow. I am really excited to see you."

Lorraine sounded a little cool, "This we stuff is bothering me. I can't imagine what is going on. I'm really looking forward to you getting here so we... I... can figure out what is going on."

Sam tried to reassure her, but he realized until he told her the whole story, or most of it, she would not be satisfied. He didn't blame her. They continued a desultory conversation that gradually wound down, said goodbyes and hung up.

Later that evening while Cherie watched TV in the motel, Sam called his brother. "Hey Roger, it's Sam. I'm in Cleveland headed sort of west."

Roger answered, "Great, will we be seeing you soon?"

"I have to stop in Chicago. I met a girl, woman, and I want to see her for a while. Nothing negative about you and Janie, I just need to see what develops, plus I've got another situation I need to take care of. I'll explain it all later. Are you two and the kids okay?"

Roger was used to Sam's cryptic messages. "We're fine, and whenever you want to get here is okay. I hope you've found someone good for you." They talked for a few minutes and ended the conversation.

Sam took the iTab and typed out a message to Allo: <Allo, how are you coming with your bank hacking? I might have an idea for some fun, Sam>

Allo quickly answered, <I've made some headway. We will need to talk directly. I can get a throwaway cell. I'll let you know the details soon.>

They ate a quick breakfast in the Best Western and drove down the street to the Ford dealer. They walked into the dealership, and Sam asked for the sales manager. A man came over and introduced himself. Sam told him the model of SUV he wanted. The sales manager asked him what color he wanted. Sam turned to Cherie, and said, "What color do you like?"

She looked bewildered. "What colors are there?"

The sales manager showed her a display and said we have one of each color.

Cherie looked thoughtfully and said, "I like the silver one. I like silver things."

The sales manager turned to Sam and said, "I'll have one brought out front. Do you want to drive it?"

"No, thanks, I want it with every option though."

"This one fills that bill." The sales manager walked away and talked on the phone to someone. He walked back. "It'll be right here. Do you want to make an offer? Are you prepared to buy today?"

Sam gave the man a slip of paper with a name and number on it. "Give this guy a call. Whatever the price is, tell him. He'll get you a check or whatever you need. I want to drive the car out of here in an hour. We need to get on the road. You can give me whatever the car out front is worth in trade."

The sales manager gawked at Sam. He took the paper and went off to his office. In about fifteen minutes he came back. "Mr. Dancer, everything is arranged. We will have the car prepped for you and ready to go. I must say, you are a great customer. The bank called our bank and a check is there. Wow, this is a great way to start the week." He was all smiles and obviously flustered.

Within the hour Sam and Cherie had put their things in the SUV and were on their way. Sam wouldn't even let the sales manager show him all the features. Sam figured Cherie would have a good time reading the manual and telling him how everything worked.

# Chapter 22

On the same Monday Sam was buying his SUV, Wilson Quaker was getting worried. Burns had not shown up for work. Burns was a very reliable employee. He always got to the bowling alley a few minutes early and made sure everything was ready to go and organized. Besides being a good worker and organized, he was a nice fellow. The customers liked him. He always had a good word and a new joke for each day. Today was the first time he had not showed up. Wilson decided he would have to wait and see if he showed up. He had a cell phone number but Burns didn't answer. He got behind the counter and began to check out everything. Normally, he would be counting the weekend receipts. It was very unsettling.

A mile down the road, Adnan Rasil was having similar thoughts. Rafi had not shown up for work. Adnan really liked Rafi. Rafi was also a minority in this new country and seemed to share Adnan's work ethic. In fact Rafi was responsible for a significant decrease in pilferage from the 7-Eleven.

Rafi seemed to have a sixth sense when someone was about to try to take something. He foiled two attempted robberies by calling the police before the robber began the robbery.

Rafi called the police, telling them there was a robbery in progress and when the cops pulled up, the robber was caught standing there with his gun held out.

In both cases Rafi reached across the counter and hit the robber's gun hand with a pipe kept behind the counter for such contingencies. The robber dropped the gun, tried to run out, but into the arms of a policeman. *Where could he be?* Adnan wondered. He tried to call Rafi on his cell, but no answer. Adnan shook his head. Good employees were so hard to find. His nephew was worthless, but family. When his nephew came in that afternoon Adnan would have to see if he could find Rafi.

Fred, actually Federico Bacelli, was having a bad day too. All the rain had increased business at the car wash. Lamont hadn't showed up for work. Lamont was not the best employee, but he showed up each day and worked hard. Sometimes Fred had to make sure he was wiping the cars completely, but Lamont tried hard. Another employee, Corman, had broken his wrist while trying to fix one of the machines, so Fred was short two men. *Arrrg, the joys of a small business,* Fred thought. Lamont didn't have a cell phone, and Fred wasn't sure where he lived. If Lamont didn't show up soon, he would have to see if he could find another employee, always a difficult job. The pay was low, the work laborious and boring. *Shit,* he thought. *Mondays suck!*

About 7:00 p.m. Wilson Quaker walked out of the alley and got into his late model Mercedes. He drove the five miles to where he knew Burns lived. He knew Burns lived with two other men. They had been in and bowled some games occasionally and had a few beers. They were regular guys.

Wilson knew they all were ex-cons. He had taken on Burns at the request of a business friend he knew, Doc Kidd. Doc had gone to the Parole Board and set up the whole situation. Doc would let them live in his parent's old house and vouch for them as far as getting a job. Doc was a successful importer/exporter and Wilson had bought several collectibles from him.

Wilson pulled up in front of Burns' house. The van was in front, but there were no lights. Wilson thought this was funny. He walked up to the front door and knocked. There was no answer. He peered through the front window into the living room. There was no sign of life. Wilson couldn't figure out what was going on. *Maybe they had an emergency or something,* he thought. He left a note stuck under the door telling Burns everything was cool with him and to call Wilson when he could. He left.

Adnan drove by the house the next morning on the way to work. He hoped Rafi might have a twenty-four-hour virus or something. He walked up to the front door and saw the note sticking out from the front door. He pulled it out and read it. Apparently someone else was missing one of the men too. He had met Burns when he came in to pick up Rafi and buy some milk and other supplies. He wasn't sure what to do. He went back into his car and sat for a while. Well, he would just have to wait and see if Rafi would show up. He would have to hire his sister's son now. A bleak prospect.

**********

Doc was pissed. He had tried to call Burns several times during the week. He had some business for the three. It had a short fuse. "What the fuck is with him," Doc fumed. It had been over a week since he last talked to Burns, a Friday. He decided he would have to drive to the house to see what was going on. He had set up the whole thing, and Burns owed him big time. Doc did not like to leave his shop. He had living quarters in the building and rarely ever left. Belonging to Rotary was hard enough, even though the meetings were only weekly. His gross weight of 420 pounds restrained his movements. He pushed himself out of his chair, lumbered to his Hummer, and laboriously climbed up into the driver's seat. The seat was specially fitted for him to accommodate his bulk. Nonetheless, he rarely drove the vehicle. When gas got low, one of his employees would go and fill it for him.

Doc arrived at the house and was instantly puzzled. The van was there. Burns never went anywhere without the van. He opened the Hummer door and slid out of the seat to the ground. It was mid-morning and no one was around and there was no sign of activity coming from the house. Doc walked slowly up the walk, paused and climbed up the three front steps. He saw a white slip under the door, but it would require too much effort to pick it up. He knocked on the door loudly. "Burns open up, dammit." The knock sounded hollow to Doc. He was concerned. He tried the front door; it was locked. "Shit, I'll have to walk around the back." He knew where there was a key in the back.

Doc was breathing hard by the time he opened the gate on the left side of the house and walked around to the rear. The key was hung under the rear railing leading up to the back door. He took the key off and took a few deep breaths and climbed up the five steps to the back door. He fumbled with the key getting it into the lock. As he turned the key, he realized the door was unlocked. *That's funny*, he thought as he opened the door and pushed it in.

The kitchen door was closed, but the basement door was opened. He frowned trying to figure out what was going on. He opened the kitchen door and as he did, a disgusting odor wafted out. At the same time he saw the pile of bodies. He gagged and threw up on the floor landed on all fours at the same time. He crawled backwards and sat down. *What the fucking, fuck, fuck?*

He sat there for several minutes thinking about what to do. His first thought was to call the police, but then quickly rejected that thought. He didn't want to be involved in whatever had happened. He pushed himself up the wall to stand, reached into the kitchen for the doorknob, and closed the door. He went out the back door and closed it and locked it, taking the key with him. As he walked out to his car, he looked around to see if there was anyone around. He got back into the Hummer and drove back to his warehouse. He would lie low and see what happened.

The house sat for two weeks. The power company bill was not paid and the power was shut off. The men's employers figured the three must have moved on. Burns' and Lamont's paroles had run out six months before and were off the state roster. Rafi had three months to go. His parole officer, Nelson Crockett, was overworked, as they all were, and had let his monthly visit slip to five weeks.

He had tried to contact Rafi on his cell phone several times. He called the 7-Eleven and asked Adnan how Rafi was doing. Adnan explained Rafi seemed to have disappeared. Crockett was not happy about this news. Rafi had been a model parolee and had required little work. Now, Crockett would have to research the situation, write a long report, and let the police know Rafi had disappeared. First, though, he would have to go to the house to verify Rafi had gone.

He pulled up in front of the house about 10:00 a.m. The van in front of the house bothered him; the guys should have been at work. Crockett had been the parole officer for Burns, too. Burns had been the leader of the bunch. Consulting his records, he saw a Robert Kidd had been the sponsor of all three. The progress of the three working into an ex-con, productive life seemed to be working. There was no sign of life at the house, but Crockett felt he should at least see if he could find out anything. It was a very cold November day. He walked up the sidewalk to the steps of the house and noticed a piece of paper slipped under the front door. A small porch roof covered the landing in front of the door. He bent down to pull out the paper. He noticed the writer had put a date on it of two weeks before. He paused—a smell he hadn't experienced in over twenty years hit him.

Crockett was fifty and approaching retirement. He had been in the military during Desert Storm and been up the "Highway of Death". The smell of decaying corpses was one you never forgot. He smelled it now. Something was very wrong in this house. He walked down the steps and looked at the house for several minutes, and made his decision. Taking his cell phone out of his pocket, he called 911.

"What is the nature of your call?"

"I want to report a dead body."

"Are you standing with the dead body?"

"Yes, it is decomposing. I need to have the police come immediately. The address is 142 Poplar Lane."

"What is your name?"

"Nelson Crockett. I'm a parole officer visiting a parolee. I need police support immediately. I will be here in front of the house."

"I'm sending police support immediately."

Nelson stood at his car. Within five minutes a police cruiser pulled up with an officer in it, lights flashing. He walked over to the cruiser and the officer got out. He was a tall, heavyset young man with a short burr haircut. He was very businesslike. "Who are you?"

Nelson pulled out his official ID and told him. The policeman responded, "I'm Officer James Willenski. Where's the dead body?"

"I was trying to see a parolee of mine. When I walked up to the front door, I smelled a rotting body. I was in the army and know what they smell like."

The officer looked at him skeptically. "Okay, let me check for myself." He walked up the sidewalk, inspecting the house. When he got to the front, he took a big sniff and recoiled. He turned and yelled to Crockett, "Whew, there is certainly something dead here. Why do you think it's human?"

"I have smelled that before." Crockett yelled back.

The officer knocked on the front door several times. "I'm going around back."

Crockett leaned against his car. This was going to be a long day.

Officer Willenski walked down the narrow passage on the right side of the house to the gate leading to the rear. He pushed open the gate, and walked cautiously around to the back steps. Everything was very quiet, but the smell was becoming stronger. He walked up the back steps and tried the back door. It was locked. He knocked on the door. He could see a corridor through the back door window. There was a window to his left, but it was covered with a curtain. He decided he should verify there was a dead human body inside. If it turned out to be a dog, his watch commander would make him the laughing stock.

Willenski was only on the force six months after leaving the Air Force as an Air Policeman. It looked like the lock was only a twist lock on the inside. He took his elbow and smashed the lower left pane in the door. The smell whooshed out the pane. Willenski gagged.

He put his hand over his nose and reached inside and unlocked the door. He stepped into the corridor. There was an open basement door to his right, a closed door to his left. The stench was overpowering. He decided he needed to open the closed door quickly and then get out.

He twisted the knob and shoved open the door. A thousand flies buzzed around his head; he saw a pile of what appeared to be bodies. He reeled backward, dizzy and confused. Without realizing what he was doing, he fell back into the open basement door and fell down the stairs, knocking himself out on the steps as he fell.

Crockett was becoming impatient. Willenski had been gone for a half hour. He hadn't seen any signs of life in the house, no noise, movement, nothing. He decided to go to the back of the house to see what was going on. The back door was open, but no sign of Willenski. The stench was coming out of the back door together with a thousand flies. Crockett raced back to the front and opened the cop car door. He sat in the driver's seat and picked up the police microphone and called the dispatcher. "Hello, this is Officer Willenski's car. I have a police emergency."

By 5:00 p.m. there were ten police cars, a Crime Investigation Unit vehicle, and several investigators in white suits with gas masks. They had been there for five hours. Crockett was sitting in his car with the heater on. He had called his wife and told her he would be late for dinner. He had watched as an ambulance came and took Officer Willenski away on a gurney. One of the officers told Crockett Willenski had fallen and hit his head. He would probably be all right.

One of the bunny suits came down the walk, taking off his gas mask. He motioned for Crockett to come out. Crockett met him and stood there while the investigator stripped off his suit. "I'm not going back in there. The other guys can finish up. Your name is Crockett, right?"

Crockett nodded.

"You were here to check up on one of your parolees?"

Crockett nodded.

"Was his name Rafael Martinez?"

Crockett nodded.

"Well you can close his file. He is one of the dead bodies."

Crockett looked at him. "One? There are more?"

"Oh, yeah, two others and two dogs. They were all piled up in the kitchen. Someone really wanted everyone gone here."

Crockett shook his head. "Were the other two named Burns and Mason?"

"Yeah, that's who they are."

"I was Burns' parole officer too, until he came off parole. Mason had been a parolee too. The three lived together and were getting their lives together."

"Well, their lives are over now."

*********

Police Chief Runfallo was reviewing the State Police report. He had suggested they take over the investigation when he realized his meager Township resources would not be able to really do a credible crime scene investigation. It had taken a few weeks to wrap up the basic findings. The most astounding revelation of the investigation, besides the deaths, was the discovery of the snuff DVDs. There appeared to be four women who were raped and killed by the three men in the house. The basement room apparently was used as prison and a studio for the murders. The three men's faces were never shown on the DVDs, but there was no mistaking who was doing the murders or where they were taking place. The police had published pictures of the women's faces. So far only one had been identified, a coed from Swarthmore. The bodies had not been found. The FBI had been called in because it looked like the DVDs were distributed across state lines. Bank accounts with over $500,000 were found in the names of the three men. Runfallo shook his head in disbelief.

The murder method had everyone puzzled. Two of the men were stabbed to death while the other and the two dogs seemed to have been killed by either an arrow or crossbow bolt. The State forensic pathologist was pretty certain it was a crossbow bolt. Why that was used remained a mystery.

There was no certainty where the men were killed. If anything had happened outside, several severe rains and snow had washed away any clues. There was also a complete lack of the motive of the murders or who may have committed them.

The fact there were two methods used suggested at least two persons. The involvement by the three men in the snuff videos also may have had some relation to organized crime.

There was a bit of luck. Fingerprints on the back-door knob and the kitchen door were found belonging to a Robert Kidd. He was the owner of the house. It had belonged to his parents, and he had kept it and then rented it out to the three victims. He admitted he discovered the bodies and vomited in the kitchen. His decision to not contact the police was the subject of another legal procedure; however he did not appear to be a part of the murders. The whole murder investigation had petered out. The FBI was having a lot of luck following the DVD sales. The State Police had released the details of the murders to great sensation in the press. The national press media, TV and newspaper, had several days of sensational coverage, but it, too, had gradually waned as no further information appeared.

# Chapter 23

They had about an eight hour drive ahead of them before they would reach Evanston. Sam realized he was getting excited to see Lorraine. As they drove Cherie read the manual and set up the radio. "We have a satellite radio," she said excitedly, "and it tells you what the road conditions are and where there are accidents and everything." She began punching buttons and tuning in stations.

Next she found the GPS. "What is the address of the lady?" she asked. He told her it was in the Contacts list. She punched in some data, and a display on the dash began showing their progress. "We only have four hours and thirty-three minutes to go," she announced. "You can also access the Internet with this display. What do you want to know? I can also link the iTab to the car computer and display all kinds of information on how the car is doing."

Sam thought for a while. "When do we need gas and where can we get it?"

She played with the display for a bit. "We'll need gas in three hours and fifty minutes if we continue at this speed, and we can get it at Exit 39A just outside of Chicago. I've never been to Chicago. I've been to Cleveland, though, just today." She was very excited. "Actually this whole thing can be activated by your voice, but you have to train it. Do you want me to do that?"

"No you just work with it and let me know the things you find out." Sam was afraid he had allowed a monster to be created. The next thing she would have the car driving itself.

They stopped for gas and a quick hamburger and were on their way. As they drove, Cherie kept a running commentary on what they were passing and the sights and places of interest. She was getting all the information from the display and the iTab. A lot of what she was relaying was interesting, but Sam was more interested in getting to Lorraine.

They got off the interstate and followed the instructions from the GPS. They had arrived about 7:00 p.m. and it was dark. They drove down streets lined with trees and older houses. Everything seemed well-kept, neat, and clean. Cherie was looking at the houses as they drove. "This is a really nice area. Everything is really clean and nice. This lady we're going to see, is she your girlfriend or something?"

Sam smiled. "Or something. I met her in Florida and we had a nice time together. She wanted me to visit her, so we're going to. I told her I was bringing you. She's excited to meet you."

"I'll be real good, Sam. You just tell her whatever you want. I'll keep quiet."

"Don't worry. I know she'll like you. She's a nurse and knows a lot about helping people."

The SUV pulled through a set of brick pillars with a sign proclaiming Seaton Towne. Lorraine lived in a small townhouse development in a very nice area. They stopped in front of a landscaped line of three-story brick townhouses. Lorraine's house was an end unit. Large evergreen bushes stood on the end, and there was a small area of rose bushes in the front. The plants were covered for the winter. Low evergreen bushes were also in a bed in front of the townhouse. Everything looked like it had been tended with someone's care. He parked in a public space next to the townhouse.

They got out of the SUV and walked up a set of steps next to a two car garage to the second floor entrance. The ground floor was taken up with the garage. Sam rang the doorbell. He heard someone's steps approaching the front door. It opened and Lorraine stood there.

All Sam could do was stare. She was so lovely, he could not speak. He had forgotten the effect her eyes had on him. They were laser-like. He had a lump in his throat.

Lorraine looked at him. She was in better control than he. "Well, you have less hair, but I still recognize you. Do you want to come in? Or just stand there?"

He stepped into a landing. There were a few steps leading up into the house. Lorraine stepped back and onto a step. She looked over his shoulder. "Is this the young lady you mentioned would be with you?"

Sam was flustered and not sure what he was doing. "Uh, yes, this is Cherie, Cherie Latham. She's traveling with me. I… uh we… will explain everything." He stepped forward and Loraine went up to the steps.

"Come on in Cherie. Sam appears to be a little lost."

Sam could see Lorraine was not going to make it easy for him. Sam and Cherie walked up the steps into the living room of the house. It was decorated in a contemporary manner. There were several paintings obviously expensive and of high quality. A small lit gas fireplace was in the center of the room. Lorraine led them to the back of the house. They passed a dining room to a kitchen and a small dinette table. Everything was very understated, but elegant in a way. Lorraine obviously had an eye for decorating. Sam had not been in many civilian homes, having mostly been on ships or Navy quarters or grubby hotels, but he could see this woman was someone who knew what she was doing. It reminded him of his parent's home.

Lorraine told them to sit down at the table, and she offered them coffee, iced tea or lemonade. Sam asked for coffee, and Cherie asked for lemonade. "I've made lasagna for some dinner if you feel like that." She smiled at Cherie who made a small whoop.

"I just love lasagna." Cherie said.

"Well, we can also have a salad with it if you want."

Sam was still fighting his discomfort and just nodded.

Lorraine served the meal and sat down at the table. "Well, Cherie, you look like you could use some food. How are you doing? Has Sam been treating you well?"

"Sam is my guardian angel. No, really, I mean it. He saved my life. I don't know what or where I would be if he hadn't found me."

Lorraine looked at Sam. "I didn't realize guardian angel came with your list of qualities." She was still non-plussed about the whole situation. Sam could see they needed to cut to the chase on this, but he didn't want to discuss everything in front of Cherie. Emotionally, she was still pretty raw about what had happened to her.

He smiled at Lorraine. "There's a lot you need to find out about me. Let's talk after we eat." They ate in silence with Cherie commenting on how delicious the meal was and how she had just discovered lasagna.

Lorraine cleared the dishes and put them into a dishwasher. "Cherie, would you like some dessert, ice cream? You can go downstairs and watch some TV while Sam and I catch up on what he has been doing."

Cherie nodded. "I know you need to talk with Sam. I love ice cream, and I'll be happy to watch TV."

Lorraine fixed a bowl of vanilla ice cream with chocolate syrup. "Would you like some cherries on top?"

Cherie looked at her. "I guess. What do they look like? Sam would I like them?"

Sam smiled at her. "You'll love them. They're very sweet, and red."

Lorraine was puzzled by a girl who didn't know what cherries were. She topped off the ice cream and led Cherie down a flight of stairs. When she returned, she asked Sam if he would like another cup of coffee.

I certainly would, he thought. I need to get everything out on the table.

Lorraine fixed the coffee. "You take two spoons of sugar as I remember from our breakfasts together, right?"

"Right," he answered.

Lorraine sat down opposite him and looked him in the eye. "Okay, guardian angel, talk."

Sam began by telling her about his parent's deaths. He wanted to see his house and his parent's graves before going to see his brother in Idaho. Then he met her, but he still wanted to take the trip to Pennsylvania. He just couldn't share it with her, especially because of the way they died.

He told her after leaving the house he was driving through an area outside of where his parent's house was, and it was raining. Suddenly, he saw this girl run out in front of his car and trip and fall on the side of the road. It was night, and he stopped and picked her up.

She was hysterical. He put her in the car and tried to calm her down. She told him she had escaped from a house somewhere and had been kidnapped and raped by three men. He suggested they go to the police, but she was crying and said she just wanted to go home. Her clothes were ripped and torn.

He tried to understand where she lived, but she couldn't make any sense. He decided to go to a motel and see if she would calm down. She told him she hadn't had anything to eat for several days. He got her a MacDonald's and rented a motel room. She collapsed in the bed and fell asleep.

Lorraine shook her head in disbelief. "You didn't call the police?"

"Well, she was so distraught; I thought the police would just make her worse. Besides she had no idea where she had come from or how far she had been running. The next morning she told me the men had grabbed her near her mother's apartment in West Chester. I suggested we go see her mother and that seemed to be okay with her."

Sam was trying to move the story into what actually had happened after staying in the motel.

Lorraine seemed to be mollified by this. "What happened next?"

Sam told her the whole story and what he had learned about Cherie.

After he finished with their arrival, Lorraine looked at him seriously. "What's next? What do you want to do with her?"

"Lorraine, I spent many years overseas getting rid of bad people, rescuing people, and mission after mission, I felt there was something waiting for me back home.

When my parents were murdered, I felt like I had wasted my time overseas, when there was just as much evil here and no one was fixing it. When I met you, it was like a light was turned on inside me. I had the possibility of someone.

"But when I picked up Cherie, it was like I was back overseas rescuing again. Cherie is a good person who has had nothing in her life, but she has a beautiful attitude about life. The fact she has continued on after being raped by her mother's boyfriends and three degenerates is staggering to me. She still believes there is good in the world, and she can find it. I think I would like to be her guardian. I think that is a legal possibility. I also think she should have some medical attention. She could have STDs and she seems malnourished. She also needs to continue her education. Despite everything, I think she's worth it. As far as how it affects you and me, I don't know. I want you in my life. I need you in my life. When I saw you in the door, I was stunned. I didn't realize how much you mean to me."

Lorraine had been looking at him intently throughout his speech. She leaned across the table held his head and kissed him firmly and leaned back. "You just hit a home run, buster. You got me. I was prepared to toss you and your little bunny out, but I can't. I will help you do what needs to be done with her." Tears flowed, but she didn't sob. She reached across and held his hand. "You are even a better man than I thought. I was really uncertain about what had happened in Florida, but I think we can build on that if you want to."

He came around the table and pulled her up into his arms. "There is nothing more I want." They stood for minutes just holding each other.

They turned as they heard Cherie coming up from the downstairs. She had a large smile, "I guess you two worked it out? I thought we might be leaving soon."

Lorraine extended her arm, "Come here." Cherie tentatively walked over. Lorraine put her arm around Cherie's shoulders. Sam did the same. "I will help you Cherie," Lorraine said. "We three will stick together and work something out."

It was late, and Lorraine suggested they all go to bed. They went upstairs, and she showed Cherie to a room with two twin beds in it. "This is a guest room for my niece and nephew. They're thirteen and fifteen. They come and sleep over sometimes. You can sleep in either bed. You can use the bathroom in the hall."

Cherie was amazed at how neat and clean everything was. "Is this really your house? It's so nice and clean."

Lorraine smiled. "Well sometimes it isn't this clean, but yes, this is my house. Maybe tomorrow you'll meet my niece and nephew." She turned to Sam. "I'm not sure how we want to arrange our sleeping. With Cherie here we may want to keep the doors open in case she needs anything. I have tomorrow off, and we can make plans in the morning."

Sam considered this. "I'm willing to do whatever you want. We can take it slow if you want."

"I think it's a good idea. I have a foldout couch in the third bedroom. I use it as an office. Let's do that."

Lorraine went into her bedroom and closed the door. She called her sister.

Her sister answered the phone before it stopped ringing once. "What's the deal sis? Quick, tell me everything. Who is this girl he dragged along? Is he staying there? Do you still like him?"

After about ten more questions, Lorraine broke in and told her the entire story. At the end of their conversation, her sister suggested, "How about if we come over tomorrow and talk? I think Michael can take the morning off. I think you need some legal advice."

Lorraine agreed and said they would be ready for them. Lorraine hung up and got ready for bed. She opened the door to her bedroom and walked down the corridor to Cherie's room. Cherie was sitting on the edge of one of the beds. "Are you okay, Cherie?"

"Yes, I just am so disoriented. I can't believe I'm here with two people who are so nice, and care about me. At least I think you do. You are so nice. I've never met someone like you. You are so pretty and nice. I hope you like Sam. He is my guardian angel. He rescued me from hell."

Lorraine's heart went out to this poor girl. She had seen horrible things in Africa, but Cherie's story rivaled anything she had seen there. She sat down next to her and put her arm around Cherie. "Don't worry, Sam and I will work something out. You can stay here until things are clear, and yes, I like Sam a lot. I 'm glad he's your guardian angel." She hugged Cherie, "Now, get some sleep. We have a lot to figure out tomorrow."

Lorraine walked down to where Sam was folding out the couch. "I would like us to be together tonight, but until we see how Cherie does here, I feel better if we keep things simple. Plus, I agree she needs a physical exam for STDs. I am very concerned about that aspect of her story. I can arrange something with my father or through work. What do you think?"

Sam looked at her with a serious expression. "She's so thin. I'm concerned about her health. She needs a complete physical, also probably a good dental exam. I can pay for all those things."

"Don't worry about paying. I have a lot of people who owe me things. I think we need to keep the police and authorities out of this. We'll have to be very circumspect as we get her looked at. I can make that happen. I talked to my sister on the phone. She and her husband are coming over tomorrow. They can help us a lot."

Sam turned to Lorraine. He reached for her and pulled her to him. "We may not sleep together tonight, but I demand a good night kiss."

Lorraine willingly complied. After several minutes, they both stepped back and laughed.

"I think we'll have no problem resuming our Florida relationship. Good night, Sam." Lorraine walked back to her room out of breath.

# Chapter 24

Sarah and Mike McConnell parked their SUV in the space next to Sam's new SUV. Their kids were in school. They had been discussing what Lorraine told her sister about Cherie the night before. Mike was a bit concerned Lorraine had jumped into something without thinking about the ramifications. Sarah had poked him in the ribs and told him he was just being a lawyer. Mike responded there was nothing wrong with that. They rang the doorbell, and Lorraine opened the door.

Sam was pleasantly surprised to meet Sarah; she looked like a slightly older version of Lorraine. As he chatted with Mike and Sarah, he realized there was a difference between the two women. Sarah was more academic and analytic; Lorraine much more instinctual. Mike was a tall man, slightly graying hair and stood very erect. He had played basketball in college and projected an air of confidence. Sam guessed he would be formidable in a courtroom.

After introductions they settled into the living room. Cherie sat on the floor next to Sam's chair. Lorraine sat in a chair next to Sam, and Sarah and Mike faced them on a sofa across a coffee table. Mike spoke first, "What concerns me most is the status of Cherie. She's a minor, but old enough to declare independence from her mother. Of course she has to have a sponsor, whom I assume could be Sam."

Sam nodded.

Mike continued, "I have an associate who can help us. I'll get started tomorrow. I need to get some personal information about Cherie to begin."

Sarah leaned forward. "Cherie, what grade are you in?"

Cherie answered, "I was going into the eleventh grade. I'm taking all advanced courses."

Sarah said, "That's good. I might want to give you some tests to see where you might fit here in Evanston."

Cherie shrugged. "Okay. I don't mind tests."

The four adults continued talking about what things they needed to do to settle the situation. Lorraine said she had arranged for Cherie to have a complete medical exam the next day. Mike and Sarah rose to leave.

Cherie stood up. "I want to thank you for anything you can do to help me. I realize you don't have to, and I can't pay you for anything. But someday I will make it all up to you."

Mike and Sarah were startled by this. "Cherie, you have a lot of time to worry about that. Let's just get your status figured out first," Mike responded.

The couple left and Lorraine and Sam sat for a while.

"Cherie, I want to look at what clothing you have. If I see something you need, we'll go shopping." Lorraine looked at Sam. "When a girl doesn't know what to do, she goes shopping, and I think Cherie and I need to do some of that. She needs to learn how to be a girlie girl."

Cherie giggled and looked at Sam.

"I'll drive you to whatever stores you need. This is all new to me." Sam looked bemused.

The next day Lorraine took Cherie to have a complete medical exam through a female doctor friend. Lorraine's work and school schedule would normally have her out of the house for most days and evenings. Her school exams were coming up in a week, and she was debating whether to take some the next semester. With all that was happening, she thought she would take some time off. Her work schedule usually had her at the hospital four days a week for ten hours. She could adjust. She needed to be with Sam and get to know him. Her whole world was changing.

After Cherie's medical exam, Sam took Cherie to Sarah's house each day for the next week. Sarah had an office at home. Her children were at school for most of the day, and Sarah spent each day with Cherie trying to evaluate her scholastic skills. She also had extensive psychological counseling education and training. She wanted to use this experience to evaluate Cherie's mental state.

Lorraine worked and Sam went to the gym. He wasn't sure where he was or what he was going to do. In the past when he had time between operations, he worked out, so this was nothing new. The three of them tried to settle into a routine. It was new for them all.

\*\*\*\*\*\*\*\*\*\*

The following week the four adults got together in the morning to discuss what Mike and Sarah had found out. They all sat as before, Cherie on the floor beside Sam. Cherie's physical exam had found she had Chlamydia and some severe vaginal lesions; she was also severely malnourished. The doctor said everything was treatable and fixable. She also had a visit to a dentist who said it was remarkable she had only two cavities. He cleaned her teeth and filled the two teeth. He also counseled her on proper tooth care.

The most interesting news came from Sarah. "I gave Cherie a succession of tests. The results are interesting—no, amazing." She looked at Sam and Lorraine. "Cherie tested out with an IQ of 173. This is a genius level IQ. I've talked to her about this. She really didn't know what that meant. She explained to me she didn't want to be a show-off at school, so she just tried to be at the level she was suppose to be. Her mother would have yelled at her for being a smarty and a cheat and the kids would bully her. At any rate that's behind her. I gave her the GED, and she maxed it. I also had a sample of the SAT, which she maxed. I want to take her to Northwestern to see if we can find a fit for her. She likes math and physics so we may start there. I have to say, I have never met someone like her. I almost want to take her on as a project. She can have an incredible future ahead of her."

They all looked at Cherie. Sam put his arm on her shoulder. "Well I'm glad I rescued her. She can help us all make the world a little better place."

Cherie beamed. "That's what I've wanted to do all my life. I don't care about what has happened to me. I'd like to do something with my life to make sure no one has bad things like happened to me."

Lorraine thought for a minute. "Will it be all right for her to stay here, Mike, for the time being?"

"I don't see any problem with that. We need to have someone declared as her guardian. Sam, do you want to take that on?"

Sam looked a bit stunned. "I have no problem, but am I the best one to do that? I mean, are there considerations that might make someone else a better one. Like, I don't know anything about education. Would it be better to have Sarah as guardian? I know you have two other children. I guess I just want to make sure we do this right."

"Sam, all you have to do is be financially responsible for her and for her upbringing: school, clothes, food, shelter, etc. I'm sure between Lorraine and Sarah she will have a lot of mothering and guidance. Don't be put off by the education part of it," Mike said reassuringly.

Sam nodded in agreement.

"Okay, then, I'll begin the process. We'll have to contact Cherie's mother and the state of Pennsylvania, but I know people who can manage those things. In the mean time Cherie can stay with Lorraine or us as we try to work everything out."

Before they broke up, Lorraine said she wanted to make an announcement. "Christmas is coming soon, and I would like to have a Christmas party here on the twenty-fourth with both our families. I know our parents would like to get together with all of us and meet Cherie and Sam. Is everyone okay with that?"

They all nodded enthusiastically. Thanksgiving was in a week, and Sarah said they would be getting together with Mike's parents. Lorraine and Sarah's parents were just returning from a Mediterranean cruise. Lorraine said she would be taking their parents out for Thanksgiving and she hoped Sam and Cherie would want to join them. Sam and Cherie both said they would like that.

Mike said he had to get to his office. Lorraine took Cherie upstairs to sort through some clothes, and Sarah indicated to Sam she wanted to talk to him. They went into the kitchen.

"Sam, I just wanted to talk to you about something I have learned about Cherie. It's nothing bad, but she is rather unique. I couldn't imagine how she could have gotten through all the sexual and physical abuse her kidnappers put her through, as well as her very poor home environment."

Sam nodded. "I've been wondering that myself. She seems to have been able to either accept it without any trauma or somehow just repress her feelings."

"It's more than that. She has developed some way of almost entering a trance-like state. She can do it very quickly. She told me she had read several books on self-hypnosis and meditation. They helped her to ignore what was happening around her. She uses these techniques to disassociate herself from whatever is going on around her or to her. I'm not sure whether it's good or bad, but she seems to have blocked out all memories of the abuse. When I asked her about it, she said she knows what happened to her, but she has processed it and rejected any negative impacts. I'm not sure what she means, but she seems to be unaffected by any of the abuse. She has assessed her mother and decided her mother is just a biological aspect of her background. She doesn't seem needy in that respect. She's almost like Spock in Star Trek. Another thing, she uses this technique when she studies or reads or takes a test. She can rapidly absorb an entire complex text book and understand it and apply what she has learned. I'm very excited about her mental abilities."

Sam digested what she had told him. "I guess the fact I was able to rescue her is a real blessing. I guess I was her guardian angel. Fate is strange. I'll do what I can to help her, but it sounds like professional help can be much more useful to her. Go ahead and do what you think will be best for her. You have much more experience with kids than I do. Does she get along with Michael and Lilly?"

"They are entranced with her. She has been very good with them, and they treat her as part of the family. She has already been helping them with their school work. She seems to have no ego about her intelligence.

She just wants to help. In some ways she is very mature and in others, perhaps because of her home environment, very young. Lilly is using her to help with her social life in school. Lilly is only twelve and likes having an older sister. Michael Junior is in the teenager cloud and is just rolling along. I think we will just have to observe her and let her progress. She's very eager to go to the university. She wants to move quickly into more advanced studies. She has an insatiable curiosity and desire for knowledge."

Sam and Sarah talked for a few more minutes as Lorraine and Cherie came down the stairs. "Lorraine thinks I need a few more warm clothes, especially in case it snows," Cherie announced. "And you know what? Sarah has a dog! I've never really been around a dog. Her name is Happy. She really likes me. Whenever I sit down, she comes and sits with me. I didn't know dogs were like that."

Lorraine smiled. "I'm trying to get her organized for living with us. We're getting settled with her personal items and just need to round out her wardrobe a bit. I need to get to work, but Sam you could take her to the Sports Chalet and get her these items I have written down."

"After you do that, Sam," Sarah injected, "I'd like you to bring her by our house. I have an appointment for us with the Dean of Admissions at 4:00. I know the dean personally. As you know I work with the university a lot in placing students."

"I'll bring her by as soon as we finish. The store is on the way to your place," Sam replied.

As Sam and Cherie drove to the store, Cherie began acting very nervous. "Sam, I need to tell you something. Something I read."

They were just pulling into the parking lot, and Sam parked the SUV. "It's okay Cherie; you can tell me anything you want."

Cherie pulled her iTab out of her backpack and turned it on. "Look at this news item," she said as she handed Sam the computer.

The item said, "Police mystified about multiple murder." It went on to describe how police in a small township in Pennsylvania had found three ex-convicts and their dogs murdered in a house. It also described how they believed the three men were involved in the murders of several women and how they had created "snuff videos" of their crime and they were suspects in several other crimes.

Sam read the article carefully. "Are these are the men who had you?"

"Yes, and not only that, they were going to murder me. I didn't realize they were as evil as they were. One of them, Rafi, said they were going to let me go. I believed him. I don't know what to think. I realize you did what you did, and I thank you for it. You saved my life. They were so terrible. I can't believe what they were doing to the other women. Oh, Sam I'm almost sick thinking about this." She began to cry.

Sam reached over and put his arm around her. "I don't know what to say. I had no idea they were doing what this says. Do you know why I came there?"

"No, I've tried to just forget about the whole thing. I never thought about why you were there. When I think about it now, you didn't know I was there. How did you know about them?"

"Cherie, I will tell you, but we need to continue keeping this to ourselves. They murdered my mother and father. I learned about them. The police couldn't do anything about them. I decided to do something. That's all. You realize if the police connect me to that, I will go to jail for murder."

"Sam, I will keep this secret to my grave. What you did saved me. They didn't deserve to live. They were evil, evil men. I will not even discuss my imprisonment with anyone in case they connect that with these men. Thank you, thank you for my life." She held on to him.

They sat there for a few minutes and then got out of the SUV and went into the store. They finished their shopping and Sam took Cherie to Sarah's. He gave her a big hug. They didn't have much to say to each other, both thinking hard about what Cherie had gone through and what Sam had done.

Sam returned to Lorraine's house. He logged on to his new iTab and sent Allo a message:

<Allo, what's going on?>

Allo again replied quickly: <I've got a cell number call me in one hour. See you then.>

Sam called the cell phone number Allo had given him. "Okay Allo, what have you got?"

"First of all, I saw the news about those three men. I guess they're no longer something to worry about."

"Yeah, it's a real sad loss."

"Well, I was able to hack into their Cayman accounts, also into Doc's account. There's a lot of money in them. I think I could maybe move it elsewhere. Do you have any ideas? I wouldn't put the money in my name. It could come back and bite me if anyone found out."

Sam thought about Allo's suggestion. "I have someone who could use the money. If you could set up another account in the Caymans or somewhere else and put it there, could you then move money into a US account?"

"I think I could. Let me check banking laws and see what I can do. Who do you want to get the money if I can work something out?"

"I have a young girl who is parentless and could use some money. I can set up a US account for her, and if you can put money into it without raising suspicion, it would be a good thing. If there's other money, we could have it anonymously donated to some good cause—cancer research, Alzheimer's, whatever. I don't want any of it either."

"Okay, I'll look into it. If I can make it work, just give me the details of the US account."

"Another thing Allo, if you can anonymously alert the police to one of Doc's operations, do it at the same time you move his money. It would be just great if he tried to run and had no money to do it with."

Allo laughed. "That's a great idea. I'll work on that too."

They chatted for a few more minutes and agreed Allo would call Sam when he had more information.

The next morning Sam and Lorraine sat at her dinette table. Cherie was spending the day and the night with Sarah. "Lorraine, I need to talk to you about what's going on... between us... or me... or whatever."

Lorraine looked at him with a raised eyebrow. Sam had learned that expression meant, "You are making no sense."

Sam continued, "What I mean is I need, and you do to, to figure out where we're going and how you want to proceed. I know we haven't had any sex since I got here, and I don't mind that. I feel you want to have some idea of what I'm thinking before you get any deeper into whatever we have, if we have anything."

"You're right. I was afraid I was getting too deep into something. I don't mind helping Cherie, but she's not us. I need to understand where you want to go with this. I'm not going to push you at all, but I don't really know what you see as your future. Where do you want to go with yourself and us?"

Sam collected his thoughts for a while. Having talks like this with anyone, let alone a woman he thought he was deeply in love with, was completely new to him. "First, I want you to know I'm in love with you. I would like to have a permanent life with you; I mean marriage. I'm old enough to know that's what I want, but I want you to understand what you will be getting. I am forty years old. I haven't lived in a house or permanent place for the last twenty years or more. I have no college education or skills or trade or career other than what I did in the Navy.

"I know how to do a lot of stuff, but I don't really know what or where I would like to do with myself. I do know I want to do it with you, for the rest of my life. If you want more time to decide what you want, I can deal with that. I'm unsure of who I am in this environment. It's all new to me. The idea of having someone in my life more important than me is new. I like it. But you really don't know me. I am afraid of messing up with you since I've never really had a chance like this before."

Lorraine looked at him, uncertain as to how to answer.

"You don't have to answer or comment," Sam continued. "Also, I want you to know I am independently wealthy."

Lorraine looked at him as if he were nuts. "Right, what did you do, steal some gold bars from some sheik or just save your Navy pay?"

Sam smiled. "I know it sounds silly, but while I was in the Navy, I had an opportunity to invest based on an individual I met on an operation. I made a lot of money. I know I told you my parents died. I haven't told you all about that, but they left me and my brother a great deal of money. It just added to my financial independence. I don't want to sit here in your place and eat and sleep without paying my way somehow. If we were to become permanent, we can either stay here or get something else. My mind is just spinning around with all of these thoughts."

Lorraine looked at him and nodded. "It's been a little bit of a whirlwind for me too. When you brought Cherie into the equation, it added a lot of considerations. I know you have a real feeling of ownership of her, in the sense of responsibility for how you got her. I think I know something about your parent's death, too."

Sam looked at her with a wary frown.

"When I was on the plane flying back, I looked up Dancer and Philadelphia on my laptop. I saw the article on their murder. I realize why you didn't want to go into it with me then."

Sam looked relieved. "I was really upset. I had just come back from an operation when my CO told me about their murders. I called my brother. He had pretty much taken care of the funeral and disposed of the estate. There are a few things left for him to do, but my parent's lives are over. I had hoped to see them at Christmas. I hadn't seen much of them over the past twenty years because of the life I was living. I was always very close to both of them, but somehow life slipped by and then they were gone."

"I'm very sorry for you. I wish I could have met them."

"I do too. If they knew I had met a girl, they would have been very happy for me. I know my mother was worried I would let life slip by and I would miss out on what she considered a very important part of life."

"I don't want to be nosy, but are you sure you really have enough money? You know, it's maybe a little more expensive than you realize to get by in the US. It is not like being in the Navy and having everything provided for you."

Sam smiled. "As best as I can tell, I will have something between $30,000 and $40,000 a month coming in. That should buy enough underwear and hamburgers for my daily activities. Of course I don't have to spend it each month, but it will keep coming in. My father had a very successful medical practice; he was a very smart investor; he was part owner in several local businesses. He had his coin collection, which has disappeared of course. And he had relatively large insurance policies on him and my mother. Also, the fact there are no inheritance taxes helped too."

Lorraine looked at him. "You really don't have to work or do anything for the rest of your life, do you?"

"Yeah, and it's a bit disturbing. I've never had to do nothing. For the past twenty years, it has been operation: plan operation, do operation, and so forth. I had a lot of training in how to destroy and kill, but not much on how to live a civilian life. I'd planned to visit my brother in Arizona and see if I could somehow work for or with him. All of a sudden I have a beautiful woman in my life and a teen-age girl to watch over. It's a bit bewildering."

Lorraine thought for a while. "We need to get to know each other. I don't feel like there are any issues keeping us apart. I'll never have any secrets from you. I won't ask you about your Navy career. You can tell me anything you'd like about that."

Sam looked at her seriously. "There may be some things I need to tell you, but it will take some time for me to figure out how to tell you them. One thing bothering me is the money and how it relates to you. I know you're used to being on your own. I will share anything with you, but I think you want to be independent of me financially. I don't think you want to quit your career and then have to come to me and ask if you can buy a new dress."

Lorraine hadn't considered this. "I think if I tell my girl friends I walked away from this incredible man because he had too much money, they would think I was crazy."

She smiled. "I'm kidding. You do have a point. I hadn't even thought about our life together. Everyone I know has to work. I think we need to consider what we'd like to have as a lifestyle. If we are to continue, we need to work out some arrangement. The last thing we need to come between us is money arguments."

"Yeah, there's a lot to consider. Right now, I'm not in the mode of giving everything to some charity and getting a job in a car wash. I just wanted you to be aware of my situation. Do you have any vacation time coming up? Once we get Cherie settled I'd like to go see my brother and have you meet him and his family. I know I have talked about marriage. I'm not going to push anything. I can go out and get a ring, but that's just the superficial stuff. We have a lot to organize. I know you're an organized person, and I am too. We now have been together for about eleven days total between here and Florida. I'm willing to work on refining our relationship for at least a few more days." He smiled wryly.

"You sure know how to sweet talk a girl." Lorraine chuckled. "But you're right. We've only known each other for a very short time. I don't know why, but from the moment we met, as you ran up the beach, I felt in my heart we were meant to be together. It sounds corny and schmaltzy, but that's what happened to me. I never believed in this soulmates stuff, but there is something between us that meshes. I think we both have been alone for so long and hurt before, we don't know whether to trust our senses."

They sat there for a while, silent, and then Lorraine looked at him. "You know, Sam, you're a lot more analytical than I am. I like to plan, but I also like spontaneity. I have a great idea."

Sam looked at her, expecting a profound insight.

"Let's go upstairs and make love. I think we need to recapture some of our Florida time." She reached across the table, took his hand, and escorted him out of the kitchen and up the stairs.

**********

Several days later Sam and Lorraine were lying entwined in each other's arms as the morning sun lit her room. Sam had been sleeping with her in her bed for three days. He rolled on his back and looked at the ceiling. He was amused.

He realized he had not stayed in a house as long as he had with Lorraine since he left home after high school. It was a funny feeling; no ship's bells and announcements or sounds of people in small spaces.

When he was in Florida for short times, he had stayed in the Bachelor Quarters, and when he was on an operation he might be in a hotel, a tent, or a sleeping bag. He hadn't had a permanent place with a roof in over twenty years. He had stayed at his parent's intermittently, but not for long periods.

Lorraine rolled toward him and snuggled her body against his. "What great thoughts are running through that brain?"

He smiled, "I was just thinking I could get used to this. Living in one place, having a beautiful woman with me in a bed, waking up with her." He turned to her and gave her a kiss which degenerated into another lovemaking session. "I could get used to waking up like that every day too."

"Well, maybe on weekends like this, but if I continue working, we may have to rearrange our schedule. This reminds me, Mom and Dad are coming in from their cruise today, this afternoon. I've been talking to her on and off, and she's aware of our relationship. I'd like you to come along with me when I pick them up. Do you mind? I mean, I don't want to force you to a meeting that may be…I don't know. I don't know why I think you wouldn't want to come."

"You're sounding silly. Of course I want to meet them. Since I won't be a surprise to them, I'm sure they're eager to decide whether you've gotten yourself into a mess or not. I'll even shower and wear clean underwear."

Lorraine socked him in the arm. "Okay, okay I'm being dumb. I just am so happy I want everyone to know how happy I am."

"Well I'm very happy, too. I think once they see us together, they'll realize we are two moony, dopey lovebirds. At least that's how I think we're behaving recently. I feel like I'm in high school with an infatuation. I don't think it's infatuation though. It's a deep love that continues to grow."

Lorraine gave him a deep kiss and rolled out of the bed. "I've got to get going so we can get there on time, and you need to take that shower and find your clean underwear. You might wear some clean clothes too," she said sarcastically. Secretly, she was very happy with his personal hygiene habits. His years in the Navy had produced a very clean, organized individual. He even folded his underwear when he put it away.

As they drove to the airport, Sam began to think through the meeting. "You know, I have one concern about your parents, and maybe your sister and even your friends. Everyone in your life has very good educations, including you—college degrees and advanced degrees. I don't have anything like that. I'm just a Navy enlistee, not even an officer. I just hope it doesn't stand in our way. I think the reason I'm mulling all this over is I never had to concern myself with where I stood with other people. I had a rank, but I also had a status based on my capabilities, I had demonstrated with people. Do people in the real world rate you by your education?"

Lorraine considered this for a while. "Yes, they do. They also consider how you dress, how you speak, and how much money you have. My parents brought me up to look at each person and judge their character and use it as a measure of their worth.

"I can't speak for my friends or anyone else we might meet, but I believe you can hold your own. I think as time goes by, you'll find your niche in life. We'll find our niche also together. I'm more like you—an enlisted man. In the hospital hierarchy doctors are gods, brain surgeons at the top. Nurses like me are not at the bottom because I have specialized skills, but I'm not a doctor. I make a good salary. Of course, with women, their looks and age count. I'm aging out of the young hottie category, but I think I can hold my own on looks. However, I don't have the status my sister has. She's a published author with a doctorate. I don't think my parents will rate us, though. They've just always wanted Sarah and me to be happy. And with you in my life, I think they will be really happy, especially my mother. From my phone conversations so far, she is very excited to meet you. My father will go along with her judgment. He just wants me to be happy and not get hurt. So you better not hurt me."

"The only way I might hurt you is in some of our lovemaking. We both are pretty enthusiastic." They both laughed. Lorraine pulled into the parking area, and they walked to the waiting area.

The meeting at the airport went well. Lorraine's parents recognized her immediately and went to her. Sam stood aside as they hugged and greeted each other. Lorraine's mother, Celeste, looked very much like Lorraine, tall and refined. He was surprised to see how young she looked, no grey hair. Her father, Jason, was also tall and slender and distinguished looking. He also had no grey hair. Sam was impressed with the two.

Lorraine introduced him. Her father shook his hand warmly and her mother hugged him. "I'm so glad to meet you. Any man who can pass Lorraine's muster must be a really great guy."

Sam was pleased at her warmth. As they walked back to the car, Lorraine questioned them about their cruise. They had visited many ports in the Mediterranean Sam was familiar with from his time in the Navy. His time with the Group had taken him to many other areas, too.

Her parents had arrived in time for dinner, and they all decided to go out before going home. The evening went well, Sam thought, and as they left her parent's house, Lorraine turned to him and gave him a big kiss. "You passed with flying colors. You even knew which end of the fork to use. I'm kidding. My mother loves you, and my dad is okay. He just has much less to say, but you impressed him with your discussion of the stock market."

"Well, when he started talking about golf, I had to find something of mutual interest. He's a nice man, though. We've lived different lives and may never be friends, but we can get along. We have something in common—we both love his daughter."

They agreed to let things go for a while until after the holidays. In the mean time Lorraine would finish her classes and arrange her work schedule to be home with him as much as she could. She also needed to start planning for the Christmas Eve party. She left instructions for him to decorate the outside and put up her Christmas tree. Sam was amused to find the tree was artificial; he had never seen one before.

He found a dojo where he could keep up his Tae Kwan Do skills, worked out at a local gym, and found a shooting range where he could keep his firearms skills up. He didn't know what else to do, and decided to just keep his skills as current as possible until he was able to figure out his next step in life.

He called Allo, and Allo told him he had looted all the accounts, deposited money in a new off-shore account for Sam's needy girl, and donated the rest to several charities anonymously. He gave Sam the particulars so Sam could set up an account in the US for Cherie. Sam thanked him, and they decided to keep in touch just in case either of them heard anything or needed anything from the particular skills they both possessed. Sam was feeling good about things. He next wanted to see his brother and began thinking about a road trip in the New Year he and Lorraine could take.

# Chapter 25

Cherie was happier than she had ever thought possible. She had suspected there were people who had good lives, but had never really met them. Her friend in West Chester was nice and her parents were too, but they really never accepted her, and they were very negative about everything. They always complained about their lives. Her friend's parents were even very critical of her friend. The McConnell's treated their kids like they loved them. They gave them lots of compliments. There were rules, but the kids never really fought them. They were focused on their school work and stuff they did after school. Michael was on a hockey team, and Lilly took ice skating lessons. Their mother was the smartest and nicest woman Cherie had ever met. Every Sunday the whole family went to church. The family was not real religious, but they seemed to do what Cherie thought Christian people should do. Cherie liked going to church because it was peaceful and she liked the singing and sometimes what the minister had to say was interesting. She had read the whole bible one time and there was a lot in it she wasn't able to make sense of. Sometimes the minister would explain parts and Cherie enjoyed that.

The best part of her new life was her involvement at the university. She had read several books and journals on the latest advancements in genetic research. The whole subject of DNA fascinated her.

When Sarah took her to meet her friend, Cherie told the woman about her interest. The woman arranged for her to attend two courses. She began auditing the two courses in genetics and found she could easily understand the concepts. She had written a paper for each one and the professor was amazed someone her age and educational level could have the thoughts and insights she did. She began thinking about developing math models that could lead to computer simulations of the entire human genome. Her idea was to couple the math model into a demonstration of how a human being became created. If she could develop a time-based model, she could show how genetic anomalies would lead to disease or birth defects. She had begun writing her thoughts and showed them to Sarah. Sarah was so impressed she took Cherie to one of the department heads to discuss her idea.

The department head suggested she might be able to develop her paper into a master's thesis. He had already decided her thinking was advanced enough; she might be able to bypass the normal undergraduate courses and even some of the graduate courses. He offered to bring her case to the school and put her into a special program to qualify her for obtaining her master's. There were a few precedents for this action, and he thought he could help make it happen for her.

Cherie was excited about this because she had been afraid she would be forced to slog through courses she had already mastered on her own. The department head arranged for her to take several undergraduate final exams just to justify his action. Cherie had passed all of them with ease. Her reputation was beginning to attract attention in the university.

After a month Cherie heard from her mother through Sarah's husband, Michael. Sarah had talked to Cherie's mother on the phone. Her mother was willing to sign the papers so she wouldn't be responsible for Cherie anymore. An interesting aspect of the discussion between Sarah and her mother was an insight into Cherie's early childhood. It seemed she had been diagnosed as autistic about the age of two. Cherie didn't talk and would sit and watch what was going on around her, but would not interact. She would play with toys, but not in the way the toy was designed to be played with. She would also dismantle toys. Her mother thought Cherie was a possible dangerous nut case because she often pulled her dolls apart. At the age of four Cherie suddenly began speaking, not in baby talk, in perfect sentences.

When Sarah mentioned all of this to Cherie, Cherie explained she didn't talk because she wanted to do it the right way when she did. She pulled her dolls apart because she wanted to see what was inside them. She thought they might provide insight into how humans worked. Sarah said she was glad Cherie did not decide to experiment on real human beings.

Cherie said one time she tried to see if she could pull off her finger, but it hurt too much. She decided maybe she could figure out another way to learn what she wanted to. There was a TV show she sometimes could watch showing medical things. She watched it when her mother was doing something else and Cherie could change the channels. Cherie said she would channel surf when she was four and five and try to find the most interesting things she could. She liked shows describing the real world.

Unbeknownst to Cherie, Sarah and Sam had discussed Cherie living with the McConnells. Sam thought it was a good idea if the family as a whole agreed. He was concerned about any financial impact on them. Sarah assured him if there were any major impact, she would let him know. Sam had already said he would be responsible for her education, clothes and whatever else.

Cherie had been living with the McConnell family and was treated as a member of the family. Cherie decided she should take her status in the family as a serious matter. She discussed with Sarah how she should interact and what Sarah expected. They decided to present the matter in a family council meeting.

The entire family was enthusiastic and voted to include her in the family. Cherie was very excited by this acceptance. One thing she decided she would do to help Michael Junior and Lilly was to teach them how she was able to focus on things by using her self-hypnosis technique. Each day after dinner they would get together in Lilly's room, lie on the floor, and Cherie would talk them through the technique.

Cherie told them they could use it for school and for improving their sports. Sarah had not realized the children were doing this, but suddenly the two children's grades began substantially improving. Michael Junior began emerging as a leader and high scorer on his hockey team, and Lilly's skating performance improved to where she was winning some of the local competitions.

One evening when everyone was settled down: Michael Junior and Lilly were doing their homework, and Sarah was working in her office. Michael Senior was reviewing some documents in his office. Cherie tapped on the door frame to Sarah's office. She had often admired its cozy environment. There were large wooden bookcases on one wall and a fireplace, now burning, on the facing wall. The dog, Happy, was lying in front of the fire. He looked up when Cherie tapped. Sarah's desk was in front of a window looking out into the backyard. "Do you mind if I ask you a question?"

"No, not at all Cherie, what's bothering you?"

"Well, I'm trying to figure out why you and your family are living the way you are and the way I saw most of the people living in my old area. I also can't figure out those men who kidnapped me. You and your family are working hard, I guess, to improve yourselves. The other people I've seen don't even try or seem to want to improve themselves. What makes the difference?"

Sarah thought a while. Cherie never failed to come up with a question people had struggled with for ages. "You know, Cherie, I've thought about that too. In fact, many people have. I believe it depends on two things: the genetic factors in the individual and the environment they are brought up in.

"There are some people like you who come from very meager and poor environments and yet are able to overcome all that and do well. Many people who come from very good environments with good parents do well, but there are some who don't. I think it is because of their genetic factors. So maybe genetics are the dominant reason. Perhaps your modeling might be able to allow some studies on that problem."

Cherie had sat on the rug in front of the fire and was rubbing Happy's belly thoughtfully. "I hadn't thought about that as a part of the model. Yes, how does behavior factor into genetic DNA? I'll have to think about that and do some reading. Thanks, Sarah that was a good insight. Oh, another thing—do we live in a mansion?"

Sarah looked at her, puzzled by this turn of thought. Cherie was like that, thinking at an adult level and in one instant, jumping to a question that an eight year old would ask. "Well, to some people we probably live in a mansion. We do have a large house. Michael and I have worked hard to be able to live like this. You probably wouldn't believe the apartment we started out with eighteen years ago. It had one bedroom and a kitchen and living room in one area. So, everyone starts somewhere."

Cherie nodded thoughtfully.

"I've been meaning to ask you a question," Sarah looked at Cherie to see her reaction.

"What is it?"

"Well, I was wondering about your bad experiences and how you might think about them in your future."

"My future?"

"Yes, do you think someday you would like to have a family and husband?" Sarah asked gently.

Cherie cocked her head and thought for a while. "I would like to have a family, and I guess I should have a husband to have one. I know I don't *have* to have one, but I think a family should have a mother and father."

"After what you have been through, do you think you could have a good relationship with a man?"

"A man like Sam or your husband would be nice. I haven't met anybody at school who I could really like. I guess I will have to wait and see what happens." Cherie looked thoughtful and a little sad.

Sarah looked concerned. "I hope I haven't upset you. I was just concerned about the perspective you were putting the whole experience in."

"Don't worry, Sarah, I guess I was just thinking about my mom and what a sad life she had. I think I'll go and see how Michael is doing on his math homework." She walked out of the room.

Sarah thought about what Cherie said. Maybe I started her thinking about her future. She needs to eventually talk about what she thinks of men and how they could fit into her life.

The McConnell house was a classic center hall colonial in a very nice subdivision. On the right side of the entrance was a dining room. On the left side was a large living room. Behind it were two dens which Michael and Sarah used as offices.

A hall led to the kitchen and family room across the back. A small bath was behind the dining room on the right. There were five bedrooms upstairs and two full baths. Cherie had never imagined anyone lived in so much space. There were many houses in the subdivision. Cherie realized there was an entire set of people who lived a different life than she had thought possible. The fact that many people lived like this stunned her.

Another exciting part of her new life was her own room. Cherie had never had any space of her own. She now had a room with her own bed, a desk and bookshelves and even a chair to sit on. She had never in her wildest dreams thought she would live like this. It made her want to work harder to be able to understand how she could have a house of her own some day. She saw Lorraine's house and how Lorraine lived and thought how neat it would be to have something like that. She might even have her own dog. The McConnell's dog was a wonder to her. Happy was always glad to see her and be with her. She thought it was a nice way to be. People could learn something from dogs, she thought.

Cherie had thought deeply about the comparison between the McConnell family and her upbringing. Most of the kids in her old school seemed to be uninterested in what school offered them. They didn't care about what was going on in the world, and they didn't have much of an idea about what they were going to do with their lives.

She began to realize the parent's were causing this. There were some kids who seemed to be directed toward something, but most of the others were not. She noticed many of the directed kids were Asian. She guessed they had some very strong parental direction. She wondered why not all parents were like this. She tried to figure out her mother. She had never met her grandparents; they lived in other states. Early in her life she had decided she would somehow change her own life. She realized she could not change her mother's.

When she was taken by the three men, it was the first time in her life; she thought she might not live. She never gave up hope, but in the back of her mind, she had almost given up. And then Sam came and took her to safety. She really believed God had sent him to rescue her, and since he had, she resolved to do the best with her life she could. When Sarah explained to her she possessed incredible intelligence, Cherie decided this was further proof she should do something positive with her life.

She was visiting Sam and Lorraine at Lorraine's townhouse one day. She was happy for them because they seemed to have decided to live together. She wanted Sam to have a good life and someone who would love him.

Sam took her into the living room while Lorraine fixed them dinner. "Cherie, I have something to tell you. The three men who kidnapped you were working for a criminal who was directing them in their crimes. I can't tell you how, but some of the money they stole is now in a bank account in your name. I think you deserve it."

Cherie shook her head. She didn't want money that was evil.

Sam held up his hand. "Wait. I know you might think this is not good money, but I think you can consider it in a different light. You can use it to further your education, buy your own clothes, and make your own way. I know you want to do something good with your life. This can make it possible. You don't want to be asking me for money, or anyone else. I have arranged for you to have some money available each month for your own use. I will help you track it and manage it until you become comfortable. I also will find someone who can manage the tax situation. We don't want to have to explain where the money came from. I think I know someone who can do that." Sam was thinking of the man who helped him with his investments. He had told Sam if he ever needed any financial help, he could get it for him.

Cherie sat for a moment. "Okay, Sam, I'll trust your judgment. The way the money was gotten bothers me, but I never thought about how I would pay for anything. They are gone, and maybe some good can come from the whole thing."

Sam gave her a hug and told her he was glad she thought like that.

*********

The weekend after Thanksgiving Cherie began to hear her new family talking about Christmas. The two male members went into the basement and began hauling out Christmas decorations. This fascinated Cherie; she had never seen so many things for Christmas. Her mother thought Christmas was a bunch of nonsense—just a way for stores to make money. Her mother might buy her a present, but only something like a pair of underwear. She had never gotten her mother a present, but always made a card for her. The McConnell's approach to Christmas astounded her. Sarah began putting up a small village on the sideboard in the dining room. Cherie was struck with the number of little houses and people, and the scene it portrayed. It looked like a little town in a Charles Dickens book, or what she imagined such a town would look like. There were more decorations all throughout the house and on the house. She noticed other people in the neighborhood were putting decorations up on their houses, too.

Once all the lights were put up outside, Sarah announced the following week the family would go look for a Christmas tree. The first night after the lights were on the outside, the entire street was illuminated by all the houses. Cherie felt like she was in a fairyland. Her head was spinning; she never imagined there were people who lived like this.

The family drove out to the countryside to look for a suitable Christmas tree. Sarah had explained to Cherie a real Christmas tree was needed to properly celebrate Christmas. As they drove through the flat country and passed a few farms, Cherie realized she had never seen country before. They finally stopped at a roadside Christmas tree lot and everyone got out. The children were very excited; every year they had a great debate as to which was the best tree. Cherie had no idea you could buy trees like this. She thought they all were plastic and tiny. One of her mother's friends in the apartment complex had invited them over for Christmas Eve one year, and she had a small plastic tree.

The family settled on a very tall tree, at least Cherie thought it was. Mike Senior and Junior put a plastic wrap around it and hoisted it onto the roof of their SUV and tied it down. They all piled in the car and began the drive back. As they drove they listened to Christmas carols on the radio. Cherie could tell everyone was very excited about the coming holiday. She had never felt this warm and happy in her life.

Several days later Sam and Lorraine came by to visit. Sam took Cherie aside and asked her if she would like to go shopping for any presents. Cherie looked at him with a very puzzled expression. "Sam, I wouldn't know how to do that."

Sam looked over to Lorraine. "Lorraine, would you come over here for a minute?"

Lorraine looked up from where she and Sarah had been discussing something, and came over. "What's up?"

"Cherie needs to go shopping for Christmas presents, but she has never done it. Perhaps you could help her to make a list and go with her to select some presents. I suspect she'll be receiving some, and she will want to be able to reciprocate. She has her own money. I have arranged for that. So she just needs some help."

Lorraine looked very seriously at Cherie. "Cherie, there is nothing I would like more than take you Christmas shopping. We can have a blast. We can go to lunch and look at all the shops. We might also get ourselves a few things, like a Christmas outfit. What do you think?"

Cherie squealed in delight. "I think that would be fantastic."

"Well, that's settled." Sam said with a large grin.

*********

A few days later Lorraine picked up Cherie to go on their shopping excursion. Lorraine had decided to take them to the Old Orchard mall. When she told Cherie this, Cherie wasn't sure what a mall was. She had been to the store with Sam and Lorraine, but not to a mall. Her mother had never taken her shopping. Her mother might come home with a shirt or pair of pants from where she worked, but Cherie never went with her. Lorraine turned to her when they got in the car and asked Cherie, "Do you have the list of people we put together?"

Cherie nodded eagerly and pulled out her iTab. "Sam gave me $1000. I told him you said it was a good number for what we had on the list."

Lorraine drove them to the mall. The mall was an open air mall with pathways and stores scattered about. The Christmas lighting was magical to Cherie, and it had begun to snow lightly. Lorraine said it was a perfect time to Christmas shop.

Cherie's list started with the two children she lived with. Lorraine took her to several stores and helped her pick out some clothing for Michael and Lilly. Cherie was overwhelmed by the whole experience. She wanted to get something special for Sam; he was the only one she and Lorraine had not been able to figure out. As they walked by a jewelry store, Cherie's eye was caught by a silver bracelet. There were several, each with a different military insignia. "Maybe I could get him a nice bracelet. I could have it engraved with his name and get the one with the Navy thing."

"That's a perfect gift." Lorraine said. They bought it, and while it was being engraved, they continued their shopping.

Cherie was thrilled with this experience. She had never had anyone she really wanted to do something nice for. They stopped for a while and had lunch in one of the department stores. They continued their shopping. Lorraine also had a list, and the two of them had a great time deciding what each person would like.

Finally, they were finished and Lorraine explained to Cherie the next part was even more fun—wrapping all their gifts. Lorraine told Cherie choosing the right paper and ribbon was one of the best parts for her. It was an opportunity to show some artistic flair.

Cherie had never considered how nice Christmas could be. She had seen all the people buying presents and how excited many people were, especially the children. There was an entirely different world than she had ever believed existed.

Her world had never imagined there were people living the way she had seen during her shopping trip or the way the McConnell's street looked as they drove toward her new home. Her mind was processing all of this, and she wondered why such a country as the United States was not able to have its entire people live the way she had seen in the past weeks.

She was going to think about this as she pondered the genetic puzzle in her studies.

# Chapter 26

Clifton Burton Jamesway Senior was ushered into the President's Chief of Staff's office. Jessica Alverez was not impressed and tried not to show it. Shamika had told her the entire story of Jamesway's son and how his father's influence with the President allowed the situation to happen. Jessica was very unhappy. She was chosen to lean on Shamika to promote Clifton Junior. However, she was gracious as she escorted Senior into her office. After some short chatting, Jessica got to the purpose of the meeting.

"I realize it's unusual to be called to a meeting here on such short notice. I have some disturbing news about your son." She saw him lean forward in concern, "It's nothing about him physically, but it is very serious." She proceeded to tell him the entire story of Junior's misdeeds.

His expression changed from the initial concern, to serious, to frowning in consternation.

As she finished, she explained the current situation, "Clifton is in a special detention facility in Maryland. We have held him there since he was arrested. He met a judge in a special court set up for national security cases. He has been remanded, and the government is determining how they want to proceed. You may see him if you wish. He has a court-appointed lawyer. All the proceedings to date have been held in a very restricted, classified environment. You can appreciate the sensitivity of this."

Jamesway responded after taking a deep breath, "I am deeply disturbed by my son's actions. I am a member of the President's National Intelligence Advisory Board. I was instrumental in working to set up the Group's charter and mission. I have followed their missions. I can't believe my son was as stupid as this situation indicates. I'm not trying to give him any justification for his actions. I would like to see him though."

Jessica responded, "I will arrange for you to see him immediately or whenever you wish."

"I'd like to see him as soon as possible."

They discussed the details for his visit, and Jamesway left.

Jessica summarized the meeting in a memo for the President. She went into the Oval Office to report the results of the meeting. Elizabeth Rawlings looked up from a report she was reading.

"Madame President, I just met with Burton Jamesway. Here is a memo on our meeting." Jessica gave her a short synopsis of the meeting.

Rawlings looked at Jessica with a stony face. "Let me know what happens between the two of them. It would be very useful if we could let Junior go in Dad's care or custody. Senior would be very beholden to us."

Jessica smiled a tight-lipped smile. "After they talk, I'll talk to the Justice attorney and the judge and let you know what their thoughts are." She left the office to get on the phone.

*********

Burton Jamesway, Junior was sitting in a small, featureless room, empty except for a sink integrated into the wall, a toilet similarly integrated, and a narrow concrete slab of a bed projecting from the wall with a pad and pillow on it. A door with a two-by-three-foot window pane of thick plastic looked out into a blank wall. The room was painted a light green. Burton tried to scratch it, but it probably was epoxy paint; it couldn't be scratched. A small slit of a window, four inches by three feet was along the rear wall about eight feet from the floor. Burton couldn't see out of it. A light from outside the room provided diffuse light. Burton was wearing a red jumpsuit made of some material he couldn't rip or tear. He knew there was a camera monitoring him as he sat on the cot. He reflected on what had happened to him. He was terrified beyond words.

When the state police picked him up, they took him to the nearby state police station on Route 50. Waiting there for him and Carlita were four men. Two of them took him to an unmarked van, placed him in a seat in the back of the van, and handcuffed him to the seat. As he walked to the van, he saw Carlita being led off. He had not seen Carlita since.

There were no windows in the van, and he had no idea where they took him. He could not see anything outside the van. He knew they could see him because he could see a small camera pointing at him from the front of the vehicle, but he could not see into the front of the van. Two men sat across from him and looked at him in stony silence.

They drove for about two hours and stopped briefly, seeming to go through a checkpoint. They stopped, and the back door to the van was opened. They were inside a large garage. He was taken into a blank room with a table at one end with two chairs anchored to the floor, one on each side of the table. A man was sitting on one side of the table. Burton was handcuffed to the other chair and his two escorts left.

The man said, "I am your court-appointed lawyer. You will be seeing the judge in a few minutes. Do you know what you're charged with?"

Burton decided to be enraged. "Do you know who I am?"

"Yes, you are the Deputy for Special Programs, a special office reporting directly to the President. You are charged with unauthorized revelation of classified information to a foreign intelligence service and espionage against the United States, a crime that could lead to a life sentence or death."

Burton turned white and began inhaling and exhaling. The lawyer looked at him. "Are you all right?"

Burton nodded. "What are you talking about? What foreign intelligence service. I don't know anyone like that."

"Your girlfriend, Carlita, works for a foreign intelligence service. The government has videos and recordings of you telling her about the existence and mission of a very secret United States' operation. She passed that information to a man who works for a country hostile to the United States.

Because of your revelations, you were responsible for the death of one of the operatives on a special mission. You will have great difficulty explaining yourself. I need to know how you intend to plead when we see the judge."

Burton was having difficulty in maintaining his original indignation. "What do you suggest? I would like to have an opportunity to explain my actions."

"In that case I suggest you plead 'Not Guilty'. You will then have an opportunity to lay out a defense. You don't have to use me at all. You can pick your own lawyer. I'm here because I have the necessary security clearance. If you select your own lawyer, he or she will have to go through a security background investigation and lie detector examination."

Burton thought for a minute. "I will plead Not Guilty."

Burton sat on his bed slab and tried to figure out how he could get out of this mess. He was innocent. He didn't know Carlita was a secret agent. He thought she was just a dumb illegal immigrant. How could she betray him? He had treated her well, even given her some expensive presents. The death of the operative didn't faze him, soldiers did dangerous work. He needed to talk to his father. His father would understand. He had always rescued him when things went bad. He had been in the prison—he called it a prison, but he really didn't know what it was or where he was—for about five days. He was getting worried. He needed to talk to his father. His father would know some really smart lawyers who could get him off. He knew his father would be on his side.

The light began changing on the other side of his door; that usually meant a guard was coming down the corridor. There were two guards standing on either side of the door as electronic bolts slammed into the wall, and the door opened. They escorted him down the corridor to the room where he had met his lawyer. They opened the door and escorted him into the room. His father was sitting at the table. Burton was overjoyed; he now had a chance for freedom.

His father was not smiling. Burton realized this was not a good sign. They sat looking at each other for a while. His father finally spoke, "Burton,"—This also was not a good sign. His father always called him Junior.—"I have reviewed the evidence they have of your involvement with this woman Carlita. You are in a great deal of trouble. I can't believe you have behaved so foolishly. You have disgraced the family." His father stopped and looked at him.

Burton wasn't sure how to respond, "I was tricked…" He trailed off as his father waved at him impatiently.

"It doesn't matter how it happened. You violated the trust the government placed in you. You have failed miserably. I don't know what the government will do at this point. They could conceivably charge you with treason and ask for the death penalty. You caused the death of one of America's finest special operatives." His father alternated between anguish and anger as he looked at Burton.

"I, I had no idea. I never wanted…I am so ashamed, Father." Burton trembled.

"Well, at this point, I will have to talk to your lawyer to see what alternatives there are. I just wanted to see you and let you know the enormity of what you've done. I will see if there is any way we can reach a plea that will not end with you in prison for life or your death." His father stood up and the door opened. The two guards escorted him back to his cell.

His father stayed in the room, and Burton's lawyer came in. He introduced himself and explained his father could get another lawyer.

"I understand," Burton Senior said, "but I would like you to stay in it for a while." He assumed the lawyer had experience in this sort of case.

"Actually, I have usually dealt with foreign terrorist suspects. This is the first case of its kind I have been in. I've talked with the Justice lawyers, and they would like to talk to you. They're willing to meet with you at the Department tomorrow at ten o'clock."

Burton Senior nodded. "I would like that opportunity. Tell me where to be and I'll be there."

The next morning, as Burton Senior rode in his limousine to the Department of Justice, he reflected on his situation. He was the heir to a family who had great wealth, but used their position to help the United States. He had served in the Marines during Vietnam. He had been Ambassador to Brazil and Secretary of the Navy.

It was his time as Ambassador that led him to think about the need for a special clandestine force, reporting directly to the President.

The force, which became Group 5, could be used by the President to perform needed actions known only to him and a select few congressmen, senators, and other selected senior government individuals.

He had two daughters from his first wife who died of cancer. His second wife was much younger than he, but she gave him great joy when she gave birth to Burton Junior. He doted on his son and now realized he had spoiled him to the point he was ineffectual. He had let his family ties blind himself to Burton's inabilities.

The limousine let him off in front of the Robert F. Kennedy DOJ building. He walked up the stairs to the main entrance and walked to the guard's desk. He was a bit put off by this lack of respect. He was usually picked up by a government limousine and met by an escort. He realized his son's stupidity had caused him to fall down steeply in the respect hierarchy of Washington politics. He had a lot of crow to eat before he could command the perks he was used to. Well, he had a lot of friends, and contributions to the right politicians could create a lot more respect. His main worry was he might be taken off the prestigious President's National Intelligence Advisory Board. He wrote his name in the entry log and the individual he was to contact. He waited about fifteen minutes and an attractive young woman walked up and introduced herself. He was given a badge requiring an escort and followed her to the elevators.

He was surprised, instead of meeting with a middle management person he had been led to believe he would be dealing with; he was taken to the Attorney General's office. He was ushered right in. The AG was standing near a couch and chairs. They shook hands. "Burton, come on in. I'm sorry we have to meet for such an unfortunate circumstance."

"Hello, Jack, it's good to see you," Burton replied. He was mystified by this welcome. He had expected to be treated like a pariah, but here was his old friend from college and business acting as if this were a casual visit, even offering him coffee.

"Burton, I don't have a lot of time. I heard about the situation and discussed it with the President. We both agreed it would be best if you and I could figure out a positive resolution to avoid embarrassment to you, but allow some leeway in the legal area. I would like to make an offer to you and see if it can work out a solution to the situation."

Burton Senior replied, "I'm willing to listen to anything. I'm very upset with my son's naivety and stupidity. I'll work with you in any way I can."

The AG indicated Burton Senior should sit down in one of the chairs. He sat down in the other. "Burton, we've known each other for a long time, but this situation is unlike any I've ever experienced. From what I can determine, your son was, as you say, extremely naïve, but that doesn't excuse his gross lapse of judgment. His actions caused the death of one of our best operatives, a young man with a wife and family. If this had not happened, we might be able to finesse this situation.

However, I believe we can find a way to move beyond this. If Junior is willing to allocute regarding the charges against him, the government will impose only parole. We will release Junior into your custody. He will serve ten years in that status. What you do with him is up to you, but I suggest you bury him somewhere. The fact he caused the death of an operative has caused some very hot feelings. As far as anyone will know though, he is serving time in a special jail reserved for national security offenses. I believe this is a very lenient resolution of this situation, but the President wants you to know she wishes to help you through this difficulty."

Burton Senior was taken aback by this offer. He had not expected any leniency of this order. "This is extremely generous and thoughtful. It will help me with my wife. She doesn't know anything about this, and I'll be able to explain the situation to her. I'll explain to Junior the situation. I understand if he doesn't comply with whatever I do with him, he will be subject to returning to prison. I believe I can find someplace to satisfy your aims. I have a small factory outside Chicago. A man running the shipping department is a trusted family friend and owes me a great deal. He is also very discrete. I can send Junior there. I'll have a very rigorous conversation with him. He has brought disgrace to our family, let alone committed a very serious crime, and I don't see any way for redemption. As far as I'm concerned, his future is very limited."

The AG nodded sympathetically. "I'll work out the arrangements and try to get this over as soon as possible."

They chatted for a few minutes, and then the AG escorted Burton Senior out of his office. As he walked with his escort down the hall and into the elevator, he was discouraged for the first time in his life. He knew Burton Junior was not that bright, but he had no idea he was so limited in his street smarts. In fact he had none, no common sense. He was a complete loss. His two girls were much different: brainy, independent, and successful. The girls were older, and when his new wife gave birth to Burton Junior, he had high hopes for his new son. He realized his hopes had blinded him. He had given too much leeway to Junior. He should have paid more attention to him. He was just not bright enough to be trusted in any position of responsibility.

He walked out of the DOJ and got into his limousine. "Take me back to the hotel," he told the driver.

**********

Several days later a man came to the door of Burton Junior's cell and opened it. He handed Burton his clothes and told him to get dressed. The man then escorted Burton down a hall to an office. His lawyer and his father were standing in the office with another man. His father turned to him and said, "Burton, listen to this man. He is from the Department of Justice. They are offering you a deal. You must take it."

The man explained to Burton he was released into the custody of his father. Burton was on parole for the next ten years. He would have to do exactly as his father said. He pushed some papers forward on the desk and told him to sign them. Burton looked at his father and the lawyer. They both nodded. Burton signed the papers.

His father escorted him out of the building. Burton had never seen the outside. He had no idea where he was. It was a one-story concrete rectangle surrounded by double chainlink fences. His father's limousine was waiting for them. His father opened the door for Burton and pushed him inside. His father went around to the other side and got in. His father tapped on the window separating the driver, and the car began to drive off.

His father turned to him and began to explain to him his new situation. "Burton, you have disgraced me and the family. I was given no choice. Either you would be in a maximum security prison for the next ten years or be released to me. I had to think long and hard about that choice. I misplaced my trust in you, and I'm going to try to rectify the mistake. I'm taking you to the airport where we will get on the company plane. I'm sending you to a town outside Chicago where the company owns a small factory. You will work there for the next ten years at a wage set by the factory. You will work as a shipping clerk. You must find yourself a place to stay. I will not communicate with you, neither will your mother or siblings. I will be monitoring you. Your boss is a trusted friend of mine who understands the situation. Do you understand?"

Burton was in tears by this time. He didn't know what to say; he just nodded. All he could think about was his life was over. His father had just disowned him. The car drove through the Maryland countryside toward a private airport. There was silence as they drove. Burton couldn't begin to talk his throat was so constricted.

**********

Several months later Shamika Johnson dropped into Jessica Alverez's office. "Sorry to bother you Jessica, but I was wondering what ever happened to Burton. He seemed to drop off the earth."

Jessica looked up from her desk, "As far as I know he was brought to trial and is serving a sentence in a remote prison. Because of the sensitivity of the situation, the whole thing was kept very quiet. Trust me, Burton is being punished."

"Thanks, Jessica, my troops and the Group have been wondering if justice was done. Losing one of our own was very painful. It'll help if I can give them that feedback." She left and went back down to her office.

# Chapter 27

Burton had worked several months in his new job. His supervisor was not friendly to him, but made sure he understood his duties. The other people in the shipping department were nice to him, but reserved. They weren't sure who he was. He didn't tell anyone his real name. His father had told him he was hired as Burton Clifton, and he better be very quiet about any relation to the Jamesway's. Burton had decided his best chances for survival and not returning to jail lay in doing his job and being very circumspect. The job was not complicated, but it was the first time he ever had to actually work. His summers after college were always at the Island and all he did was sun and play.

The factory was a small manufacturing firm supplying specialized machined parts for a variety of customers: automobile manufactures developing prototypes, automobile racing teams, vintage airplanes and automobile reconstruction enthusiasts. They had a team of designers, engineers and master machinists and a small foundry for casting precision parts. Burton was not involved in this, but his job required him to make sure when an order came in it was routed to the proper department and sent out according to the schedule established with the customer. Burton began to feel he was doing something useful for the first time in his life.

Usually at quitting time, Burton would walk the mile to his small bachelor apartment. His supervisor recommended the place and it was affordable with his salary. Once in a while he would go down the street to a small diner and have dinner. He was lonely, but had a lot of time to reflect on his life and mistakes. He began to realize he was a part of a privileged class living so apart from the people he worked with there was no way to describe the gap. His class of people lived like the royalty of old. They had people who cleaned their houses, drove them to work, private airplanes for travel. Burton had never seen the way most people lived. He had to budget his money for the first time. He began to feel ashamed of the way he had treated Shamika. His supervisor and several of his co-workers were black—African-American, he corrected himself.

They were all nice people. They seemed to enjoy each other and the other workers: African-American, Hispanic, and white all got along with each other. They all ate in the small company cafeteria, and the table sittings were along department lines instead of color or other divisions.

At first he sat by himself, but one of the African-American men who worked next to him in a cubical invited him to come over and sit with his table. There were five other people at the table: a female African-American, the man who invited him, two male Hispanics, and a younger white woman. He sat down next to one of the Hispanics and the white female.

The man who invited him seemed to be the table leader. He said to the table, "I thought it was time we got to know Burton. He looked like a lost doggie sitting by himself. Burton, my name is Clifton, Clifton Burns," and he chuckled as he said it. "People this is Burton Clifton. No relation." He laughed.

Clifton began introducing each of the table members and a little about them—where they were from, if they were married, who had children. He then said to Burton, "Tell us a little about yourself, Burton."

Burton had been dreading this moment for a while, but he had thought through a story that made sense. "I'm twenty-five and originally from Boston. After I graduated from high school, I worked in a Walmart warehouse. Last year I decided to try something different and a different city so I applied on line for this job and got it. So far I like the company and everyone I've met. I'm not married and not into a relationship, at least not yet." He smiled. Everyone seemed satisfied by this story. They all began chatting with each other and discussing some of their work problems. Soon they all got up and went back to the shipping room.

Several weeks went by and one of the Hispanics, Rodriguez, asked him if he would like to stop for a beer after work on a Friday. Rod lived close to where Burton did. He seemed to like Burton. They often joked about things that happened as they processed the paperwork and made sure the machined parts were packaged properly.

Burton was often reminded of Carlita when he heard Rod's accented English, but he tried to put those thoughts aside and agreed to have a beer with Rod. They had a good time, and Burton began to hope he could have some life even under his circumstances.

The white girl, Jenny, who worked in the department with him was unmarried, but going with someone. She asked him if he would be interested in going on a blind date with a friend of hers. Burton decided he would like to have some female companionship and agreed to go out. Burton had no car so he had to take a cab to the restaurant where the date was to take place. He met Jenny and her boyfriend at the entrance to the restaurant. A girl walked up to them. She was small with long dark hair and sharp features. She wasn't beautiful, but looked nice and was dressed in a nice dark pink sweater and dark blue skirt.

It was cold and she was taking off her coat as she walked up to them. "Sorry I'm late, but the office had a pile of records to finish." She continued talking as they walked into the entrance of the restaurant. "Hello, you must be Burton. Jenny has told me about you from her work. I'm Alice." She reached out her hand, and he shook it.

Jenny looked at Burton and laughed at Burton's bewildered look. He obviously was not used to a woman who acted so forwardly. "Well, I don't have to worry about introducing Alice. This is my boyfriend, Hank. Hank, Burton, Burton, Hank."

They went into the restaurant, an Italian one, and were seated at a table. The evening went well.

Alice kept the conversation going and Burton enjoyed her company. She was different than any woman he had ever met. She had grown up on a farm in rural Illinois and when she graduated from high school went to a community college for two years where she got an associate's degree in data base management. She worked for a firm processing health records for various doctors. Burton had a very good time and when they rose to go, he asked her if he could see her again.

She looked him in the eye and said, "Burton, you are a quiet guy, but I can see you are a nice man. I've been looking for a nice guy to go out with, and I will be glad to go out with you again."

Burton was excited. It was the first time in his life a girl agreed to go out with him not knowing anything about his father, his family or his wealth.

Burton and Alice began going out several times a week. He had given her a fictitious background: his parents died when he was young; his brother and sister and he lived in foster homes until he graduated from high school. He was not close to them. Alice seemed to accept this. They were not having a sexual relationship. Alice told him she had two relationships that went nowhere. She was determined to better know who she went out with before getting deeply involved with someone. Burton respected this. He actually felt the same way based on his experience with Carlita.

They continued going out intermittently. Burton did not have much money, and Alice often worked late hours. She was friendly, but a bit distant. Burton realized she was waiting to see who he really was. Christmas week was a holiday week for the company Burton worked for. When Christmas came, Alice went to her parent's house near a small town outside Chicago. He was left alone. It was the first Christmas he had ever spent alone.

During the Christmas break, Burton realized something profound had changed within him: He cared about someone else more than he cared about himself. Alice had become the center of his life. He realized he was in love with her. Never before had he thought like this. His father had taught him women were not important. They were just objects to be used for a specific purpose. He had never reflected on his two half sisters and how they fit into his father's thoughts. His mother was not close to him as he grew up. He mainly had nannies watching him when he was younger, and his mother was often out with her friends shopping or doing charity things. When he was older he went to a private boarding school. His relationship with Alice was more real than anything he had ever experienced.

# Chapter 28

The President of Venezuela sat at the head of a small table off to the side of his desk in his office. The office was the size of a small house without any walls. Ornate tapestries hung from the walls. The floor-to-ceiling windows were hung with rich gold and emerald green drapes. The marble floors were covered with several elaborate, deeply piled rugs. His desk was size of a dining room table. Two large gold lamps sat on a table behind the desk. Everything was designed to provide the impression of great power.

The table he was at was not especially ornate, but the chair he sat in was two inches higher than the other three chairs on either side of the table and more ornate. He felt it helped him to project an aura of command. At his left was his chief of internal security. Next down from him, his chief of external security sat, and across from those two, another man was seated.

"Well gentlemen," the President began, "it sounds like our little plan is progressing as we desired." He gestured to the chief of external security. "Juan, tell us of your progress."

Juan looked at the other men around the table and began to describe the ongoing operation. The chief of external security was equivalent to the Director of the US CIA. "Mr. President, as you all know, in working with our friends in Iran we both came up with a desire to embarrass the United States and further create its isolation from the rest of the world.

"Its attempts to prevent terroristic acts around the world have made it especially unwelcome in the Moslem world, and its attempts to disrupt the drug trade, caused by its own internal moral corruption have brought hardship and trouble to its southern neighbors."

He went on, "I will let Senior Borzin explain how they have selected and trained their personnel, and then Hector will explain how we have been able to ship them to the US. I will end by describing the intended operation."

Borzin was the man to the President's right. He sat forward and began speaking in halting Spanish, "Mr. President, I would first like to extend the hand of friendship from my president. He is very much in favor of your desires for putting the United States at a disadvantage. Our other projects with your country are proceeding very nicely from all the reports."

The President nodded with a large smile.

"To start, we selected twelve individuals. Our planning called for four sets of three, but as the training went on, we eliminated three for a variety of reasons.

We used Al Qaeda as our cover in recruiting. Al Qaeda has no knowledge of what we are doing though. As we recruited individuals, we offered them the opportunity to become as heroic martyrs as the men who participated in the 9/11 operation. We selected individuals from Saudi Arabia, Yemen, Jordan, and several other Mideast countries.

Two of these were from the US and had gone to Yemen eager to have revenge for whatever reasons. They were eager to participate. We were very careful to make sure, as we explained the potential. We did not expose who we were or what the nature of the operation was. We eliminated the ones we decided were unsatisfactory. By eliminated I mean they are no longer around." Borzin looked meaningfully at the President who nodded in understanding.

"Next we took them to Iran. They had no knowledge of where they were. We blindfolded them and flew them to a secret site in a remote area of our country. Anyone they met spoke Arabic and as far as they knew they were working for someone from Saudi Arabia. We were very careful to maintain this façade. They were taken into our training facility. It is a very large old warehouse. There, they were provided initial physical fitness training and training in firearms and explosives handling. We spent three months with this activity.

"We were able to observe them and decide who worked best with each other and how reliable they each were. We then divided them into units of three and separated them from each other. This was to ensure they did not get knowledge of each other's targets. As I said, we eventually eliminated three of the original twelve due to them not measuring up to our needs.

For security purposes we believe if we tried to have a larger number of individuals, it would have made it more difficult to infiltrate them, and possibly make security more difficult. Each of the three units was trained against their particular target.

"We used pictures, mock-ups, and target run-throughs, as if they were actually at the operational site. We are very satisfied they are able to do the operation. They are very motivated and dedicated and have no fear of sacrificing their lives for this effort.

"We also were successful in training another two individuals for a truck bomb attack. This activity was completely separate from the other nine. Once we were satisfied with their capabilities, we put them into two cargo ships and sent them to your country. Your very capable Chief of Internal Security will tell you of the next step." Borzin gestured to the other man across the table and sat back.

The man to the President's left leaned forward with a smile, "Mr. President, I am very excited by this activity. We have managed to transship the individuals through our ports with no observables by any individual. The individuals were moved using special containers outfitted for human transport. The containers originated in Iran, but were then sent to Hamburg where they were placed on a German freighter and sent to our port. Throughout the voyage our agents were there to check on the individuals and on the ship. These agents did not know details about the mission; however, they did know there were humans in the containers.

"Once they arrived in our port, the containers were placed in three different warehouses and the individuals allowed to exit and relax. A doctor examined them and we allowed them to get some exercise and have some good meals. Their morale and dedication seemed to be excellent.

"We only allowed Mr. Borzin's representatives to speak to them to ensure they did not know exactly where they were. Any problems with the containers were fixed and improved for them. We then made sure the containers would have some disguise if anyone became interested in what they contained. They were shipped as machine and steel parts en route in three different ships to three locations in the United States. My men made sure there was no unusual interest in these containers as they were moved to our ships for transport to the US. At that point my colleague, Juan, took over the operation." Hector sat back in his chair.

Juan pursed his lips and looked serious. "Mr. President, this is the most difficult part of the operation. We seem to have been successful in inserting our operatives into the United States. They were shipped to three entry points in the US: Houston, Charleston and Chicago. The reason for this diversity was to place them as close to their operational targets as possible. The actual targets were selected by our agents traveling to the US as tourists about a year ago. We evaluated ten sites, but eliminated several due to operational factors. We now have three: Chicago, Washington, DC, and Scottsdale, Arizona. Our 'tourists' rented safe houses for the individuals to stay in and provided transportation for them. Once the operatives left their ships, they were put in closed vans and driven directly to their safe houses near each city. The drivers know nothing of their mission other than to transport the individuals. At this point the operatives are in their safe houses; their arms and explosives are with them. They are now waiting for the day. In three days they will be activated and terror will be visited in America."

The President smiled broadly. "Bravo, gentlemen this is historic. The Americans will be running around like ants around sugar and will have no idea of who or where this calamity came from." He began to laugh. He stood up, and the three stood up with him. "No, no, sit, sit." He walked over to a chest and opened the top and pulled out a bottle of scotch. "Let us toast our success. He looked at Borzin. "Can you join us?"

Borzin smiled. "Of course. A toast is certainly in order."

# Chapter 29

On Christmas Eve Sam gave Lorraine a diamond engagement ring. She was very surprised, but happy. They had discussed where they wanted their relationship to go and both realized they wanted the stability of a marriage and not just to let their relationship drift along. They also both wanted to have children—not immediately, but in the near future. They announced their engagement that night at Lorraine's Christmas party. Everyone was excited and happy for them. Her parents were overjoyed, her mother especially. They hadn't decided when or where they would get married, and Sam wanted Lorraine to meet his brother and family before they got too tied into decisions. He really missed his brother, whom he hadn't seen in over two years.

Christmas and New Years passed and Lorraine and Sam planned a trip to visit his brother. Sam was living with Lorraine in her house. They had agreed, until they worked out their life together, they would take one thing at a time. Sam was still considering what sort of career he might like. He was still looking at a medical field. He had thought he might like to be an Emergency Medical Tech, but then thought he wanted to be with Lorraine more.

He knew he had to have something to do, but when he introduced Lorraine into his life, he realized how much he had missed in his personal life. He saw how much her sister had with her two children and what fun it was watching Cherie figure out her new life. She was almost like him. They both had something they never thought they would ever have.

Sam suggested they take a leisurely trip to Sedona to see his brother. Even though it was winter, they wanted to drive there. Sam had never seen the western US and thought a road trip would be fun for the two of them. Lorraine agreed. She had never been past the Mississippi River. They both thought they were a bit provincial about the United States.

Her sister had an engagement party for them before they left. Many of Lorraine's work friends wanted to celebrate her engagement, and her parents wanted to show Sam off to their friends. She held the affair in the party room of a local hotel. Following the party Lorraine and Sam talked about what sort of wedding they would like. Both agreed they did not want a giant affair, but when they started talking about who they would like to attend, they realized they were talking about several hundred people. They really didn't want something that large.

Sam thought of Allo and Heck and some of the other people he had worked with. Lorraine did the same about her friends. They decided they would try to work out the whole thing as they took their trip.

Lorraine had taken a six month leave of absence from her job with the surgical team. The head doctor was not happy with her decision, but he understood. He assured her whenever she wanted to return, she was welcome.

They started out on a wintry February day. Light snow was falling, but it was the back end of a storm that had already passed through. Conditions were expected to be good for the next week. The roads were clear, and as they drove along Interstate 80, the sky brightened and eventually the clouds dissipated and the sun broke through. They were both in high spirits. Sixties music played on the satellite radio and they laughed at the old tunes. Some they recognized and some were new to them.

Lorraine couldn't stop looking at her engagement ring. She had never expected to see one on her finger. While she knew she was attractive, after Paul, she never thought she would have reason to get involved with anyone. There had been something so appealing, no, not even appealing, breathtaking, about Sam as he ran toward her on the beach in Fort Myers. She was in love before he spoke. She knew that was silly, but ever since they had been together, desire for him had only grown.

They had almost a silent communication between themselves. She would be amused by something and look at him and know he was laughing too. She knew he felt the same way. When he surprised her with the ring at Christmas, she knew it was the right thing to do. They would be married, and both their lives would be better for it.

Sam was driving and noticed her looking at the ring. "Do you really like it? I'm not being funny. The man started asking me square cut, emerald, round, baguettes, all kinds of stuff. I had no idea what he was talking about. I just got something I thought you'd like." He had finally selected a three-carat diamond with three stones on either side. He couldn't remember all the details, but he thought the ring was very nice.

"My love, I am just admiring it. I can't tell you how much it means to me. I'm not a jewelry person, but you have done well. I wish I could give you something that would show you how much you mean to me."

Sam drove for a while thinking about this. "I guess for men things like that aren't as important. It isn't that I need you to give me something as a token or sign of your love. The fact you're with me and want to be with me for the rest of your life is so overwhelming to me. It's enough. I'm glad I got something to symbolize my devotion to you. I'm glad it means something to you. It means a great deal to me."

She leaned over and gave him a kiss. "I understand. I'm just thrilled and excited."

Their first stop was near Omaha. Sam wanted to see the Strategic Air and Space Museum in nearby Ashland. While Lorraine was at work, Sam had planned their trip and the hotels they would stay at. He researched each place they stayed and what there was to see. Omaha had a nice older hotel in a district called Old Market. A good steak restaurant was nearby. Omaha was famous for its steaks.

"I think the hotel is a nice one, and we can have a good meal, look around the city, and then drive down to Ashland where the museum is. We'll stay in Lincoln tomorrow and then go on to Denver." Sam was enjoying his new job as tour director.

"I don't care about where we stay as long as the room is clean and the bed is comfortable and we are together."

"You would have done well on board a Navy ship, although some of the beds were of questionable comfort." Sam responded with a laugh.

It was dark by the time they drove into Omaha. "I didn't realize that Omaha was as modern a city as it is." Lorraine observed.

"It looks like we can have a nice visit tomorrow." Sam replied. He signed in and they went up to their room. Sam was a little tired; he was not used to driving for so long in one day. Lorraine looked at him and said, "You know Sam, I have a driver's license too. I'd like to share the driving, if you want. You don't have to be macho in the car."

"That would be nice, and I could sightsee a little bit. It just never occurred to me. My dad always drove wherever we went. It's not a macho thing with me. I know you're a good driver."

They had a nice dinner at a restaurant nearby and went to bed.

The next day Lorraine drove out of Omaha to the museum. She had enjoyed Omaha and its shops in the old town part of the city. At the museum Sam was impressed by the aircraft displays and space hardware. Lorraine tolerated his passion, but was ready to continue onto Lincoln where they stayed that night.

As she drove out of Lincoln, she began thinking of their life ahead. It was exciting to consider. They would have enough money to live anywhere or anyway they wanted. Her townhouse was worth about $380,000 and she had about $110,000 in savings and another $300,000 in an IRA. She wouldn't be able to live independently of Sam's income, but they had discussed this. They could work out something, but she didn't want him to think she wanted to live off of his money. She thought she might be too proud, but she had been financially independent since she was about twenty-two. These thoughts swirled through her head as she drove. As they left Lincoln, the land began to get very flat and lonely looking to her. Most of it was snow covered with a few bare patches. It was part of the great prairie extending from the Mississippi River to the Rockies. She realized she liked scenery. She was looking forward to seeing the Rockies. She had been to Africa and parts of Europe. Since she returned from Africa, she had been living in stasis—going to work, taking classes, coming home, not thinking about the future. Now there was a whole new future ahead.

Sam was lying back in his seat listening to the satellite radio. Today it was '70s music. The Beatles had just finished a song. He realized he was dozing. It was a unique experience to be relaxing like this, he thought. He had usually been thinking about a coming operation or one that had passed.

He thought about Rico and how Rico never had a chance to move on in his life. He had kept in contact with Rico's wife a few times, but she was immersed in her children and her new life.

He could tell from her responses she really didn't want to have much to do with him. It was probably too painful for her to be reminded of what happened. He became aware of the countryside as Lorraine drove on.

"How're you doing? Need to change yet?"

"No, I'm okay. I was just thinking about things. It's almost as if we're starting out on a new life right now. I was also thinking about places to live. I'm not hung up on staying in Evanston or Chicago. I just landed there after I got back from Africa, and sort of went into a remote control mood. I was thinking we could stop in North Platte for lunch and change there."

"Sounds good. Where would you like to live? I guess I haven't thought much about it. I wasn't thinking about leaving the service for another ten years and really hadn't thought about where I would end up." The prairie stretched out before them; farms and farmland passing them by. I've never been to the Rockies or West Coast. They might be interesting to consider. I'm not sure about Europe. I can speak fluent Spanish, some Portuguese, pretty good in French, and some Farsi or Iranian and some Arabic. I'm not interested in any Mideast countries. I did like the European Mediterranean coast—Spain, France, and even Italy."

Lorraine considered what he said. "I speak pretty good French and some Spanish, but I'm not sure about living overseas. There's just too much turmoil there. If we think about having a family, I think I would like to raise children in the US.

I've seen too much violence overseas. I don't know about Europe, but there've been some pretty terrible terrorist events: London, Paris, Lisbon, and even Denmark and Belgium. There doesn't seem to be anyplace there safe from the nuts intent on getting their forty virgins."

Sam nodded in agreement. They were both silent for several minutes, then Lorraine asked him a question, "Could you tell me about one of your operations? I don't want you to spill any secrets, but I'd like to understand what things you did. Don't worry about scaring me or grossing me out. I think I told you about being rescued by a SEAL team while I was in Africa."

"Yeah, I think you mentioned it. Hmm, I guess it wouldn't be a national security leak if I told you about the one in Brazil."

He paused for a moment. "A team, six of us, was in Brazil working with the Brazilian armed forces to help them develop an internal security team to deal with terrorist incidents. We were at a Brazilian base when we got word from our headquarters the Ambassador and his wife and entourage had been kidnapped. It was just the kind of thing the Brazilians were trying to guard against. Our embassy security team was ambushed as the Ambassador and his wife and entourage was going to a birthday party for the Brazilian president's daughter.

"They disappeared from Campo Grande, a smaller city in central Brazil, into the jungle. They were in Campo Grande because the president was from there. We were on the coast at a Brazilian army base. The Brazilian government asked for our help. "

We agreed to take two of their officers along as observers. There was some negotiation. Apparently the Brazilians were concerned we might kill some of the kidnappers. The Brazilian Defense Department ruled we could operate as Brazilian police and had the authority to use deadly force."

Sam took a deep breath—all of a sudden he was back in the action as the memories arose. "We were air evacuated to Campo Grande. The kidnappers didn't know we knew exactly where the Ambassador and his family were. They all had tracking devices planted beneath their skins. Even if they were stripped, we could find them. We had launched a small drone when we were activated and tracked them into the jungle. The fact of the devices was a very closely held secret, but we had to share that information with the Brazilians. Our headquarters was not happy about that. Anyway, we landed in Campo and made preparations to enter the jungle. Our drone provided us with pictures of the area the kidnappers were in. The area was in a jungle, the Mato Grosso, which is a combination marsh and deep jungle. We had often worked and trained in that kind of environment."

He paused for a moment. Lorraine was silent, concentrating on what he was telling her as she drove. She spoke up, "Why don't you stop your story there? We're close to North Platte."

Sam agreed, and they took the exit to North Platte where they saw a MacDonald's sign. They both got a burger and fries at the drive through, and Lorraine parked the SUV. As they ate Lorraine, who had been listening intently asked Sam, "How could you react so quickly? Did you have equipment with you?

"We're used to having to react quickly. We got as much intelligence about the area as we could. We carry a lot of specialized equipment with us whenever we travel and wherever we go. One of the Brazilian officers we agreed to take with us had been a guide into the Mato Grosso. He was invaluable for our planning."

After they both stopped in the restroom, Sam got into the driver's side and they started off again. "We took two boats down a river and put ashore where we knew the kidnappers would not expect us to come from. We didn't know if they had any communications with spotters either in Campo Grande or at our jumping-off spot. So far the Brazilian government had no communications from the kidnappers, and no one knew what their intentions were. We had to assume their demands might lead to the murder of one or more of the Ambassador's party. We broke up into two companies; one went to the west and one to the east of where we knew the kidnapper's camp was. It was early morning and our plan was to surround their camp, but start from about a mile out, assuming they were concentrated in one spot. Our drone had infra-red sensors, and we were able to identify what we thought were most of the kidnappers. Unfortunately there are large animals, jaguars and such, in the jungle and we had to determine which might be the kidnappers and which were animals. By evening we were in place. We had hiked about ten miles into the jungle. Of course we were in communication with each other. Our communications gear could not be detected or intercepted."

Sam stopped talking for a minute in exasperation as he came upon a large truck in the right lane and a slow-moving set of cars in the left two. "Our plan was to come as close to the camp during the night as we could. We rested for four hours—slept, nodded off, ate some rations, whatever. At midnight we began moving forward. We were all spread out. We could track ourselves on our GPS displays in our comm units—they're the size of a smart phone. Also on the display were the locations of what we thought were sentries and the camp. The jungle was very dense, but there were some trails leading toward the camp. I moved along one until I got to what I thought was about fifty yards from one of the sentries. I had my night-vision goggles on and there were a lot of monkeys in the trees and other animals—a large anaconda which I managed to avoid. It was also a bit noisy with the monkeys and birds. Our plan was to remove the sentries and work our way to the camp by daybreak. Daybreak is the best time to attack. The sentries are tired; people are just waking up, going outside the camp to pee or whatever. My sentry was sitting against a tree, smoking a cigarette."

He paused, "How much detail do you want to hear?"

"Keep going, I have seen gore."

"I carried a crossbow with me as a weapon. We have specialized crossbows are very powerful and accurate. I was about twenty yards away. I shot him through his left eye. The bolt pinned him to the tree. I ran toward him; he was thrashing as he died. I rammed a knife into his chest. I checked him to see if he had any communication device.

"Apparently the camp was relying on him yelling for help. We were about one hundred yards from the camp. I whispered into my comm device, 'Ghost One, one down.' I had a nickname of Ghost Dancer. My friends thought it was funny. At the same time the other six members called in they had taken down their targets. We knew there were four others. I was supposed to take down the first one and then another to my left. I moved to the left. The next sentry was about fifty yards from where I was. I had to move slowly because of the thickness of the jungle. Part of the reason they called me Ghost was I had become an expert at what was called 'Close Operations'. I could get anywhere and not be heard and eliminate people very quietly. I had a friend nicknamed Tonto who was a full-blooded Cherokee. He had similar skills. I found the other sentry standing in front of a tree, peeing. I came up behind him and cut his throat. Again, I called in. By this time all the sentries were eliminated." He paused.

Lorraine asked, "I never thought about it. You must have extensive training on how to eliminate people."

"We trained to silence people by rendering them unconscious or killing them, depending on the situation and the plan. It becomes a skill you don't think of. I have killed many people. I don't think of it with pride or regret. It was part of my job, and I was trained to do it quickly and effectively."

Lorraine considered this. "I see. It makes sense, but I had never thought of it like that."

"Most people don't realize the only reason for a soldier is to kill people for the United States or whatever country they work for. They are authorized to do that. They are unique just like the police. Deadly force is authorized.

"Anyway, we were now surrounding the camp and daylight was beginning. The monkeys and birds were screeching so much the kidnappers wouldn't have heard us if we walked up with a brass band. We were about ten yards from the camp. In the center of the camp was a large wooden cage with the Ambassador and his party sitting on the ground inside.

There were twenty more kidnappers. There was a small tent with a cook fire outside to my left. Five were standing around the fire. Five more were standing in front of the cage with their backs to me and Tonto to my left; another one of us, Grey, was to Tonto's left. We figured the rest were sleeping in two open tents on the other side of the cage.

"Tonto and Grey said they could take care of the guys around the fire and help me with the guys at the cage. We decided we would each fire a crossbow bolt which would create consternation, and then use our silenced handguns. The guys on the other side would take out the two tents. The two Brazilians were with them. Our lieutenant was with them, too. "

"A flashing light on our GPS was the signal to go. I shot the one in the middle in front of the cage. He fell against the cage, and the other four looked at him as if he were nuts. I shot the next two on the right and they went down. The other two were looking around to figure out what was going on.

The ones around the fire were all down, and then the other two were down. Tonto and I both shot them. On the other side of the tent, the guys had to get a little closer in since the kidnappers were lying down, but they killed all of them. There was silence. Well, the jungle was still noisy, but we all ran into the camp and made sure the kidnappers were all dead. The Ambassador looked at me, and I gave him thumbs up. I broke open the cage and told him we were American SEALS. The lieutenant came up beside me and told the Ambassador to get his party out of the cage. We were going to get them back to civilization."

Lorraine exhaled deeply. "Wow. I was living that with you. I'm not surprised at what you did. I was kidnapped with two Americans and twenty-five aid workers and patients in Africa. The same thing happened. Suddenly, our captors were all on the ground and there were, I don't know how many, Americans in battle gear protecting us. That's how I met my friend Jason Cloud. He's a SEAL in San Diego, has a wife and family. I don't think he still does field operations."

"I've been in many operations. That's how we're trained. Come in quickly and get it done with as little fuss as possible. Of course sometimes things don't work out, but that's another story. Did I answer your question?"

"Yes, you certainly did. I have no problem with what you told me. I just was interested in how you lived, or worked, or whatever. I understand the training and tension you must have lived with. I do want to share something with you.

"After I met you in Florida, I called up Jason and asked about you. I wasn't sure whether you were real or not. I had fallen for you so far and fast, I began to distrust myself. He told me you were a real person and even sent me a picture of you with much less hair than when I first met you. He also told me you had won a Silver Star."

"I'm impressed with your background check and with the way you welcomed me when I got to your townhouse with my little bunny, and yes, I did receive a Silver Star for that operation. It's also where I got the tip that got me my first three million.

"It turned out the Ambassador was an oil company executive who had contributed a lot to his political party. He had been a Marine officer in Vietnam. As we were getting his party back to where we could exfiltrate them, we began to chat. He asked me about my background and we became sort of friends. He told me he would like to stay in contact. I gave him an email address. I went back to our training camp in Brazil with the rest of the team.

The Brazilians were ecstatic with the results. Since all the kidnappers were dead, there was no need to announce anything. They were deeply embarrassed by the event. When I was preparing to return to the US, the Ambassador asked me to drop by his office.

"I did, and he told me two things: he had recommended me for a Silver Star, and he wanted to make me wealthy. He told me to take whatever money I had saved up and put it into a Brazilian oil stock. I had about $50, 000, and I put it all into what he suggested.

"Within two years it was worth over a million dollars. It has continued to rise to where it is worth about five million. I've kept in touch with him intermittently and he has passed on a few more tips; none as successful as that one, but still good ones. And that is my story about Brazil."

Lorraine shook her head in disbelief. "Again, wow. You never fail to amaze me with things that have happened to you."

They were getting close to the Denver city limits and the sun had fallen behind the mountains. "I've picked a unique hotel for us tonight. My suggestion is we stay here for two days. Tomorrow we can ride around Denver and the next day go up into the mountains. Of course you may not want to leave the hotel."

Lorraine was excited. "What's the name of this hotel? Wait,"—she looked at the GPS on the dash—"the Brown Palace? We are going to stay in a palace? Whoopee! I've never stayed in a palace." Her iTab was in its mount on the dash in front of her, and she pulled it toward her and began tapping on in. "Oh boy, this is a nice place. They even have a spa. My mother used to treat me and Sarah when we were younger to a spa once a year in Chicago, but lately we've been too busy to do it. But, you want to tour also. Maybe we can do both."

They arrived at the entrance to the hotel. Sam turned the start fob over to the valet and arranged for their overnight bags to be taken up. They had organized their clothes in Omaha in their bags so they didn't need to take their other bags up.

Lorraine was enthusiastic about the room. Sam had arranged for them to have a room in the older part of the hotel. All the rooms were nice, but in the older part there was a bit more like an old time hotel; all the rooms were decorated as in Victorian times. They decided to clean up and have a really good dinner in the Ships' Tavern dining room. Sam had gotten them a reservation for 7:30. By the time they finished their meal it was almost ten o'clock. They were both tired and fell into bed.

The next morning began with a slow and tender lovemaking and they didn't get out of bed until ten o'clock. By the time they had showered and gotten themselves ready, they decided to drive around Denver and find a place to have a brunch. They explained to the concierge they wanted to see the nice areas of Denver and get something to eat. The concierge gave them a map on which she had circled several areas.

They spent the day driving around. They wanted to get a feel for the city. As they drove, Lorraine acted as the navigator. She explained to Sam they should see if they liked living near or in a city and one like Denver. Most of the city was covered in snow, but they could see there were some beautiful old houses in one part and some beautiful newer neighborhoods in other parts too. Sam commented, one of the nice things about Denver was it was near some really nice ski areas. He had received ski training in preparation for one operation, but it had never come off. He had enjoyed the skiing part though. Lorraine had never skied, but thought it might be fun. They both agreed they might put Denver on their list of possible places.

They ate dinner at the Buckhorn Exchange as recommended by the concierge, but passed on the rattlesnake, alligator tail and Rocky Mountain oysters. They both had excellent steaks. Once again they returned to their room exhausted by the day and food and wine. The concierge had recommended they take a trip into the mountains and have an early dinner at the El Rancho restaurant where they could see the Continental Divide.

Again, their resolution to get up early was interrupted by serious lovemaking, but they were on the road by noon. It was not a long trip to the restaurant and they decided to drive farther on to Georgetown. Lorraine had been looking at her iTab and found if they drove a little farther they could also see the Loveland ski area. Neither of them had ever seen a real ski resort.

There was some traffic, but they parked in the Loveland lot, and got out and had a Danish and cup of coffee. Neither of them had eaten breakfast yet. They were fascinated by the skiers and the whole scene. It looked like something they could enjoy together. Lorraine was not intimidated about learning to ski; it was the one sport her father had not exposed Sarah or her to.

They drove back to the El Rancho, but because it was still early, drove to Evergreen. It was a quaint, but upscale little town. They parked and walked around looking at the stores and checking real estate prices. Several of the pictures of houses appealed to them. From what they could see about the community, the lifestyle here was relaxed with a lot of outdoor activities.

The surrounding mountains were covered with snow and the whole environment was beautiful. They drove back to their restaurant and talked about the day. The sun had set over the Continental Divide, but there was just enough light to see its outline. The restaurant's rustic ranch style interior was just what they needed.

"I think this is a possibility," Lorraine observed, "I like the environment: the outdoors, the views, the houses we saw in the real estate windows. It's close enough to Denver we could get there for the activities of the city, but retreat to the solitude of the mountains."

"I agree. I even saw schools in the area. So it's not as remote as it looks."

They decided to throw caution to the wind and order the wild game meatloaf with a bottle of merlot. It turned out to be delicious. It was a perfect day. After coffee they returned to their hotel. The day had been beyond their expectations.

They decided to get up early the next day. Sam had planned a short trip to Colorado Springs. He had picked out another really nice hotel to surprise Lorraine with. He was really enjoying the trip with her. He had never expected to meet someone he was so compatible with.

Felicia was different, but she was definitely a big-city girl. She had talked about the two of them living in Paris. She liked to travel, but was not outdoorsy. She would have gone to the ski lodge and had toddies while he skied. They got along well, but this relationship he had with Lorraine was so different he couldn't really compare the two women.

As they drove south, Lorraine was again sitting in the passenger seat looking at her iTab. "What's your plan for today? There are some interesting things to see in Colorado Springs."

"I really hadn't thought about it beyond the hotel. I thought we could explore the area a little. Is there anything on the iTab to see?"

"Well, on the way there's the Air Force Academy. Would you like to see it? I would, just for fun. I've never seen a service academy."

"Sure, let's do it. I've never seen one either. It can't take too long. How do we get there?"

"It's right off the interstate. We'll be passing it in about twenty minutes."

They turned into the North Entrance, and as they drove along the highway toward the academy, they passed a large aircraft. It was obviously part of a display. "Wow, what is that?" Lorraine asked.

"I think it's a B-52," Sam answered. "Let's stop and check it out."

As they walked around the large aircraft, Sam thought about his involvement with the Air Force. In several of his operations B-52s had played a major part. In one of them they were chasing a terrorist lord and his band that had just attacked a police barracks in Afghanistan.

A single B-52 was loitering waiting to support them. The hope was the terrorist band would retreat to a mountain stronghold. They did and Sam's unit was able to pinpoint the location. The B-52 dropped a single bomb designed to penetrate the mountain. There was an enormous explosion and part of the mountain disappeared. There were no more problems with terrorist band.

Lorraine was very interested in the aircraft and there was an elderly man and his wife looking at the aircraft too. He had actually flown that very plane and Lorraine asked him a barrage of questions. The man said his grandson was flying B-52s and his son had too. All three were graduates of the Academy. As they went back to their SUV, Lorraine chatted on about how some families had the legacy of military service. This was foreign to her.

Sam agreed. He was the first in his family to serve in the military.

They drove up to the Academy and parked in a lot next to what looked like a planetarium. They walked out to a broad area ending in a wall looking over the Academy area. As they walked along, a female cadet walked by them. She was obviously of oriental descent. Lorraine stopped and called to her, "Could you answer a question for me please?"

The cadet stopped and said, "Yes, ma'am."

Lorraine smiled at the ma'am. She didn't think she looked that old, but realized the cadet was just responding as she was taught. "What is the area in front of us and what are the buildings?"

The cadet pointed out the dormitories, the dining hall, academic buildings, and the chapel in front of them. "The area where the walkways are is called the terrazzo. That's where we form up when there are parades or we have to march to the dining hall. I have to go to get to class."

Lorraine responded, "Thanks a lot. Just one more thing—what rank are you?"

The girl smiled at her. "I'm a cadet colonel. I'm the wing commander."

Lorraine stared at her. "Do you mean you're the most senior cadet?"

"Yes, I just became the wing commander. There is one for the fall semester and one for the spring. I'm sorry, I really need to go." And she turned and walked away hurriedly.

Lorraine watched her go. "Wow, I hadn't thought about what women could do here. I almost wish I'd gone here. I could have flown and done things I can't imagine."

"I think you would have been a wing commander, too." Sam smiled at her. They turned to go, and as they walked to the car passed several displays memorializing famous airmen and Air Force units.

By this time they were both hungry and decided to see what they could find in downtown Colorado Springs. Lorraine searched on her iTab and found a small French restaurant specializing in crepes and had several five star recommendations.

As they drove along the streets, they passed many older houses. Some looked like they had been fully restored. They had a light lunch in the restaurant. It was excellent, and they decided to see what else Colorado Springs had to offer. As they drove through the center of the city, Lorraine was obviously not impressed. "It looks like they had a battle between the people who wanted to tear down and build new and the people who wanted to restore the old. I think both won." The city was neat and clean, but there were newer buildings scattered among older ones. They drove through the Garden of the God, an area of large reddish rocks and a beautiful housing development surrounding a golf course. "This is nice, but not as nice as Evergreen," Lorraine observed.

Sam decided it was time to check into their hotel. "I hope you like this as much as you liked the Brown Palace. It's called the Broadmoor. It's another very old hotel, but supposed to be very nice."

As they drove up the mountain toward the Broadmoor, they passed through some very upscale housing areas. "This is very nice. I like the old trees and the diversity of the houses." Lorraine was observing everything in detail.

They drove up to the front entrance and were met by a bellman. Sam turned everything over to him. He and Lorraine walked into the lobby and checked in. The clerk suggested they take the escalator up to the mezzanine lobby to see the view.

They were both mesmerized by what they saw: a lake with twinkling lights on the opposite side in the trees and a row of the hotel rooms behind them. The sun was just going down behind the mountains. The lobby they were standing in had beautiful furniture scattered about; people were sitting around with drinks in their hands. "This is better than the Brown Palace," Lorraine said, "and that's saying a lot."

After a dinner in the Golden Bee pub, they walked around looking at the shops scattered in front of the hotel, commenting on what they saw. It was very cold, and snow was predicted for the next day. They returned to their room; Sam was watching the weather report, while Lorraine undressed in the bathroom. "It looks like we'll see some snow late tomorrow," he called to her.

"Do you want to stay or try to get somewhere else tomorrow?" she replied. "I love this place, but we could drive south to our next destination and possibly miss the snow. Is the snow going to the south, or will it be to the north?" She came out of the bathroom with a washcloth in her hand.

"Our next stop is Santa Fe. It's about a six hour drive, and it looks like they'll get just a dusting. Do you want to explore more of Colorado Springs, or just move on?"

"I think this is a beautiful hotel, and it might make a really nice honeymoon spot, but I've seen enough of Colorado Springs. So far Evergreen is the nicest spot we've passed through. I have always wanted to see Santa Fe, so let's get up slowly tomorrow and be on our way after breakfast." She looked at him with a speculative eye.

Sam thought her idea was fine. He even suggested they go to bed slowly. This had become their own private code for lovemaking.

Lorraine drove the first leg of the trip to Santa Fe. Sam enjoyed watching the scenery. As they drove by Pueblo he remarked, "You know, I forgot, but we had some mountain training near here. Fort Carson has a special mountaineering training area up in the mountains. We were flown here, taken to the training area where we lived for a month, and then flown back to Coronado."

"You lived in Coronado? That should be a really nice area."

"Yeah, it was, but I never spent much time there after a lot of training. I did spend some time in Monterrey in language school. I guess, I did spend a bit of time in California, but it was never particularly pleasant. I was either swimming, running, learning fighting skills, language studies, and then overseas." Sam contemplated this for a minute. "I think we might enjoy California as civilians more than as a military family."

"Don't start thinking about re-upping. I'm not ready for the military life," Lorraine said with a wry smile.

"No worries, I've done my time. It's time for me to figure out how to be a civilian."

The drive to Santa Fe wasn't too exciting for the first leg. The interstate followed the mountains south, and the land to the east was fairly flat. The mountains were picturesque, and Sam provided Lorraine with a commentary about the names and heights of the various ones as they traveled—getting his information off the iTab. They decided to stop in Las Vegas, New Mexico for a quick lunch.

"This is a cute town, but a little small for me." They were sitting in a small restaurant. Lorraine had been studying the people and surrounds.

"Lorraine, are you on some sort of homestead search?" Sam looked at her with a puzzled look.

"I hadn't thought about it, but I guess I have been. I've been thinking about our life together. Once you gave me the ring, it became real to me we will have a new life that could be anywhere. It's very exciting to me. I don't want you to feel threatened or I'm pushing you into anything."

Sam shook his head. "I'm not concerned. I was just trying to figure out what you were thinking. I like the way you think. You are systematically considering what our new life could be. There's a lot in that and you're bringing up thoughts I wouldn't even have considered. Just keep me informed, so I can keep up with your thought processes."

Lorraine pursed her lips. "My thought processes are a bit scrambled with all I've been thinking about, but I'll keep you informed."

They finished their lunch and got on the road again. Their stop in Santa Fe was cut short to one night. Sam's brother called him and told him he and Janie were going to be in Scottsdale for the next several days on business. He wanted them to meet him there so he could show them his new studio in a mall there. He was very excited about the opening and wanted them to see it when it opened. They were staying right in Santa Fe, and they decided to leave the next morning instead of sightseeing.

Before they left Lorraine wanted to walk around the city for a while, and since it was about a nine hour drive, they decided to leave around ten o'clock after getting up at six. In Arizona they were going to take the Holbrooke exit from I-40 and head for Payson. It had lightly snowed the day before, and the road conditions on the Internet said the roads were clear.

Lorraine drove the first leg to Heber, Arizona where they stopped for gas. It was late afternoon and the light was waning. Sam said he needed to go to the head and get a cup of coffee. Lorraine said she would pump the gas and then go to the bathroom.

As Sam came out of the small convenience store with his coffee, he saw Lorraine standing with a man. They had pulled into the set of pumps farthest from the store. The SUV was facing to Sam's left. Lorraine had apparently finished pumping and the man looked like he was crowding her.

Without making a sound, Sam approached them. As he got closer he could see the man had hold of the front of her coat with his left hand. Sam got within three feet of them and yelled to the man, "What's going on here?"

The man turned with a startled expression on his face and a large knife in his hand. "I'll show you what's going on!" He extended the knife toward Sam.

Sam threw the coffee in the man's face. The man let go of Lorraine and lunged at Sam. Sam stepped to his left and caught the man's arm under his left arm. With his right hand heel he hit he man's jaw and at the same time kicked the man's legs from under him.

As the man fell, Sam held on and dislocated the man's shoulder. The man let out a screech as he fell on his face, and Sam landed on his back with his knee. The man's face was smashed into the concrete. He lay there moaning.

"Are you okay, Lorraine?" Sam asked.

"Yeah, yeah. He was trying to carjack our car."

"Go tell the guy in the store to call the police."

Lorraine ran off and within five minutes a sheriff's car pulled up next to the SUV. Sam was still kneeling on the man's back. The knife was lying on the ground about five feet away. It was a large hunting knife. The sheriff got out with his gun drawn.

"What's going on here mister?"

Sam explained to him what had happened and told the sheriff his name.

The sheriff looked at the man on the ground. "What's your name, you on the ground?" The man mumbled something. The sheriff told Sam to get off him. The man rolled over, his face bloody and arm hanging at a funny angle. The sheriff looked at the man and turned to Sam. "You've just done a public service. This guy escaped from the sheriff's department jail in Globe. He was just arrested for murder."

Sam shook his head in thought. *Why couldn't I just have a quiet day's drive?*

Lorraine came out of the convenience store as the sheriff put cuffs on the man on the ground and put him in the backseat of his car. Another sheriff's car had driven up and the two conferred. They were there another hour while the sheriff wrote up the incident and took their personal information. He wished them well as they got in their SUV and drove off.

Sam gave a big sigh as he turned onto the highway. "I don't think we need any more excitement today. Shoot, I forgot to get a new cup of coffee."

Lorraine looked at him in wonderment. "After all that all you can think about is a cup of coffee? I don't know whether to cry or shake. That was a scary situation."

"Don't cry or shake. We're all right. We're only about three hours from Scottsdale. Call my brother and tell him we will be there soon. Ask him whether he wants to meet us tonight for dinner or tomorrow morning."

Lorraine couldn't believe how composed Sam was after what happened, but she called Roger and told him what had happened. Roger told her he and Janie were at a reception and wouldn't be able to see them until tomorrow morning. He would meet them in their hotel lobby around ten o'clock.

The rest of their drive was uneventful. Lorraine leaned back and turned on the satellite radio to songs of the 40s. She thought it might take her mind off the crazy incident. A song by Peggy Lee was playing, "The Folks That Live on the Hill". As the song played, Lorraine said, "That's the way I'd like to live our lives."

Sam looked at her. "I think we should. It sounds like an ideal life."

"When I was a little girl, my grandfather lived with us. He was eighty-five and was in the Second World War. We would sit in the den on the floor, and he would play records, records not CDs or anything else, on his old record player he brought with him. That was one of the songs he played. He told Sarah and me when he was going with my grandmother, who was dead by then, that was their song. They had met at a dance before he was going overseas and decided to get married before he went. She told him if he had her to come home to, he would come back safely. He did, and they settled in Chicago and had their family, my mother and two other girls, my aunts. You haven't met them. One is in Seattle and one in Texas. I often would think about how that generation met and married with such uncertainty in their lives, but with such confidence. He was a great person. You'd have liked him. He landed at Normandy the second day and fought all the way into Germany under Patton. He even liberated one of the concentration camps." She was silent for a while thinking of all she had experienced with that man of another century.

They entered Scottsdale and drove into their hotel, the Valley Ho. They decided to have a snack in the lounge and go up to bed. It had been a long day.

When they got into bed, Sam put his arm around her and pulled her toward him. "I don't know whether I talked enough about what happened or not. It was such a bolt out of the blue, I could only react. I know you were really scared."

"When the man came up to me, I wasn't sure what he wanted. Then he grabbed me and was going to force me into the SUV. I tried to delay him because I knew you'd be showing up soon, and I tried to keep his back to you. I just trusted you would know what to do. I couldn't do anything because he had knife at my throat and was holding me so close. I figured I just had to trust you would know what to do."

"I think you did everything right. There was not much more you could have done. I was thinking, though, if we're ever in any situation where I tell you to do something, just do it. What I mean is my training has led me to be very aware of my surroundings. It's called situational awareness in the military. So, if I see something I don't like, I may just whisper or say, 'Get behind me, or get down.' It would be because something might be going on I'm concerned about."

"I understand. I'll try to not look at you and say, 'Why?' By the way you do owe me a new blouse. You threw coffee on him and me too. She gave him a hug and a kiss." This led to more kissing and serious lovemaking.

# Chapter 30

Burton and Alice were walking through the Old Mill Mall on a cold February day, but the sun was out and there were a lot of shoppers because of the President's Day sales. They hadn't seen much of each other for a while due to their schedules. Burton knew they were getting serious with each other though. He was very happy.

They were walking from Macy's McCormick & Schmick's. They had decided to treat themselves to a really nice lunch when they heard what sounded like gun shots. They looked around, trying to see where the noise was coming from. It sounded like it was coming toward them. Then they heard an explosion. An announcement came on with a klaxon sound, "Attention, there are gunmen in the mall. Go immediately into a store. Stores shut your roll downs." This announcement began repeating.

They looked for a store to run to. People were screaming and running. Burton could see a man about one hundred yards away running toward them. There appeared to be a policeman chasing him. He pulled Alice toward an alcove and tried to shield her. There was another woman with three children across the way doing the same thing.

The man ran by randomly firing a machine gun at anyone he saw. His gun stopped, out of ammunition, but as he ran by Burton and Alice he dropped a grenade in the middle of the aisle.

Burton looked at it in horror. Alice could be killed. He ran out and without thinking fell on it. There was an explosion. Everything went black for him.

Burton was in terrible pain, and he could see dimly through a red haze. He was on his back. He wasn't sure where he was. He could hear Alice crying, "Burton, Burton."

He heard another voice, "Cherie, be careful."

"I will Sarah. I just want to see if I can help him. He saved all our lives."

Burton felt things slipping away. It was like being in a dark tunnel. He felt good and calm for the first time in his life. He had done something good. His world went black.

# Chapter 31

Sam and Lorraine met Roger in the lobby of the hotel the next morning. They got up and took a walk early and came back and had coffee and a Danish before Roger came. Roger told them there would be some refreshments at his opening. Sam had told her he and Roger and were different looking, but Lorraine was surprised at the difference. Where Sam was broad-shouldered and muscular, Roger was lanky. He dressed the part of the westerner—cowboy boots and hat, jeans and a western-style shirt. He had obviously been in the sun a lot because his face was wrinkled from the sun. Yet he was a handsome man, she thought. He was very cordial to her and exclaimed that Sam had found a prize.

"Janie is going to join us later. She's looking at some horses. She and Jenny have decided they need a couple to ride on, so Janie is at a horse show. There's a lot going on in town this weekend: two car shows, a golf tournament, and a horse show and auction. I'll walk you over to where my gallery is. I just moved from what's called Old Town to the mall here." He ushered them out of the hotel and they began walking toward Scottsdale Road.

He pointed out a large structure sticking up from a bridge over a canal. "That's a sculpture by Soleri. He's an Italian architect and that's one of his works." Roger continued his sightseeing tour as they walked across the street and continued along. They passed a P F Chang's.

The sun was warm and the temperature was in the seventies. It was a welcome change from the cold they had experienced in the rest of their trip.

"Now ahead of us is part of the mall. You see that large building to the left; that's Nordstrom's. It's connected by that two story bridge to the rest of the mall to our right. I call it a bridge, but you can't see into it. There are shops all along it as it goes into the main mall. My studio is in that bridge on the first level. We'll go through Nordstrom's to get up to it."

Lorraine was impressed by what she had seen of Scottsdale. It looked like a very clean, modern city. As they walked through Nordstrom's and to the escalator, she could see this must be a prime shopping day. The store was jammed.

"I picked today to open because I knew there would be a lot of shoppers." Roger continued his tour. "This is the height of the season. The season is when all the snowbirds come down here to get out of the cold and snow. There are all kinds of events that go on and this is the time to take advantage of the number of people who are here. In the summer there are a lot of tourists in Sedona. That's why I have a studio there, too."

They exited the escalator and began walking toward the main mall.

Sam was just taking it all in. He had never seen so many people jammed into such a space: young families, teenagers, older people, many Hispanics. They were all obviously having a good time and shopping.

Many were laden down with several large shopping bags. He guessed this was what modern America was all about. It was certainly different than anything he had seen overseas.

Lorraine was enjoying looking at all the shops. She was enjoying the whole day so far. The crowds were happy and excited, and this rubbed off on her. They came up to Roger's studio: Southwest Magic. Several of his large pictures of the Grand Canyon and the rocks around Sedona were on easels in front of the store. Lorraine exclaimed, "Roger, those are gorgeous. I feel like I'm standing on the edge of the canyon."

Roger beamed. "Thanks, that's the effect I try for. I want the people who buy them to put them in their living room and feel like they're looking out a window."

There was a crowd of people in the studio sipping wine and snacking on crackers and cheese. Roger made his apologies to Sam and Lorraine and began circulating among the crowd. Sam and Lorraine wandered around the store looking at all the photographs. They truly made you feel like you were looking out a window.

After about an hour, Roger came over to them and offered a suggestion, "I've got some business I need to discuss with my manager here. Why don't you two go down to the food court and have something? I'll join you there in about a half hour or so."

They nodded their agreement and walked out of the store holding hands. They needed to because of the number of people in the mall.

They walked to a railing looking over the food court. They were a floor above it. To their left was an escalator down to the food court. The food court was full of people too. In the middle was a large, circular elevated platform surrounded by a low wall.

There were tables around the outside of the platform and on the platform. Sam estimated there were about 500 people seated in the court and many others walking around eating or waiting for a table.

They walked over to the escalator and rode down to the food court level. They got in a line for a sandwich, and after waiting a bit got their food and drink and tried to find a seat. They decided to try to find a place on the platform and walked up the steps. It was jammed with people, but some were leaving and others standing around hoping to get a table. They kept their eyes searching for people about to finish and were able to get one against one of the walls. They sat down and began to eat their sandwiches.

Sam was trying to keep alert for whatever; his situational awareness training made him want to keep up with what was going on around him. The number of people made him a bit uncomfortable because of his inability to stay aware of everything.

Lorraine was chatting on about the store and Roger and how nice the photographs were. She nudged him and said, "Eat your sandwich." He began to eat it and for a minute was focused on her and her chatter.

He noticed three men walking through the tables on the platform. They were carrying hang-up bags, the kind that looked like they might have rented or bought tuxedos or nice suits, and small athletic bags. There was something about their demeanor that bothered him. They were nervous. They were clean-shaven and looked like they might be Hispanic, perhaps Arab. He studied them as they walked toward the middle of the platform. There were about 200 people seated all around them.

The men squatted down in a small open space amid several tables. This puzzled him. They had no food. What were they doing? He couldn't see what they were doing directly. He looked at the diners around them. Most were minding their own business or eating.

As one, the three stood up with their backs to one another in a rough triangle. They were holding MP-5s, a submachine gun Sam was very familiar with from his time in the SEALs and the Group.

"Get down under the table," he said quietly to Lorraine. She was so immersed in her sandwich she blinked at him. He pushed her down. At the same time he took his tray and threw it like a Frisbee at the man facing him. This all happened in a few seconds.

Sam jumped from his chair and carried it in front of him as he ran toward the men. They started firing randomly into the crowd.

People began screaming and falling backward; blood spurted into the air. The tray Sam had thrown at the man facing him had caused him to reel back and fire into the air. Sam was upon him before he had a chance to recover.

The other two were concentrating on their bloody chore. Sam rammed the chair into the man facing him and at the same time wrested the MP-5 from his hands with his left hand. He heard the man's trigger finger snap as he did. The man screamed in pain. The strap was around the man's right shoulder and it prevented him from easily freeing himself.

Sam smashed his right palm into the man's nose; crushing it into his skull. The man fell to the floor. Sam shot him with a burst. The MP-5 has three settings: one shot, three shots, or full automatic. The gun was set to three; otherwise the entire magazine would have emptied in a few seconds.

Sam turned the gun to the man on his left. The man was just turning to see what was going on. Sam leveled him with another burst. The gun was out of ammunition and needed another magazine.

The remaining man turned and saw what Sam had done, but his gun was out of ammunition. He swung the gun at Sam's head.

Sam fended it off with the MP-5 in his hand. He lunged at the man, who turned and crashed through the tables and knocking aside bodies and injured people. He ran toward the wall surrounding the food plaza and jumped over it.

Sam ran behind him. When the man jumped, he fell into another table and people hiding behind the wall. Sam followed him, but jumped into a clear spot.

As the two of them recovered from their jumps, there was a terrific explosion sending them to their knees. A massive cloud of dust drifted toward them.

Sam was temporarily deafened and he turned toward the explosion. It had come from the direction of the bridge and Roger's store. Sam turned to look at the other man who was slowly getting up and began running for an escalator.

He turned and pulled out a grenade, pulled the pin, and threw it at Sam.

Sam caught it and threw it into a pool next to the escalator. It exploded, but the force of it was contained by the water.

Sam was bearing down on the man as he ran up the escalator. Sam caught him with his left hand by the back of his coat and hit him in the side of his head with his right fist. It stunned the man.

He grabbed the bottom of the man's coat with his right hand and turned and threw him over his shoulder down the escalator over two bodies on the escalator, a mother and her small child. Sam jumped over them as he went to the man lying face down at the bottom of the escalator. He knelt down to see if the man was conscious. He was not.

A man came running up to him and showed him a police badge. "I saw what you did. I'll take care of him, you better see to your wife."

Sam shook his head. It was almost as if he had been in a trance ever since he saw the three men arrive. His training had kicked in and his focus was entirely on taking them down and not allowing any more carnage.

He ran back to the food court and ran up the stairs to the platform. There was Lorraine lying by the wall where he had left her. A man in an undershirt was leaning over her. He walked quickly toward them, stepping over bodies and almost slipping several times on the blood all over the floor.

The man looked up from Lorraine. He had put her coat under her head and was pressing what appeared to be his shirt on her chest. He looked up at Sam. "I'm an EMT. She was shot in the chest and shoulder. I think by a ricochet. I can't tell how serious it is, but I've tried to stop the bleeding."

Sam felt faint. "I was a Navy medic. I'll take over. You go see who else needs help." The man nodded and stood up as Sam knelt beside Lorraine and put his hand on the shirt. Sam slowly pulled the shirt away. A hole was close to her lungs and chest.

It was too difficult to tell how much internal damage might exist. There was another hole at the top of her shoulder. The man might be right. A bullet could have hit the floor and a fragment hit Lorraine. He ripped the shirt in half and pressed one part to her chest and one to her shoulder. He kept the pressure on her front.

He looked around. There were bodies everywhere—young, old, males and females. Some people were trying to help others. He looked toward the bridge and could see daylight streaming in. He suddenly realized Roger would have been in the middle of the explosion. He was overcome with fear; what more could happen? This was not Kabul; this was the United States. What the hell was going on?

# Chapter 32

Sam knelt next to Lorraine. He had kept pressure on both wounds and had peeled back her shirt to better examine the wounds. The blood seemed to be staunched, but still oozing. Unhurt people were coming up onto the food court platform and trying to help the wounded. Finally, emergency workers began to show up.

A male medical technician walked his way through the bodies, checking for vital signs on each one as he did. Several others followed him. He was indicating which ones could be helped and which ones couldn't. He looked at Sam, "Is she alive?"

"I think a ricochet went through her breast and out her shoulder. I can't tell how bad it is. She's been unconscious since it happened. I was in the military and have seen many bullet wounds. I think it may have been a fragment rather than an entire bullet."

The tech stooped over. "Let me see." He delicately pulled the shirt on her front away. "I don't see any bubbling. It probably missed her lungs. I'd rather not move her until we get a proper stretcher."

"Yeah. I put the other half of the shirt on the hole in her shoulder. There wasn't a lot of blood coming out."

"I think she may have hit her head and that's why she's unconscious. The gunshot doesn't look serious enough to have caused her to pass out."

The tech slowly raised her head. "I can't tell exactly, but she may have a bruise on the back of her head." He lowered her head back onto her coat. He waved two other men over. "Let's get some dressings on this lady and get a stretcher to get her out of here."

Sam looked around. There were EMT's carrying people out in a steady stream being careful not to slip on the blood or trip on the bodies. The two other techs came over and carefully placed dressings on both wounds. He felt silly that he hadn't thought of her hitting her head.

Lorraine opened her eyes and moaned. She focused on Sam. "What happened?"

"You were shot. Don't try to move. They're taking you out of here to get some treatment."

The techs lifted her onto an emergency stretcher and carried her toward an exit. Sam followed them as they walked out with a stream of other techs carrying people on stretchers. They walked out into the street where there was a line of stretchers waiting for transportation.

"Where're you taking all these people?" Sam asked.

One of the techs answered. "They've set up emergency rooms in school gyms and cafeterias around the area. They'll take her to whichever one is next. There's a pretty good plan in effect for such an event as this."

"I'll stay with her until they take her."

"Okay. We've got to get back inside."

There were some people on stretchers who also had civilians watching them. Others had EMT's trying to stabilize people until they could be relocated. Sam realized there were probably hundreds of victims. He suddenly thought of his brother. *Oh God! The explosion! It was where his studio was. I have to go find him. I can't leave Lorraine.* He was faced with a dilemma unlike any he had seen in his operational career.

About an hour later Sam was standing next to Lorraine who was lying on a cot in a middle school gymnasium with several tens of other people. Nurses and doctors were moving among the people trying to prioritize their injuries and determine what treatment was needed.

**\*\*\*\*\*\*\*\*\***

Two days later Lorraine was in a hospital room. Her injuries had required surgery to remove bone chips from her collar bone and setting it and suturing up the two holes in her. The bullet fragment had shot up through the top of her breast, bounced off her collar bone and then come out the top of her shoulder. She told everyone it was the classic "flesh wound of the movies" which she said with a smile.

Sam found his brother in another hospital not in as good shape. Roger had been near the explosion under the shopping bridge from Nordstrom's to the mall. The bridge had broken in two and collapsed on the road below.

Roger was trapped in the rubble for fourteen hours until he could be rescued. His right leg was crushed and his back broken. He would require extensive leg surgery and therapy to recover. Sam was relieved that he was alive. Roger was trying to keep his spirits up, but he had never had any physical problems before and was in a lot of pain.

They all had decided that once they were well enough to leave the hospital, they would go back to Sedona and try to recuperate in Roger and Janie's house. Janie and Roger's kids were with Roger all day, trying to come to terms with this new situation. Sam and Lorraine realized they would have to provide a lot of support to the family. It was going to be a long time before everyone was feeling comfortable with their life.

Sam was partially unhappy that he was no longer working for the Group and might be able to help find out who was responsible for this attack on his family and homeland. He also realized that he now had someone else to worry about more than himself. These conflicting feelings were something he would have to work out. He was used to being able to right a wrong directly. This situation would require some thought.

# Chapter 33

*AP: Breaking News: President's Day, February 22. Three major US malls were the target of three separate terrorist attacks.*

*A mall in Vienna, Virginia, a suburb of Washington DC, was attacked by terrorists. 382 people were murdered and 123 others injured. The three attackers were chased into a store in the mall by a SWAT team. The three blew themselves up with grenades.*

*A mall in the Chicago suburbs was also attacked by three terrorists. 216 people were killed and 92 others injured. The son of one of the wealthiest men in America, Clifton Burton Jamesway Junior, saved the lives of over ten people by shielding them from a grenade. The three terrorists were cornered by a SWAT team in the mall and blew themselves up with grenades.*

*A large mall in Scottsdale Arizona was also attacked. A truck bomb destroyed a major portion of the mall killing at least 278 people. Rescuers are still trying to find people buried in the rubble. Three other attackers killed 27 people and wounded 35 before they were killed by an ex-Navy SEAL who happened to be in the food court where the terrorists started their attack.*

*No terrorist organization has announced responsibility for the attacks. The FBI and Homeland Security are investigating the attacks.*

# About the Author

Donald Kingsley is a graduate of the United States Air Force Academy and retired from the Air Force. He also served in the Central Intelligence Agency for eighteen years. After retiring, he decided to try his lifelong desire to write fiction. He lives in Arizona with his wife Mary Jo and their two small dogs.